THE TRAIL
OF FEAR

ALSO BY ANTHONY ARMSTRONG

The Secret Trail (1928)
The Trail of the Lotto (1929)
The Trail of the Black King (1931)
The Poison Trail (1932)

Other Books

Lure of the Past (1920)
The Love of Prince Raameses (1921)
Wine of Death (1925)
Patrick, Undergraduate (1926)
Apple and Percival (1931)
Britisher on Broadway (1932)
Easy Warriors, Etc. (1932)
Ten Minute Alibi (1934)
Without Witness (1934)
Cottage into House (1936)
The Pack of Pieces (1942)
The End of the Road (1943)
When the Bells Rang (1943)
No Higher Mountain (1951)
He Was Found in the Road (1952)
Spies in Amber (1956)
The Strange Case of Mr Pelham (1957)
One Jump Ahead (1973)

THE TRAIL OF FEAR

ANTHONY ARMSTRONG

A Jimmy Rezaire Story

WILDSIDE PRESS

To Aphra Wilson.

Published by Wildside Press LLC.
www.wildsidepress.com

CHAPTER I

DOPE

The evening crowds of Piccadilly drifted to and fro under the lights like colored artificial leaves in a stage-ballet. All the usual types were there; early theater-goers slipping from taxis into restaurant doorways under the eye of haughty commissionaires; young men with questing eyes searching for an evening's amusement; girls with prying glances under the paint, moving in a haze of patchouli and silk-clad ankles; match-sellers, beggars, and newsboys; shop-girls on their way home; old gentlemen walking to the club for their evening pick-me-up; bus crowds, shop-window drifters, bar drifters, and a sprinkling of poor people come to the free display of window-dressing and electric signs. All were there, always the same yet always changing, the innumerable kaleidoscopic units that went to make up the Piccadilly crowds.

But on this particular March evening there were three units that, though separate, appeared to be bound together by invisible strings, so uniformly did they follow behind one another. The first was a seedy look-ing man in ragged clothes shuffling along by the wall-side as if afraid of the more open spaces of the pavement. The second about six or seven yards behind was a girl of the Piccadilly class who though originally go-ing in the opposite direction had at some sign turned and followed. The third man, square-shouldered, in clothes that seemed to hang from him like a military tunic, with keen eyes and a short close-clipped moustache under a hard bowler hat, was a further ten yards behind the girl.

The three drifted on, together yet apart, the pace set by the ragged man in front, till at last he turned a corner into one of the side streets on the north of Piccadilly. At their varying intervals the others followed, till at last, leaving the shops behind, the first man stopped and turning in toward the railing, drew a cigarette from behind his ear and lit up. The flare of the match illumined his vicious, unintelligent face for a moment and his shifty eyes flickered to his right toward the following girl. Then he threw away the empty match-box and shuffled on. The little box lay white in the light of a street lamp, an isolated bit of jetsam on the smooth, hard pavement. The girl drew close. As she passed, she dropped her vanity bag and stooped to pick it up. When she straightened herself, the discarded matchbox was no longer there.

The square-shouldered man some way behind quickened his pace. He knew very well that the match-box was not empty, that it held a little packet of white powder—cocaine. He knew very well too that a little further on the ragged man would be found begging on the curb and would receive from the girl a far bigger sum than beggars usually received. That was only one of the many tricks for the disposal of "dope" and on his evidence he could easily convict the woman of being in possession and the man of supplying. But it was not for that that he, Detective Inspector Harrison, had been put on to this by Scotland Yard. At the Yard they had latterly held a theory that the growing menace of the dope traffic in London was now almost entirely due to the operations of one gang who smuggled it in cheap from the continent and distributed it down through an elaborate chain of agents, ending eventually in men such as the loafer who had just thrown the match-box away. To convict and imprison him, therefore, would be but to attack the symptoms and not the cause—like doctoring one spot on a person infected with measles. There were hundreds of other spots and, even if they were all doctored, the disease would break out elsewhere. Tonight Harrison was after bigger fish; for nothing could ever be learned from these small fry, a fact which had confirmed Scotland Yard in its belief that there was some big organization behind. But try as he would, amid all these veins and capillaries, so far he had found himself unable to put his finger on the central undiscoverable heart.

He walked on, overtaking the woman, who little knew what she had escaped, secure in the ignorance of the small fish who swims through the big meshes of a net. Harrison was now following the man ahead, as he had followed his kind for two or three nights before, trying to discover whence he got his supplies. At the corner he passed the man, cap off, on the curb edge, and without turning he knew that behind him the "beggar" had received an "alms." Waiting for him under pretence of lighting a cigarette he again took up the pursuit and followed him round into Bond Street, where another signal passed and another match-box was thrown away. Then back again into Piccadilly where a small packet was affixed secretly to a lamp post by means of chewing gum and detached a moment later by a haggard young Jew who stopped there to light a cigarette.

With his other nights' failures behind him, Harrison began to get furious. Here was the "dope" being put out under his very nose and he was doing nothing, because he was after something bigger. He *must* find out where the fellow renewed his stock of "snow," but though the man was obviously not clever, he possessed all the cunning of the drug fiend in procuring his supplies. Harrison followed him for ten minutes, till he came to the entrance to the Piccadilly Tube in Haymarket. Here the detective's keen eye again spotted yet another transaction, this time with a man selling papers. He swore to himself at the futility of it all,—and then suddenly drew a sharp breath. He believed he was on to a clue at last. The paper man was a thin lanky fellow with cunning eyes and a furtive look, but Harrison was fairly certain he was not a drug addict. In that case, perhaps what he had thought was another "delivery" was really a deal the other way. The paper seller was another link in the chain and this time one higher up. He did not peddle to anyone, he passed out the cocaine to those who did, and without doubt received it from someone else.

Harrison at once let the first man go and set himself to observe the paper seller. It seemed a forlorn hope because probably the fellow fetched the stuff from his suppliers at some secret and prearranged time, but still he might learn something of interest. He bought a paper from him, studying him carefully the while, then went and leaned against a wall, the paper held in front of his face. The crowds flowed past him, laughing, chattering, intent on their own affairs, heedless of the little drama that was being played out at their elbows. A few yards away at the road junction stood a policeman solidly protective. Harrison thought cynically that if one could see into the heart of every person who passed Piccadilly Circus that policeman would not have much time left for mere traffic directing.

Several people approached the paper man, bought papers and went away. No one suspicious. The man, who was evidently on a higher mental plane than the first loafer, kept his eyes darting hither and thither in a shifty manner that betrayed consciousness of guilt. Twice he looked narrowly at Harrison and once lounged round the corner out of sight. But the detective was too wise to be caught by that, though he had to take the risk of the man meeting his accomplice unobserved. Had he in turn moved so as to get a view of him in his new position, he would have given away the fact that he was watching. He stayed unconcernedly where he was and after a short while the man reappeared on his old pitch, though glancing occasionally at Harrison as if still doubtful of him.

At last his vigilance was rewarded. A small well-dressed man came up, hand outstretched for a paper. Harrison caught the faintest flicker of an eye from the man he was watching and was instantly on the alert. There was some understanding between the two. He grew more and more certain that he had hit upon yet another link in the chain which he was striving to break and this time an important one.

The paper was purchased, and the two men stood talking for a moment quite openly. Harrison moved forward a pace; he did not know what to do. Even if he were able to eavesdrop, he knew he would learn nothing. He gave them credit for having a story ready,—probably a "tip" for tomorrow's races—which would explain any furtive conversation. If only he could see something passed or could catch them—particularly the more important one of the two—with something on him. But by the jerk of the paper-boy's head he knew that he was already under suspicion. Nothing would be passed and yet he was certain that the newcomer had it. But he now had to deal with a cleverer type of brain. To follow him would effect nothing. By himself he could soon be thrown off the scent in this crowd by any of the old tricks. He could do nothing without proof and, certain though he was, he had nothing to back his suspicions.

The smaller man turned and began to walk away. In another moment he would be swallowed up in the crowd. Harrison had a sudden inspiration. He might yet try to bluff. With a clever man, certain of himself, he knew this would not work, but he was calculating on the other man's appearance. Despite his cunning eyes, his air of gentility and his self-confidence, there were lines of weakness about his mouth which hinted that in an actual clash of personalities he might be overcome by the stronger. Besides his fears had probably been aroused by what his accomplice had told him and he would not know how much the detective really knew.

Harrison walked quickly round the corner and before the other could lose himself in the crowd was at his side. He was staking everything on the next few minutes.

"A word with you," he said shortly.

The other started at the touch of Harrison's hand on his shoulder, but it was only for a bare instant. He turned with a politely inquiring expression, as if he had been asked to direct a stranger: "Yes, can I do anything?"

"You can," said Harrison grimly. "You can come along with me to Scotland Yard. You're caught at last, my friend."

"Caught? Scotland Yard?" The other was curious, yet uninterested, as if the matter did not concern him, but Harrison fancied he saw a flicker of fear in the depths of his eyes. "I'm afraid I don't understand."

Harrison spoke with the assumed impatience of the man who is exasperated at waste of words and futile pretence of misunderstanding.

"Now it's no good trying to bluff," he said sharply. "I'm an Inspector from the Yard. We know who you are and we've been watching you for several days. You're wanted for dope running—being in possession and disposing. We know from whom you get it," he went on confidently, "and we know where it goes to." He spoke with an air of unconcern as though to humor the other in all his pretence of not knowing what was the matter. He hoped that by thus appearing to fling all his cards on the table, as if they were invincible, his opponent would not see that they were by no means all trumps.

"All this is absurd," began the little man, still with an easy air of tolerance. "You've got the wrong person. I fear you've made a mistake. Good-day."

"Stop!" said Harrison. His hand shot out detaining the other by the coat. "It's no good bluffing, man. I know you've got the stuff on you."

"Look here, my good sir, this is past a joke. You can't stop respectable citizens in the street and accuse them of extraordinary crimes without any proof."

"Oh, I've got proof enough. Someone's snouted on you," he added cleverly.

"Nonsense," said the other quickly, and then he bit his lip. He realized he had made a false move. Had he stopped to think, he would have seen that the ordinary respectable citizen would probably not have known a slang word current amongst criminals and detectives. Having guessed that the other was bluffing, it had given him a false sense of security. He tried to cover up his slip; for he knew he had only to walk away and the detective would be helpless.

"Even if your absurd statements were true," he went on quickly, "you can't search me on suspicion." He turned on his heel, but the man from the Yard spoke quickly in compelling tones, drawing a small whistle from his pocket as he did so.

"You can either come with me without making a scene or else I'll blow this whistle for the policeman on point duty and have you arrested as a pickpocket." He stepped back a pace. "A moment ago I slipped a watch into your pocket which I can prove to be mine. In the search for my property I shall ensure of course that—er—other things will be found."

The mask of politeness dropped suddenly from the other's face. He looked furtively around. There were two policemen near by and many people; also the detective was bigger and stronger than he was. He clapped a hand to his pocket, wondering whether he might not have time to throw the incriminating watch away, but the whistle at once went up to the other's lips.

Two minutes later, accompanied by a policeman, they were in a taxi being driven to Scotland Yard. Harrison had in his hand four or five little packets containing white powder which he had taken from under a secret flap in the other's cigarette case. He had laid a finger on one link in the chain and from his knowledge of character he was fairly certain that it was a weak one and that he would know of others before the hour was out. The man at his side who had been so easily worsted did not seem to him to be the type that would refuse to give away his friends if he had the opportunity and was suitably "persuaded." And Harrison was privately of the opinion that the next link in the chain above would no doubt be the organizer of the whole gang, the master mind that was importing the "dope" and putting it out through his agents—in short, the one man that they were after.

CHAPTER II

THE WATCHER IN THE STREET

About the same time that some officials in Scotland Yard, rejoicing over Harrison's captive and the long-sought information that had been squeezed out of him, were hurriedly issuing certain orders, a man was standing before the door of a tall dingy-looking house in one of the narrow streets between the Strand and the Embankment. As he fitted a key to the lock he gave a swift and almost furtive glance up and down the street as though expecting pursuit or observation. The next moment he was inside, making his way along the ill-lit hall to the stairs at the far end.

The hall was that of a lodging house of unprepossessing character. There were two or three doors on either side of the passage, one of these with the name of the occupant pinned up on a piece of paper. At the end of the passage where the stairs to the basement began, a stout slatternly woman was carrying a tray loaded with a pot of tea, a fried kipper, and bread and butter.

"Evening, Mrs. Gibson," remarked the man. "Are there any letters for me?"

"Three," replied Mrs. Gibson shortly. "Two of 'em big 'uns," she added with a touch of asperity. She did not approve of struggling authors renting her rooms and this one, though he paid his money more regularly than her other lodgers, seemed certainly to be unsuccessful enough, judging by the amount of "big 'uns" that came by post. Mrs. Gibson had had authors and journalists before and knew what a returned manuscript looked like.

She put the tray down and fumbled in the large pocket of her dirty apron.

"I suppose you wouldn't be wanting any tea?" she asked as she handed the letters over.

"No, thanks," said the man already half-way up the stairs, and Mrs. Gibson sniffed. The fact that he had no meals from her, but always cooked what he wanted on a gas ring in his bedroom was to her an unattractive proposition, if not a positive insult; though it was mitigated by the fact that he hardly ever required anything done. He never wanted a jug of hot water or the loan of a paper or similar things that were not "included." Except for the click of his typewriter she would hardly have known he was in the house. The door of his room was invariably locked, whether he was in or out. She was only allowed inside for an hour in the morning to clear up the place under his eye, and half the time he wouldn't allow her to touch anything for fear of dirtying his "mannyscrips." It was certainly rather mysterious, but then writing gents were apt to be mysterious. Though just as curious as the rest of her sex, Mrs. Gibson had in Mr. Carlyle struck a wall which she could not scale. Many times had she tried to read his letters or get into his room when he was not there, but each time she had been baffled. At last she had given up trying. After all, the possession of a lodger who gave such little trouble and paid so promptly without querying his bill was an asset to be carefully guarded.

She sniffed again, and picked up the tray.

"Well, good-evenin', Mr. Carlyle," she said, and resumed her journey with the hall bedroom's tea.

Mr. Carlyle went slowly upstairs to his room on the first floor. He was a small man well made and carrying himself well, with a sharp featured face and restless bright eyes. The spring in his step showed that despite his sedentary occupation he was in perfect health. He looked, and was, very clever—certainly cleverer than Mrs. Gibson knew.

Arrived at the first floor, dimly lit by a half turned gas jet, he unlocked the door of a room on the front side of the house. Once inside, his first act was to lock the door behind him and slide a bolt across. He had long ago guessed that Mrs. Gibson had another key, and he had particular reasons for never wishing anyone else to enter his room, till he had in a measure prepared it for the inquisitive stare of outside eyes. Then he took off his hat and heaved a sigh of relief, before lighting the gas and looking at his watch. It was noticeable that he softly drew down the blind while the room was still in darkness.

Seen in the light, it certainly was not an ordinary room. On a table by the window stood a small typewriter surrounded by masses of typed pages and manuscript, some of which had drifted to the floor.

A half-finished page was actually in the machine. A pile of dusty books stood on a shelf and despite the air of work just left for a moment, all this paraphernalia of the author's craft seemed to be but little used. In addition to the usual appurtenances of a bed-sitting-room there was against the wall opposite to the door a big wardrobe; while a table in a corner piled high with some objects under a big cloth completed the furniture.

Whistling softly to himself Mr. Carlyle went across to this table and lifting the cloth displayed a large number of oblong cardboard boxes. One of these he picked up in a casual fashion for a moment and looked at it with a smile on his face. It was a box such as toy soldiers are packed in, labeled on the outside "The Warwickshire Regiment." All the other boxes on the table had the same label, almost as though Mr. Carlyle had a partiality for that particular branch of the Service. On the end of the box, very small, were the words "Made in Germany." The boxes were all of them empty but a big basket in the corner contained the lead figures that once had filled them, all of which strangely enough were headless. Either Mr. Carlyle was a harmless maniac with a passion for decapitating in miniature the Warwickshire Regiment, or else—there was something inside the hollow figures, put in by their maker in Germany, which Mr. Carlyle seemed anxious to obtain. It seemed to be rather a mystery, and Carlyle smiled to himself again as he looked at the results of his labors.

Then he looked at his watch once more and walking across the room to where the typewriter stood, took out of a drawer a small machine that looked rather like a clock. This he wound up and fixed onto the keyboard of the typewriter. Releasing a spring a small whirring noise was heard, and the room was at once filled with the steady clicking of the keys actuated by this small machine. Anyone listening outside the locked door would have said that the struggling author, Mr. Carlyle, was hard at work on his latest masterpiece.

The author, however, was quite differently engaged at the moment in very obviously changing his appearance in the most intimate fashion. A dark morning coat and grey trousers instead of the baggy untidy brown suit, smooth-back hair, instead of a ruffled head, clean linen and a tie pin. From a tumbler he took little rubber pads which, put into the mouth, filled out his cheeks from their normal hollowness to the puffy fatness of the man who takes little exercise; while a few almost invisible touches with paints brought his other features into conformity. Further pads increased his person to match, particularly in the waistcoat region across which now dangled a prosperous gold chain. Within a very few minutes Mr. Carlyle the author had ceased to be and a new personality was present in his place. A cheery-looking short stoutish gentleman, one of many hundreds in business in the city, well groomed, correct in every detail. Nothing was wrong save perhaps that the wrists and ankles where they showed under cuff and trousers were a bit too bony for a man of his apparent build.

With a final look at himself in the glass the late Mr. Carlyle reduced the gas jet to a blue pin point and opening the wardrobe door pushed aside the clothes hanging there and fumbled with a catch behind them.

In a moment the whole back of the wardrobe swung out and he stepped through a concealed door out of the darkened room into still more complete darkness.

Evidently, however, he knew well where he was, for in a moment a gas jet sprang into life lighting up the new room. He then closed behind him the secret door by which he had entered from the next house, which in this room wore the guise of a large file cabinet set against the wall and sat down in a chair by a central desk.

The room was furnished like an office, with desks, trays, typewriter, file cabinet, and all the other fixtures. It had two doors on the opposite side of the room, one being of ground glass on which was painted on the outside "James Robinson, Agent." Stacked all over the room and on two more tables were the same long boxes of soldiers that had been piled up in the room in the other house; but while here they comprised nearly every regiment in the British Army, there were none of the Warwickshire Regiment. It appeared that, though James Robinson's Agency dealt with a German firm in the supply of toy soldiers to the English public, that particular regiment had some cachet which gave it the right of instant entry into the room of Mr. Carlyle the author in the next house.

Mr. James Robinson, stout, prosperous-looking owner of an agency importing German toys into post-war England, looked into a pocket mirror and finally adjusted his person. Then strolling to the window he peeped stealthily out. Previously he adjusted the light so that it did not fall directly on the blind and also approached the window from the side. Then he gave a little start of surprise and annoyance.

The road outside was nearly empty. It was not at the best of times a busy street, being lined with decayed offices, cheap lodgings, or empty houses; but to James Robinson's practised and prejudiced eye it at the moment might have been as crowded as Piccadilly, for besides a stray passer-by there was on the opposite pavement, leaning up against the railing, a man. James Robinson studied him carefully. He was to all intents just a loafer, for he was dressed in rags, had hands thrust deep into his pockets and smoked a short clay pipe. He was apparently staring vacantly into nothingness, but returned to this world at intervals in order to expectorate. Innocent though he seemed, it was obvious that Robinson did not like him at all. A man does not loaf in a half-deserted side street off the Strand on an April evening, looking at nothing special, but always opposite the same house, unless he has some reason for doing so; and if there is a reason the occupation ceases to be loafing. Nor was there any object in his watching a house made up exclusively of offices and storerooms at a time when it would be normally empty, unless he was watching for something rather particular. Also the fellow's shoulders seemed squarer than was usual in men of his type and his attitude rather more tense than natural. Robinson readjusted the blind noiselessly and went back to the chair where he sat with a frown on his smooth puffed out face.

He was worried. There was no doubt in his mind as to what the presence of the watcher meant. In a word, the police were at last wise to him. He sighed, for he had not expected it quite so soon. Something in his carefully organized scheme had gone wrong. However, he was quite ready; his line of escape was prepared; it only remained to put it in final working order. He took up the telephone, and asked for a number. After a while a Jewish voice answered him.

"Hullo!"

"That you, Levy?"

"Yes, Mr. Carlyle."

"Got my check?"

"Yes, and O. K. The deal is through about that motor launch that you asked me to get. She's a war-time M. L. twenty tonner."

"What about crew?"

"I've got hold of Smithson—the man I spoke about—as mechanic in charge and two others. They went aboard this morning. They're now lying at Southampton and ready to do anything you want."

"Southampton?" Robinson hurriedly drew toward him a map of the south coast and studied it. Then he said softly: "I would like to go a trial trip in her tomorrow evening."

"In the evening?" There was surprise in the other's voice and to allay it Robinson fell back upon one of his old tricks, that of confessing to a small crime in order to put people off the scent of a big one.

"Yes. I want to go on a night cruise. You understand, eh, Levy? I may have a little—er—friend with me."

"Oh!" A fat chuckle came down the phone. Robinson could imagine him wagging a fat be-ringed finger. "You boys!"

"Well, you understand. Secret, eh?"

"Yes. Smithson shall be clearly instructed. He's a good man on a job like that. Mum as an oyster. When and where?"

Robinson, who had just pulled a letter from a pocket and glanced through it, leaned forward and in a soft voice spoke very carefully and distinctly: "About half a mile down the Beaulieu River from Beaulieu and five miles from its mouth in the Solent, there is a small quay—a flat gravel jetty…"

"Here, half a minute," came the other voice, "let me get that down… Right!"

"Got that. He can't mistake it. Going up the river, it's just before"—he consulted the letter again—"before he comes to the first house of a bunch on the right hand side—called 'Joyner's End.'"

"I expect he'll know it. He knows all that part."

"Good! I want him to be there by eleven o'clock and wait till I come. There is a double tide, but he can lie at the quay even at low water. Oh, and he should have some provisions on board, in case I'm away a day or so. Is that quite clear?"

"Right!" replied the other. "It'll be done. Good-night, Mr. Carlyle. I wish I was an author and could afford these luxuries."

Robinson smiled to himself as he replaced the receiver, and put the letter down on the table. Author indeed! His writing did not bring him in much, nor did the German-made toy soldiers—as soldiers. There were indeed only four people who knew that Mr. James Robinson's most profitable source of income was the white powder that came inside the Warwickshire Regiment. But of those four even, there was only one—a woman—who knew that Mr. James Robinson and Mr. Carlyle the mysterious little-seen author were the same person, and further that both these two characters also bore the name of Jimmie Rezaire, a name fairly well known in the upper strata of the underworld. The man sitting at the desk was well aware of the value of secrecy, and knew how to ensure it.

James Robinson, *alias* Carlyle, *alias* Rezaire, unlocked a drawer and drew out a little note-book. The book seemed to be a record of the movements of various substantial sums of money. There were statements of receipts, heavy ones, from four names—"Sam, Joe, Harrap, and Vivienne" and these items were balanced by payments to a continental firm and further by other payments, also heavy, to the name of Carlyle in a well-known bank. On another page were notes of items transferred from this bank to a bank in Paris. The lines of figures made quite a satisfactory array and at all of them Rezaire looked, smiling to himself. He had not done badly for four or five months. He had expected a slightly longer run, but apparently something had happened.

There was money in the dope traffic, more than in anything else, provided one went into it properly. Half the failures came either from taking only small profits and hanging on too long or else not organizing properly and being consequently betrayed, which, however, from his experience he knew was bound to happen sooner or later. He had only gone into the matter after careful thought and several months' preparation, always pitting his brain against those who in time would be after him.

He had a rule of his own concerning the habits of detectives. Once they had become suspicious of a person's mode of life and had decided to watch him, they were, he believed, always far more suspicious if they could find out nothing about him. But if, however, they found some small thing, they often never thought that there might be something bigger as well. Hence his cloak of a slightly mysterious agency, on which he knew the police had an eye, to cover the import of the white powder contained in the Warwickshire Regiment. Once they had looked into it, the mystery was very obviously that James Robinson did not want the public to know he dealt with a German firm and they bothered no further.

Jimmie Rezaire also had another rule. During his life he had found that it always pays to do the unexpected, however bold the course. Hence his disguise in the present case. He argued that usually the criminal commits his crime first and disguises himself afterward, thus increasing his chances of being taken. He had therefore disguised himself—as a fat man—for his crime and, to make his get-away, simply became himself again, small and thin, while Scotland Yard would in all probability be looking for a stout man wearing a disguise. When not even all his agents, who knew Robinson the dope runner, knew the real man in this affair, it was improbable that the police would.

Well, they were after him at last. Let them come, he thought, as he hurriedly gathered together a few things. He had only to walk into the next room, revert to his normal self and walk out of the other house as Mr. Carlyle. He had a car of his own garaged in Jermyn Street, a chauffeur, and a launch at Beaulieu to take him to the Channel Islands. He could lie low there for a bit and then go over to France where his earnings were stowed safely away. At the garage, in a private locker, of which the key was in his pocket, were a few other important papers, notably a passport ready made out for France, a small store of French money and a revolver. His whole line of escape was planned; and as for those who had been his agents, they could look after themselves.

He went stealthily to the window again and looked out. The loafer was still there. Right up at the far end of the street he could see a dim knot of men—doubtless the Scotland Yard detectives, who would be almost sure to be conducting such a big round-up, and perhaps some of the local police.

He laughed derisively and turned away to the table. Here he lit a candle and holding the little note-book in the flame methodically reduced it to ashes. He must leave no clue behind, he thought, as he next picked up the important letter which contained the secret of the quay at Beaulieu and his plan of escape...

Then he caught his breath suddenly, for without a sound, the door had opened and a man stood in the doorway looking at him.

CHAPTER III

FORCED COMPANIONS

For a moment Rezaire's heart stopped beating; then he gave a short laugh.

"Lord, how you startled me, Sam!" he said.

"Came up quiet," said the other man stepping quickly into the room. "Had to. There's a 'busy' outside hitched up to the railings looking about as much like a loafer as a sergeant-major on parade."

He lounged against the desk, a long well-dressed figure with a coarsely handsome face, and full arrogant lips. He was one of Rezaire's four agents, "Long Sam" by name. With his "hail fellow" and yet gentlemanly air he was responsible for pushing out the "stuff," as required, to those young men and girls with whom he picked up in bar lounges and night clubs. He had a forceful personality and once he had formed his acquaintances soon dominated them by his cheery but overbearing manner.

At the moment he seemed remarkably cool, despite the fact that the police were evidently surrounding the house and would soon begin to force an entry.

"You don't seem pleased to see me," he said rather harshly.

"Oh, yes I am," replied Rezaire, though his voice was anything but pleased. At the back of his mind was the knowledge that this new arrival considerably complicated his plan of escape which was intended for one and not for two. Also, he was more than a little afraid of his companion's domineering personality, though he knew that he himself had up to now been the unquestioned leader of the gang by holding the advantage in experience and brains. He foresaw a troublesome time ahead, for he did not think he could possibly get away scot-free if Long Sam insisted on coming too, whereas he knew enough of Long Sam's vindictive and cruel nature to realize that his life would not be worth a pinch of "snow" if he tried to side-track him. A little fear began to creep into his mind, fear of the tall man in front of him.

"Why didn't you push off when you saw the 'tecs?" he asked at length.

"What! Cut and run! Why, they'd have got me in a moment. Only chance was to come up here as if I saw nothing. I guess they're wise to our meeting and are waiting till we're all here. They won't start anything till all the birds are in the net." He dropped his light-hearted manner and went on fiercely: "Looks to me as if someone had blown on us. Well, if ever I catch him, or anyone else, trying to double-cross me, I'll—do you know what I'll do?"

He advanced and thrust his big coarse face up against Rezaire. The other automatically shrank back, still holding in his hand the letter which he had been just about to burn.

"I'll cut him to pieces," went on Long Sam furiously, his big lips working. "I don't care much for a gun, but I do like this." He whipped an evil-looking long-bladed knife in a thin leather case from his hip. "No noise or fuss—and a nigger out in America taught me how to use it. And if you want to know how a nigger uses a knife…"

"Gently, gently, Sam," remonstrated the other, recoiling. "I haven't double-crossed you, nor likely to."

"That is the truest word you've spoken," said Sam grimly; then with another change… "Why, old man, I know you won't betray us. After all, it's due to your brain that we've run clear so far." The door swung suddenly open and both men jumped as a woman entered. She was of medium height and young, about twenty-four, with dark bobbed hair and wide brown eyes that seemed somehow foreign.

"Evening, boys," she said, with but the faintest trace of an accent.

"Game's up, Viv," said Long Sam tersely.

"What? Where?" suddenly gasped the girl, her face paling.

"Outside. Didn't you see him?"

She ran to the window and peeped cautiously out, then looked over her shoulder, fear in her eyes. The two men watched her narrowly.

"Someone's given us away!"

"That's what I say. But who?"

"Must be either Harrap or Joe. Why, I'll swear it's Joe. He always was a fool and a coward. But what are we going to do now, if they're outside? Why are we waiting?" She ran to Jimmie Rezaire. "Jimmie, tell us what to do."

Long Sam's voice cut into her quick sentences.

"No need to get excited, Vivienne!" he said grimly. "They won't come up just yet." He crossed to the window. "When they begin the round-up, you'll see that fellow opposite move up."

"Jimmie, tell us what to do!" urged Vivienne again, and Sam came back to the table.

"Jimmie will tell us what to do all right," he said. "I know he's cleverer than any of us and therefore he's got a plan of escape somewhere up his sleeve." His eyes rested on the candle and the pile of ashes with a look of comprehension. "All ready to go, eh? Just burning the evidence?" He stared hard at the letter in Rezaire's hand and the other made as if to thrust it in the flame, then, thinking better of it, returned it to the envelope and put it away in his pocket. "Secret?" went on Sam with a nasty little laugh. "Plan of escape, eh?" he added with a flash of intuition.

A sick feeling made itself known in Rezaire's heart as he saw the compelling eyes of Long Sam on him and realized that all his carefully laid plans were being reduced to nothing. He thought of the launch, and the car, of the precious letter in his pocket which he must not let Sam see, and groaned inwardly. What a fool he was not to have gone a few moments sooner.

"Come on, spit it out," said Sam affably. "We haven't any time to lose."

"I haven't any plan," said Rezaire between dry lips, one eye on the door where at any moment now the last of his accomplices might come in, to be followed by the police.

"Think again," almost purred Sam, his hand on the hip where lay the knife. "You with all your brains, who organized and ran this show as well as any show I've seen." Cruelly arrogant, he utterly dominated the other by now. "What's in that paper you didn't dare burn just now for fear I should snatch it? You got us into this show, you must get us away."

"Yes, yes," suddenly broke in the girl. "Jimmie, you and I have worked together for a long while. I know you," she added in a whisper, "as yourself. You must help. Surely you've got a get-away or hiding place somewhere." She stared wildly round the room.

"I—I can't help. Let Sam suggest something."

"Jimmie—Jimmie, you helped me once,"—her voice was soft— "even to your own danger. Oh, I know things are different now—there are other girls and—with me there are other men, but that wasn't so once."

"Why should I help either you or Sam? I've done the hardest part of the job. If it hadn't been for me you'd all have been roped in long ago."

"You collared the largest part of the swag for your trouble," interposed Sam.

There was a pause—a deadlock, it seemed. Rezaire stared at Sam, the man he had used as a tool and now hated because the tool was in reality stronger than the man who handled it. Then he made as if to give way.

"Go a little way downstairs, Sam," he ordered, "and see if they are coming up."

Long Sam half moved, then smiled derisively. "What? While you and Viv slip off? Why, I thought you were clever?" He moved suddenly away from the window where he had been watching the street and striding up to Rezaire hung menacingly over him. "See here," he snarled, "stop this darn fooling. You've got a bolt hole and you're going to take us down it, or you know what I'll do to you. What's in that letter?" he snapped suspiciously again.

His hand shot out but at that moment a step sounded on the stairs and all three jumped, looking at one another. Before they could move further, a little man with a scared face, rather like a white rat, stepped quickly into the room.

"They're here," he said excitedly. "Tried to nab me. Joe was caught this evening and blew the gaff! They're all round now—plain-clothes men and 'flatties' just up the road... They'll be up any minute."

Rezaire ran quickly to the gas. His mind was made up. Whether he had to take the others with him or not, he had to save himself.

"Quick then, follow me," he cried hoarsely and plunged the room in darkness. Already he could hear a knocking on the door downstairs. In the darkness he felt Sam's big hand on his shoulder.

"Just to see where you go," came the menacing whisper.

He pressed the catch of the file cabinet and the front swung open. The knocking below grew louder. He bent down and passed through into the wardrobe of Carlyle's room.

"Shut the door behind you," he whispered back, once more in charge of the situation, "and don't make a noise."

There was a little snap, the sound of the knocking faded away, and the four were in the author's room in the next house, dimly lit by the low turned gas jet.

"Someone's there," gasped Vivienne, suddenly terrified, as the intermittent clicking of the typewriter came out of the gloom. Rezaire only laughed and turning up the light very slightly, pointed to the machine which he switched off.

"I am working here," he said, "as far as they know outside." He spoke shortly to the last corner: "Now come in, Harrap, and shut that door. We're quite safe." Already he seemed to have taken charge of them all; again he was the master by virtue of his superior intellect. Characteristically, once he had found that he was forced to see that they all escaped, he set about it coolly and thoroughly.

"I think we can get out through the back garden," he went on. "There's an alley leading between the houses, and the detectives will be watching the other house."

"Well, I've got a gun and so have you, I suppose, Harrap. I'll back myself to get out of most places."

"Never mind about that," cut in Rezaire sharply. "The less shooting the better, or we'll swing. If we disguise ourselves we may be able to walk out on a bluff." He ran hurriedly to a chest of drawers and began pulling out clothes. "Sam, you take these, pull the cap down over your eyes, and… Go on; you know how to disguise yourself! Harrap, take this lot. Viv, you'd better take off those clothes and get into these breeches and things. Quick now! There's a screen there, if you're shy." For the next few minutes there was silence as the four hurriedly dressed, broken only by exclamations of surprise from Sam and Harrap as they watched the transformation of Robinson into Carlyle.

"Do you mean to tell me," said Sam, a new note of respect in his voice, "that you've been disguised the whole time we knew you and that now, while we're dolled up trying to look like someone else, you've only got to be yourself?"

"That's the way of it," replied Rezaire shortly, slipping an automatic into his pocket, his brain busy with schemes for getting out of the house, which, despite his confidence, he knew would be difficult. There would most certainly be men in the next garden watching the house they had left. Were he alone, he could probably walk out of the front door, even speaking to the policeman, it being his custom always to take the boldest and therefore the most unexpected line of action, but with these three hanging to him like lumps of lead on a float, everything was different.

Vivienne, already dressed and looking like a handsome boy, was nervously playing with the machine fixed on the typewriter switching it on and off. She alone had not expressed surprise at the transformation of James Robinson, for she alone knew the real Jimmie Rezaire. Harrap was looking in admiration at the headless Warwickshire Regiment. Sam was putting the last swift touches to his disguise. The whole affair had taken only a few minutes. Out in the street they could hear shouting and a noise of tramping in the next house.

"So this is how the stuff came in," murmured Harrap. "Gee, you're a wonder. Don't you want to hide this?"

"No, that's all done with now. Let 'em find it if they like. Are we all ready?"

"Now, listen to me," said Long Sam, once more aggressively suspicious. He walked up to Rezaire. "We're in your hands entirely. If you think you're just going to get us out of the house and then push off yourself, you're bloody well mistaken. You've got to see us through."

"Yes, yes," chimed in Harrap eagerly, closing up like a jackal behind Sam.

"That's all right, Sam," said Rezaire hurriedly, the old fear creeping over him. "I'll do my best for you and I haven't been beaten yet. I've got a plan of escape fixed, right away to the continent. If I get through I'll take you with me."

"Tell us where it is," said Harrap, "in case we get separated."

"No," said Rezaire in determined fashion, "I won't."

"But you may get caught and not us?"

"In that case, you'll never know what my plan was. See here," he went on swiftly, perceiving a way of stopping treachery on their part at any rate. "I'm going to insure that you play straight with me." He suddenly pulled the all important letter from his pocket. "This is my plan written down in this letter, and I'm going to keep it. You've got to guard it—and me too."

"Well of all the…" began Sam.

"You'll come on my terms or not at all. This is my plan and if I get caught and can't use it, you won't either. On the other hand, if you're caught, you're not going to have the chance of betraying me."

There was a tense silence in the room. In the next house noise could be faintly heard.

"Well," said Sam at last, who saw that he was in earnest, "I suppose we'll have to. But just you listen to me. As I've said before, if you try to double-cross me I'll cut you up with this knife till your own mother won't know you. You'll only get imprisonment if you're caught by the police, but you'll get worse from me. I know you well enough and I know what you're afraid of."

Instinctively Rezaire shrank away from the vindictive cruelty of the man. Sam had put his finger on his weak spot. Despite his boldness and cunning, he knew himself to be more afraid of death and physical pain than anything else in the world. A slight film came before his eyes and for a moment he felt quite sick. Then Vivienne, hurriedly leaving the typewriter, was at his side. Her warm arm twined into his as it had done often before and a little glow of courage crept back into his heart.

"Leave him alone, Sam, you great bully," she said fearlessly. "Time enough for your mouth if he does double-cross you. I trust him all right, and God knows I've had less reason to than any of you. Jimmie was a great friend of mine."

A sarcastic smile came over Sam's face and he dropped his hand from the knife.

"All right," he said, "but he knows what to expect now."

Jimmie Rezaire shot a grateful look at Viv and she smiled back at him. A tinge of remorse shook him. He had been a brute to her and she had always stuck to him. He had given her nothing and once she had given him everything.

Then a louder noise in the next house startled them all into activity.

"Come on," said Rezaire. "Follow me and take my lead."

Cautiously he opened the door and looked out.

The little passage outside was deserted and slipping out, he turned the light lower and beckoned to them. Silently they followed him step by step down the stairs. Half-way they froze into instant immobility as a man suddenly came out of a door below and went down the hall passage.

"Too risky to go out by the front with all of them in the street. We must try the back," whispered Rezaire over his shoulder and they followed him down into the hall and then along to the end where the stairs led down to the basement. A warm odor of cooking and the sound of Mrs. Gibson's voice floated up to them from the lower regions as they began the descent.

As they reached the bottom Mrs. Gibson's voice stopped in full flood, as though she had heard something. There was a breathless pause and then it resumed, to be answered by another, evidently a friend who had come in to tell her about the happenings outside: "…and there were half a dozen men, policemen and all, standing outside the 'ouse and knocking fit to break the door down, and more of 'em up at the end of the street. It might almost have been a murder, and p'raps it is. 'Oo knows, says I; in this quiet street anythink might 'appen, says I…"

A bar of light from the half open door lay across the passage between them and the friendly darkness of the scullery beyond. Rezaire peered forward till he could see into the kitchen. He could make out a table, a chair, and the latter half of Mrs. Gibson's friend. He took a chance and with one step passed swiftly and silently across the lighted space.

Mrs. Gibson's voice was again speaking as one by one the others followed him to the end where Rezaire knew was the scullery and beyond it a door which led out into the dingy back yard.

"'Oo knows, as you say, Mrs. 'Arris, what 'alf of the people 'ere does with themselves. Why, as I've told you before, there's a gent that's been in my 'ouse five munce and I've 'ardly seen 'im. Author 'e is, and works away all day in 'is room and never lets me in, except when he's there too. Cooks 'is own food, as if mine wasn't good enough," she added bitterly.

"All, there you are, Mrs. Gibson,"—the answering voice was fainter now as they reached the dark scullery at the end—"'e might be committing murders in 'is room every day and you wouldn't know it…"

With the three behind him Rezaire at last entered the scullery and drew a deep breath.

"Now, you wait here," he whispered, "and I'll go out into the back and see if the way is clear."

"Remember what I said," came Long Sam's answer, closely followed by Vivienne's: "Oh, shut up, Sam, and leave him alone. Take charge yourself if you're suspicious; only you know you haven't got the brains for it."

Rezaire touched her hand in gratitude and then began to draw back the bolts as silently as he could.

From years of experience, so skillfully did he work, that the first intimation the others had of the opening of the door was the appearance of a patch of night sky, dun-colored from the reflected glare of the Strand, appearing above the dark silhouette of the houses in the next street behind.

Rezaire stepped out softly into the dirty area of hard packed earth, littered with rubbish, which called itself the back garden and started along in the shadow of the right hand wall. There was only a very faint light from the windows of the houses behind him and he could not see more than a yard or two. At the end of the garden, he knew, was a door which opened into a narrow alley used by dustmen. This he intended to open so as to have everything ready to conduct the retreat of his three partners as noiselessly as possible, for there were bound to be police watchers at the back of the next house.

The bolt, however, was rusty and he had difficulty with it, so that despite his care, it suddenly gave way with a slight bang. At the same instant he heard a sound somewhere on his left. He was not alone in the garden. His brain, keenly on the alert, flashed him the knowledge that this could be none other than one of the police watching the other house. Instantly he took the bold and unexpected course.

"Who's there?" he called out sharply and was glad he had done so for a second later a beam of light from an electric torch flashed on him. His challenge would have carried little conviction, had it been delivered *after* the light's fall on him.

"Who are you?" asked the man behind the lamp, his suspicions already well on the way to being allayed. For surely the other would not have taken the initiative, if he had been a wrong-doer.

"My name's Carlyle," replied Rezaire glibly. "I live in this house. What are you doing here in the garden? Come on, my man," he went on angrily, "I don't know how you got in here, but out you go."

"That's all right, sir," replied the other in an undertone, turning the light on himself for a minute. "I'm a police officer. On a job here watching the next house." Apparently by the sound he got down from a box on which he had been peering over the wall into the blackness of the next garden.

"Oh, what? Burglars?" queried Rezaire, professing great interest. He realized that Long Sam hidden in the scullery must already be suspicious of him for talking to a policeman, and a fear, which the presence of the detective could not inspire, came upon him at the thought of Sam's vindictiveness. But he knew it was the only thing to do. His presence in the garden at that time was not too easily explained and at the moment, in fact, was only resting on the foundation of his bluff.

"No, not exactly," replied the man. "Something more important."

"Can I help? Perhaps they're getting away while we're talking," he suggested artlessly.

The other remounted the box swiftly. "I'll let you know if I want help," he said shortly over his shoulder and Rezaire smiling to himself turned to go into the house.

He had barely gone two paces before he realized that a fresh and startling development was taking place within the house. Mrs. Gibson and her friend, attracted by the voices, had left the kitchen and were coming nervously down the passage to the scullery, Mrs. Gibson holding an oil lamp in her hand. Wildly hoping that Sam and the others would have the sense and ability to hide, he went swiftly to meet them before they reached the door. It was imperative that he should stop the women before they got into the scullery, discovered that it was occupied, and gave the alarm. He just reached the outer door as they reached the inner.

"Oh, good-evening, Mrs. Gibson," he began pleasantly as she halted at the door, surprised at his appearance. "I hope you weren't frightened." From where he was he could see the other three hiding behind the very door at which she stood—in fact the light from her lamp shone through the chink of the door on a rough grey coat which Harrap was wearing. Another pace or two forward or an attempt to push the door further back would result in instant discovery.

"Lor, Mr. Carlyle! Whatever are you doing down here? Was that you in the garden?"

"Yes."

"We thought it might be burglars…"

"Police all over the place," interjected her friend surveying him with a fascinated horror, for had not they just decided that Mr. Carlyle, the mystery man, committed murders all day long in the secrecy of his bedroom?

"Oh, I was just talking to a policeman in the garden. He's after somebody in the next house."

"You don't say! Let's 'ave a look at 'im!" She began to move forward.

"I shouldn't do that. They say there are desperate criminals quite close by." The humor of the situation forced itself upon him so suddenly that he almost laughed. They were certainly closer than Mrs. Gibson thought.

"The man said the best thing we could all do," he continued, "was to go inside and shut the doors, and shout for help if we saw or heard anything unusual."

"Very well, then. I'll shut the scullery door."

In a flash Rezaire turned, as she again moved forward. She was perilously close to the edge of the inner door now and in another few minutes could not fail to see what lay behind it.

"Don't bother!" he said as coolly as possible. "I'll do that." He bent to the bolts.

"Funny I didn't hear you come downstairs," began Mrs. Gibson on a new tack.

"We was sitting in the kitchen with the door open too," commented her friend.

"Oh, I looked out of the window," improvised Rezaire, busy with the bolts, "and saw someone in the garden, so I came down very quietly."

They looked at him again, this time in apparent admiration of his bravery.

"Let's go up, Miss Gibson," at last suggested the friend, "and see if we can see anything. We shall be quite safe up there."

"That's a good idea," said Rezaire, and almost thought he heard a murmur of assent from the three behind the door. "I'll just finish these doors." Mrs. Gibson and Mrs. 'Arris trailed off upstairs with the lamp, chattering volubly.

Sam's hoarse whisper came out of the darkness: "Why the hell didn't you signal us to make a bolt for it through the garden instead of standing chatting to that busy'?"

"Nonsense, Sam," came from Viv. "Jimmie did the only thing possible."

"Damn cute the way he pushed those two old geysers off," added Harrap.

Emboldened by this Rezaire stepped up to Long Sam and said in a fierce whisper: "I've told you before I'm not going to double-cross you..."

"Better not," muttered the other.

"But if you think you could have handled that show better than me, I'll just walk out at the front and leave you to it. I suppose you'd have flourished a gun and tried to run out of a bolted door with two yards' start?"

There was silence and then Rezaire went on: "Now come along. It's obvious we can't get out of the back way because there's a man in the garden on the watch. I've got another plan. Anyway, so far no one knows we're here." He led the way in and silently they followed him.

But they had barely got half-way up the kitchen stairs, before they were all startled by a sudden shriek in Mrs. Gibson's voice.

"Help! Police!" it called, supplemented by Mrs. Harris. "Burglars!"

There was a rushing upstairs and a banging of doors. Rezaire already just in the hall, while the others were still on the staircase behind, met Mrs. Gibson frantically running down.

"I shouted, as you told me to, Mr. Carlyle," she gasped, breathlessly. "There's someone in your room."

"Someone in my room?" stammered Rezaire, taken aback.

"Yes, I can hear him plain," bleated the woman. "He's working that there typewriter of yours!…"

CHAPTER IV

DETECTIVES

The hall bedroom had already ejected its occupant in a great state of excitement. For a moment Rezaire was stupefied by this sudden unexpected turn. He clung to the wall, his brain working busily while Mrs. Harris and Mrs. Gibson again related their tale. A knocking began on the back door and voices were faintly heard shouting from the windows of the next house where in James Robinson's office the police had doubtless already found the birds flown.

Rezaire guessed instantly what had happened to cause the catastrophe. Viv, while playing about with the typewriter, had left the machine running and he had not noticed it when he went out. It had served him well for five months and now it had given him away at the last. He heartily cursed Vivienne. Once get a woman into any business and the first thing she does is to upset it by some foolishness.

Then a plan flashed into his mind, a bold and desperate one. Only a few seconds had elapsed since Mrs. Gibson's first frightened rush downstairs. He must play a game of bluff and play it quickly. Instantly he spoke sharply to the man who lived in the hall bedroom.

"Quick!" he said. "Go up to the landing and see he does not break out this way. I'll go down and let the detectives in at the back. You two women had better get into one of the rooms in case there is shooting."

The man, looking rather scared, demurred for a moment, then went up reluctantly. Rezaire ran down the basement staircase again, whispering to Sam as he passed: "Wait!"

In another moment he was running back once more, this time clattering noisily up the stairs and hoping they would not notice that in reality the detective was still banging at the garden door in answer to Mrs. Gibson's call for help.

"You three are detectives whom I've let in," he explained in a hurried whisper, as he passed them. "Sam, take charge and get us up to the top of the house."

The next minute they all came rushing up as though they had been let in at the back from the garden, Vivienne keeping in the shadow as much as possible so that her figure should not betray her.

The hall was empty, the two women having retired into one of the rooms. They clattered on up to the first floor, Sam leading. Here they found the man from the floor below nervously standing outside Carlyle's door. Another man had come halfway down the next flight and a woman peeped over the banisters of the floor above. From within the room came the undisturbed sound of the typewriter.

Sam was in his element. He had not much originality, but once he had been given a line to go upon he could follow it out well. Flourishing a revolver, he issued swift orders: "You, sir," he began to Rezaire, "come with me. You know the room. You, constable," he went on to Harrap, "go up to the landing above in case he bolts up that way and be prepared to protect the lady."

Harrap turned and ran up to the landing where the woman was. As he passed the man on the stairs the latter called out: "Can I help?"

"Certainly," replied Sam graciously. "Will you and this other gentleman go down, please, to the hall in case they get past us and make…"

"Hadn't we better give you a hand here?" began one of the men. "He might get…"

"Excuse me," interrupted Sam, fixing the man with his eye, "I'm a detective and I'm in charge here…"

The two went downstairs and Long Sam, with a swift upward glance to see that they were no longer observed from above, whispered: "Quick! What's the game? Road's clear to the top of the house."

"There's a skylight and a ladder. We can get out on the roof and down through another house; or else I believe there's a fire escape at the end…"

"Right… Lord! What's that?" A new noise suddenly reverberated through the house. The police, warned by the shouts of their men still vainly trying to get in at the back, had left the next house alone and were now hammering on the front door. They had found that their coup had failed and guessed that their quarry had by some means or another got through.

Sam turned without a word and ran silently up the stairs, giving the word to Harrap as he passed. As they pushed past the woman on the stairs, Rezaire saw a look of surprise and suspicion cross her face; then they were already on the landing above which was in darkness.

While Harrap struck a match to light the gas, Rezaire was already fumbling for the ladder which hung on the wall near the trap-door leading to the roof. Far below in the hall they could hear the two lodgers debating rather fearfully with Mrs. Gibson through a closed door whether they should open the front door to the insistent knocking. That on the back door had stopped, the man having apparently given up. Out of the darkness came Sam's hoarse tones girding at Vivienne: "Lord preserve me from women! You are a blasted fool, Viv, leaving that thing going! It's upset the whole bag of tricks. We'd have been away by now."

"Leave her alone, Sam," panted Rezaire struggling with the ladder as the gas flared up under Harrap's fingers. "We were just as much fools not to notice it was going when we left." A momentary return of the old brief passion his heart had once held for the girl flickered up in him, called into life again by Sam's rebuke. She had once belonged to him—and he had treated her rather badly too; but she had never belonged to Sam, and Sam, therefore, had no right to say anything.

With the help of the other two he had soon placed the ladder up to the trap. Harrap was already at the top and working furiously at the bolts when they heard the rush of men in the hall. The front door had at last been opened and they could hear the men below explaining to the police that there was already a detective upstairs.

"Quick! Quick!" urged Vivienne, wringing her hands in excitement. "They're in! They'll be here in a moment!"

"I'm going as quick as I can," panted Harrap, and gave a final heave. There was a grating wrench as the trap flew open, a glimpse of a patch of sky half-blotted out by Harrap's body scrambling out, and they were all on the ladder. Vivienne followed Harrap, agilely enough in her man's clothing; Sam and Rezaire were at her heels. The moment that Rezaire had rolled clear on to the roof, Sam's hand went to the ladder to unhook it and throw it down, but the other, with quicker moving brain, clutched his arm.

"No, you fool, pull it *up*. They'd pick it up in an instant."

As they pulled the ladder through, they heard the detectives and police, momentarily delayed in the hall, racing up the stairs. The woman on the floor just below, her suspicions finally aroused, was calling to them to come up quickly. As the last rungs of the ladder rattled over the edge of the trap, Rezaire caught a fleeting glimpse of a short man with a square cut moustache on the last steps of the flight. He was shouting something: "Stop!" he called. "I hold a warran—"

Then the trap-door closed down with a bang, shutting out the words, and the four were alone on the dark and dirty roof. They had emerged in the dip between the two roof pitches which ran right and left along the whole length of the row of houses. Broad chimney-stacks stood up out of the slope on either side. They were, as it were, in a trough, bounded by the two steep slopes, each end stretching away into darkness.

They began to run. For a few minutes they stumbled along in a silence broken only by the grating and scraping of their feet on the leads, till they had put several houses between themselves and the two where the police were.

"How are we going to get down?" panted Sam.

"Have to go down through one of the houses, if there isn't a way out at the end," returned Rezaire. "Come along."

They went along as quietly as they could, tripping and stumbling over the upstanding trap-doors in the semi-darkness, the two roofs with their big blocks of chimneys on either side of them.

At last they came to the end of the block of houses. An extension upward of the end wall formed a small parapet about two feet high. Rezaire looked back, but he could see and hear no one as yet on the roof, though without doubt their pursuers would soon be up. A thin fog was creeping up which, with the darkness, made it difficult to see far. Then he gave a low cry of joy as he peered over the parapet, for dipping down the side of the house was a frail iron structure—a fire ladder. It was the fire escape for the whole row of houses. He could see the hazy light from the lamps of the side street glistening on the ironwork. The street too seemed to be empty.

But before he could speak Sam had roughly pushed past and thrown a leg over the wall.

"Come on," he said sharply, "and don't stand gaping."

"Is there anyone at the bottom?" queried Harrap anxiously, but Sam was already on the steps of the ladder, his head on a level with their knees.

"Can't see," he replied, "and anyhow they won't stop me."

Harrap went next; then Vivienne; and lastly Rezaire. The ladder shook and trembled under their progress. Sam, as far as Rezaire could make out, had hurried on almost a flight ahead of them and was now nearly half-way down.

Then suddenly a challenge floated up to them out of the darkness from the garden at the foot of the fire escape.

Sam stopped suddenly, as did the others, shrinking back against the wall. But though their challengers were invisible they themselves must have been clearly outlined from below against the sky.

Again the voice floated up to them. There were men down there and before they could get down others would have been summoned. It was hopeless to think that they could descend into the middle of a group and yet get away. Rezaire whispered that it would be better to retreat, and as silently as possible he and Vivienne began to retrace their steps.

But Sam further down did not or would not hear him. He stayed still, Harrap just behind him. Rezaire, reaching the top once more, saw light glint on the barrel of a revolver and fear came over him, quickening his steps. The second challenge not being answered there was a sudden rush from the garden at the bottom and two or three men began rapidly to ascend the ladder. Sam leveled his gun, wavered, thought better of it, and turning began to flee up the escape once more. As Rezaire tumbled over the parapet with Vivienne, he heaved a sigh of relief and his fear left him. He had thought that Sam would shoot, and then the police would shoot back. The idea of bullets whistling round him, striking him, wounding him, had made him quite faint. Bold and resourceful in a tight corner, he yet feared physical pain more than anything else in the world, which was one of the reasons why Sam so dominated him with his threats of violence.

"Sam's a fool," snapped Vivienne viciously. "He's not as clever as you."

A little glow of what might have been gratitude came over him. Despite the way he had treated her, Viv always had stood up for him. Again he felt the stirring of an emotion that he had once thought dead. Viv in her boy's clothes, her short dark hair gathered up under a cap, looked strangely attractive; and he had once not so very long ago found her very attractive indeed. He had a sudden idea.

"See here, Viv," he whispered hurriedly, before Sam and Harrap reached the roof again. "Nip up and hide behind the chimney-stack. When the 'tecs come up they'll run along the roof after us three and there's a chance that you'll be able to slip down the escape again."

Even as he spoke, he was pushing her up the slope of the roof to where the broad chimney-stack stood up from the tiles, forming a hiding place between it and the continued slope beyond.

"You come too," breathed Vivienne, turning a white face to him in the gloom. Already she had hold of the rough brickwork of the chimney.

"No, no." He ignored her appeal. "It's only a chance for one. You shall share my plan of escape. Remember this: The village of Beaulieu... A quay on the river near a house called 'Joyner's End'... A motor launch waiting there tomorrow night. Don't give me away if you're caught."

"Jimmie, come too. You deserve to get away for helping us."

"No, I'd spoil your chance and mine. I'll join you—with luck."

"Jimmie!" she pleaded.

He shook his head. Then swiftly moved by a sudden impulse he bent down and kissed the white upturned face.

"Good luck!" he muttered, and as Vivienne with a little sob drew herself back into the friendly shadow of the chimneys, he slid down the tiles. The incident had taken barely a few seconds. Sam and Harrap were just getting over the parapet. The next minute the three of them were once more running back between the roofs the way they had come.

Sam was so busy cursing his ill-luck and also his stupidity in not using his gun after all and making a dash for it that he did not observe the girl's absence. Harrap who led a self-indulgent life was just behind, breathing in long tearing gasps, and was far too occupied with his own plight to notice anything else. Rezaire, however, was wondering what they could do next. It seemed to him that they were trapped. In a few minutes the police would be on the roof arriving both from the fire escape and probably up through a trap-door in one of the other houses. They had no hope of concealment in the long straight trough of the roof and if they hid, as Viv had done, behind the chimney-stacks, they would be discovered in a very short time. Also, despite the darkness and the slight fog, there was light enough from night London's sky to see a little distance.

They had gone about twenty or thirty yards before they heard their pursuers' feet behind them.

With a detached portion of his brain Rezaire found himself wondering whether Vivienne would be able to dodge them, and whether she would have the luck to get clear away at the bottom. Then suddenly his whole brain was alert once more. Somewhere ahead of him he heard the creaking of a trap-door and the sound of voices. As he had thought, the detectives were also coming up onto the roof through one of the houses. Their pursuers were now in front of them as well as behind, while on either side rose up the steep slope of the roofs.

In a flash he did the only thing possible. With a hurried word to the others he turned sharp to the left up the roof pulling himself up by the help of one of the chimney-stacks. Sam was just beside him and they both gave a hand to Harrap. In a moment they were all crouched in the dark angle formed by the chimney springing from about halfway up the roof. Behind them the slates sloped up still further to the top, whence the roof descended in a sweep to the back of the house. The sounds of pursuit drew close.

They lay there trying to restrain their gasping breath and thankful that the light was such that the detectives could not have seen them turn aside.

The two parties of their pursuers met just at the stack behind which their quarry lay hid and conferred together in low tones. Rezaire could catch a word here and there, but evidently they were momentarily at a loss to account for the disappearance. Then he heard one of them say something about chimneys, and they separated again going in opposite directions. They had seen that the only possible hiding place was behind the chimneys and they were going to search the whole row thoroughly from end to end, to ensure that their quarry did not slip away.

Rezaire, his face pressed against the rough dirty brickwork of the chimney, peered around the corner. In all there were more than half a dozen and they were going to begin a thorough search of the small space within the two roofs. Lying hid with the other two, he was conscious that, despite his own position, he was glad that Viv at any rate had probably got away. Nevertheless, he did not see how he himself was going to escape—and with every minute his chances seemed to be growing less.

CHAPTER V

ON THE ROOF

"Where's Viv?" asked Sam in a quick whisper, as the detectives moved away to either end.

"Don't know," lied Rezaire, and Harrap added: "She's probably pinched by now."

They lay there in silence wondering what to do next.

Then a new hope came into Rezaire's mind. If by any chance they could again get along to the end unperceived, they might be able to force their way down the fire escape which with luck might now be poorly guarded. But it was obvious they could not get past the police in the trough of the roof without being seen, whereas if they stayed where they were they would soon be discovered. Therefore, their only chance—and a poor one too—was to get along on the crest of the roof. He at once whispered this to the others, who were by now prepared for anything; in fact, they were doubtful whether they would get away at all.

"I'm sick of this eternal chatting and dodging of yours," Sam said. "The next chance I get I'm going to shoot like a man or have a go with my knife and bad luck to anyone who tries to stop me."

"So'm I," added Harrap.

"You're fools," said Rezaire tersely. "If you start shooting the police will start, and if you hit it's probably hanging instead of quod."

"Well, I'm going to get down somehow," retorted Harrap. "I'm not a blasted cat to go crawling all night over the tiles. For the Lord's sake," he added with an undercurrent of fear in his voice, "let's get where we can walk on ground level."

"Oh, shut up and come on!" interposed Rezaire tersely.

Sam was the first up, scrambling with as little noise as possible from the chimney up the last portion of the roof to the summit where he crouched down so as not to be seen against the sky. Their pursuers were still some distance away on either side working from the ends in their search behind the chimney-stacks. Rezaire next pulled himself up behind Sam and together they gave Harrap a hand. All of them were now astride the roof-pitch and the slight fog that had arisen swirled about them, giving a sense of unreality and giddiness. Harrap looking down shivered slightly. On the one side they could barely see into the dip between the roofs, but on the other the projecting dormer windows of the attics which faced the back stood up at intervals in a detached fashion, as if floating in the mist, while between them was the steep outer slope of the roof with a sheer drop into the back gardens.

Rezaire began to work himself along straddle-legged. He dared not let himself think about the drop on his right, down the steep roof past the dormers into the garden, but despite his efforts his imagination conjured up picture after terrible picture. He tried to concentrate on not making a noise. Already he could hear voices and the clattering of heavy boots on the slates as their opponents conducted their search along the roof. Would he be able to escape notice as they went past? They would search behind the chimney-stacks, but would the darkness and fog conceal a figure further up on the ridge of the roof itself with the sky behind? He doubted it but there was just a chance. Anyway there was only one way of finding out—by trial; trial and probable error. Behind him he could hear the occasional faint scrape of Sam's boots, otherwise they were moving soundlessly. Any noise they might make was being drowned in that made by the police as they helped one another up at each successive chimney springing.

They had gone some little distance along when Sam touched his shoulder and nodded.

"Harrap's afraid," he whispered and Rezaire looked back. There, some way behind, almost indistinguishable in the darkness, crouched the little man Harrap, a dim shadow pressed close to the roof. His nerve had gone and he dared not move either way.

"Damned weakling," muttered Sam.

"Go back and give him a hand."

"I'm hanged if I do. He oughtn't to…"

"Well, I will…"

"Look here," whispered Sam fiercely. "You go right on or I'll stick a knife in you. You're going to help me to escape and you can let those other two rip for all I care."

"He's getting down again behind the chimney now. The fool! That's just where they are looking. He'll be caught as sure as anything. Shh…"

The police were coming nearer. They were making a very thorough search. Surely they must see anyone on the top of the roof? Only a cat could have escaped them—unless a man could have got down the steep slope on the outer side of the roof while they passed.

Rezaire straddled on a few cautious yards, Sam just behind him. Then he stopped again and put his lips close to Sam's ear: "They'll see us when they come," he breathed.

"Well, then we'll shoot and run for it."

"They'll shoot us too; there are almost half a dozen of them."

"Can't we get down on the far side of this roof?" Rezaire shuddered. The idea had occurred to him, but it was terrifying, repugnant. He thought of the drop beneath. There was nothing, not even a parapet at the lower edge.

"We must do something quick," muttered Sam; "they're coming."

It was quite true. They could almost now see the dim figures of the Scotland Yard men. They were at the chimney-stack about ten yards away.

"Quick!" whispered Sam again. "Go over and hang by your hands from the top. It's the only chance."

As he spoke he swung himself outward and let himself slip a little way down the further side of the roof till he lay flat against it, his hands gripping the ridge piece at the top. Rezaire took a deep breath and nerved himself to follow his example. In another moment they were hanging there side by side on the steep slope of the slated roof. The noise they made had evidently reached their pursuers' ears, for their voices suddenly ceased. There was silence and then Rezaire heard one of them say: "Could have sworn I heard something."

Then another voice replied: "I suppose there's nowhere else they could have gone?"

"Unless they've gone over the roof and dropped fifty feet into the garden or the road."

The search resumed for a minute or two and then the first voice said: "Shouldn't be surprised if they've got away down one of the trap-doors. I think Harrison's wrong. Doesn't seem to me that they would be such fools as to wait behind these chimneys till we came for them."

Then the noise of their search passed on. Though they had taken but a few minutes, to Rezaire it seemed to be hours that he had hung there in terror, a terror that was inspired not by the police but by the knowledge that only the grip of his fingers prevented him from sliding down the roof and so to that terrible drop to the ground. His shoulders ached, his arms ached, his fingers ached. He pressed himself as close to the roof as he could, hoping that this position would take some of the weight off his arms, but the slates were too smooth to be of much aid. Gradually his fingers became numb and he could hardly feel. He kept getting the impression that his grip was loosening and convulsively tightened it every few seconds. So numb with the strain were his fingers growing that the cold edge of the roof seemed to glow with heat, as if he were clasping a bar of red-hot iron.

Then he was tormented with a new fear. Supposing the police should see his fingers just appearing over the edge of the roof and should creep unsuspected up on the far side and suddenly loosen their grip. He would have no chance; the first he would know about it would be that he would be slithering down the tiles, vainly clutching and grasping… There would be a slight check at the iron gutter and then he would be tumbling through the air. He did not mind the thought of death so much but it was the physical pain that would be bound to accompany such an end. To linger for hours with all his bones broken… He thought almost enviously of Harrap. Though Harrap was certain to be discovered, he at any rate was free from that terror.

The police had at length passed. He could hear Sam's restrained breathing as he moved quietly at his side. The ordeal was over. They could pull themselves up, straddle along the roof to the end, rush the man or men at the fire escape and then perhaps freedom.

He began to pull himself up. It seemed more difficult than he had thought. His arms were numb and aching with the strain they had endured, and he could do nothing to assist himself. He could not dig his toes in; he could not get any hold by drawing his knees up. The pull must come from his arms alone and they were too tired. He suddenly thought his fingers were slipping and gave a desperate jerk,—and to his horror they really did slip. It almost seemed as if the void behind were sucking him down.

"Sam," he muttered quickly. "Give me a hand. I'm going."

"Half a minute," panted Sam, pulling himself up with caution. The strain had been great even for his strong sinews. "In a moment."

But Rezaire felt it would be too late. He could distinctly feel himself slipping now. All the weight of his body was on the muscles of his fingers and they could not hold it. As Sam finally threw one leg over the ridge of the roof, his numbed fingers gave way…

He heard Sam's gasp of horror and then he began to slide downward kicking and struggling, but there was no grip to be had on the slates. Once, by pressing his whole body frantically to the roof he arrested his movement slightly but he had too much momentum to check completely. He felt sick with terror and then suddenly something came up between his legs with a bang and he found himself sprawling astride the pointed gable of one of the dormer windows that projected from the roof. For a moment he could hardly believe his good fortune and clung there not daring to move.

"My God!" floated down Sam's whisper. "That was close."

But Rezaire was feeling too sick to answer. All his courage had been shaken out of him by the accident. He could bluff the police and take the wildest risks in making an escape without turning a hair, but this was different. In one case the stakes were but prison for so many years; in the other they were lingering pain and death.

He stayed there a bit longer while the life crept back into his aching arms, rejoicing at the feeling of something solid between him and the ground. Out of the roof a small dormer, one of a line of similar windows, thrust itself, only a foot or so from the gutter edge, with a small gabled roof at right angles to the main slope and it was astride this, facing inward, that he found himself. He was perfectly safe and hidden from the police on the far side, but—he could not get up again. Above him the main roof sloped up to where Sam crouched, but it was far too steep and slippery to crawl up and without a rope Sam could not help him. Also his pursuers were on the other side and that way lay capture. It seemed he was trapped.

Sam's whisper came to him again.

"You all right?" it queried. "What are you going to do?"

Before he could answer, there came a sudden shout and a sharp challenge somewhere away to his left, followed by the sound of feet on the leads.

"That's Harrap for certain," called down Sam in low tones. Then a moment later: "The damn fool's running this way. They'll see me."

"Come down here."

"How'll I get up?"

"Don't know. You'll be caught if you don't."

The sound of feet approached. A voice shouted urgently to one "Lacey" to look out.

Sam swiftly made his mind up, swung himself over, and judging his position, let himself slide. Both feet, however, went to one side of the gable and he only saved himself from plunging onward by throwing his arms across the ridge. As he helped him to safety, Rezaire marveled at the coolness and courage of the man. Not for a thousand pounds would he have taken that risk of his own free will, but Sam had not seemed to give it a thought.

Together they sat astride the small dormer roof and listened to the sounds of pursuit and the shouts in the central dip between the pitches.

Then suddenly clear and sharp came the crack of an automatic and the sound of a cry. The running stopped for an instant and a whistle blew.

"The fool!" muttered Rezaire. "They'll shoot now."

As if in answer came two more reports and quite close it seemed to them a man's cautious "Aim low, boys!"

"Gee! Harrap's going to make a Sydney Street business of it," muttered Sam excitedly, but Rezaire only repeated: "The fool!"

From where they were they could hear the fight, though with the whole roof between them they could see nothing.

After the two shots there was silence for a space.

"Harrap's hiding somewhere and they're stalking him," was Sam's comment.

Then came a sudden shout and four more shots in rapid succession. One bullet hit something on the top of the roof; they heard the hum of it above their heads and a little chip of tile struck Rezaire on the arm. They heard a faint groaning somewhere above.

Then within a few seconds there came a quick rush of feet further over on the right, another shot, a muffled cry, and a metallic clatter. Then a hum of voices.

"They've got him," said Sam. "He hadn't much of a chance up there."

"He'll be lucky if he gets off hanging," added Rezaire.

"What are we going to do anyway? We can't sit here forever and we can't get up again."

"I've got an idea," whispered back Rezaire. "While that show was going on I looked over the edge here. This attic window, the roof of which we're on, is open. We can get into this house."

"Anyone in the room?"

"I don't know. We must take our chance. I don't think so, unless he's still asleep; if he'd been wakened by the noise he'd have had his head out of the window before now."

"I suppose it's the only thing to do. We might get through quietly and out at the back."

Sam began to let himself down the side of the gable while Rezaire watched him. The old fear was creeping over him again. But watching Sam do it seemed so easy. He just let himself cautiously down still holding the side of the attic window till his feet rested on the gutter at the edge of the roof. Then having tested the strength of the gutter he shifted his grip round to the front of the window which, as Rezaire had observed, was open, till he was at length kneeling on the sill.

Helped by Sam, Rezaire accomplished the journey with comparative ease, and in another moment they were in the absolute darkness of the room. As soon as they had entered, they instinctively drew away from the window that they might not show up against the light and waited in perfect silence, though Rezaire was fairly certain the room was empty. Anyone who had been in it, even if asleep, could not have failed to have been wakened by the noise of their entry and their climbing about on the roof.

Not a sound could be heard, not even the regular breathing of a sleeping being. By good luck they had struck an empty room.

At last Rezaire made a slight move in the direction of the door. He had not taken a pace before a girl's voice cried: "Hands up!" and a ray of light from a torch leaped into their eyes, momentarily blinding them. Just within the circle of light there appeared the barrel of a revolver.

CHAPTER VI

NIGHT OPERATIONS

They both stayed absolutely still for the space of a few seconds. The whole thing was so utterly unexpected. To creep into an empty room and find it occupied by a girl with a revolver. Rezaire realized that she must have heard them for some time and that the reason for his thinking the room was unoccupied was that she had been sitting there in the dark waiting for them.

The light and the revolver still pointed steadily at them. Then suddenly Sam laughed.

"Well done, Miss," he said, "but you've got the wrong people. May we have some light?"

With the utmost coolness he struck a match and, quite unconscious of the revolver which followed his movements, walked to a gas bracket and lighted it.

As the flame lit up the room, Rezaire gave a sigh of relief. Their adversary was only a girl of about nineteen or twenty who was sitting up in bed—torch in one hand and pistol—of an old-fashioned make—in the other.

He noted the steadiness with which she held them, but his practiced glance saw instantly that her wrists were resting on her knees as if to prevent any wavering. Her eyes he could not see properly because of the torch, but he suddenly felt certain that she was afraid.

"Put your hands up," suddenly said the girl again, as Sam finished lighting the gas, "or I'll fire."

"Don't fire at us," replied Sam, still with that easy tolerance. "We're not burglars. In fact, we're after them instead." Rezaire could see that he was going on the same line as he himself had suggested earlier when they were in Mrs. Gibson's house, that of pretending to be detectives. "Now tell me," went on Sam, "have you seen or heard anything in this room during the last hour?"

"No, I haven't," the girl answered, but the revolver still pointed at Sam's chest.

"Do put that gun down, please," began Rezaire, now taking a hand in the game. He could see that it was imperative that they got through into the house as soon as possible and that this girl was not frightened into giving the alarm. "You're a plucky little girl," he went on with a smile, "but I wish you had held up the fellows we're after."

"I don't believe you are detectives."

"Good Lord!" Rezaire laughed. "Sam, have you got your papers on you?... No? Look here, young lady, I'm sorry, but we haven't any time to waste proving to you that we come from Scotland Yard. We're after a couple of men who, we believe, got in by this window and through the room while you were asleep."

He moved round toward the door. He and Sam were now standing on opposite sides of the bed in which the girl sat. He could see the white of her knuckles as she gripped the torch and knew now without doubt that she was desperately afraid.

She seemed to be making her mind up. He gave her a few seconds that the reasonableness of his statement might sink in.

Suddenly she spoke again: "Are you really detectives?"

Rezaire nodded.

"And you want to go after the burglars?"

"Yes."

"Well, the door's locked."

"Then unlock it, please, and let's get on. The men will have got away by now."

Still holding the revolver, the girl got lightly out of bed, and took a key from a table at the bedside. Inserting it in the lock she turned it; then with a sudden dramatic movement flung it out of the window.

For a moment Rezaire stared uncomprehending, then took a quick step to the door and tried it. It was locked.

"You young fool," he began angrily. "What have you done?"

"There!" she said breathlessly with a sort of frightened triumph: "I knew you weren't detectives. I could hear you for a long time just outside my window. If you had really been after someone you'd have come in at once. Besides, when I said the door was locked, neither of you asked how the men you pretended you were chasing had got through. Now you're caught here while I give the alarm."

But she had in her momentary triumph at outwitting the two men forgotten about Sam who, standing at one side, had been imperceptibly edging behind her. Now he flung himself suddenly across the bed and as the girl opened her mouth to scream, his big hand closed over it.

There was a muffled gurgle and the girl reeled backward under his grip. Almost at the same moment Rezaire had wrested the revolver from her grasp. It was of a very old pattern, more of a trophy than a weapon. He gave a snort of disgust as he snapped it open and found it unloaded.

"Damned young fool!" snarled Sam. "Be quiet, will you!" He shook her in his grasp as a terrier shakes a rat.

"We can't break open the door," said Rezaire swiftly. "We'll have all the house on us. What are we to do?"

"Don't know," said Sam shortly. "We must stop this girl giving tongue anyway." He tore off the pillow slip and stuffed as much of it as he could into her mouth, binding it round her head with a scarf that was lying on a chair. "We'll have to go back through the window and get into another house, I suppose."

"But," interjected Rezaire, "surely…that's impossible. Isn't there anything else we can do?"

But Sam did not answer. Having gagged the girl, he now proceeded to tie her up with handkerchiefs, and other articles of clothing he took from the drawers, till she lay, helpless, on the bed.

"Otherwise she'll start to scream," he explained, "or make a noise of some sort the moment we're gone. Now, come along."

As in a dream Rezaire obeyed. He had not yet gotten over his fall down the roof and the thought of having to venture out there again brought back the same sick feeling of hopeless terror that he had experienced then. "I don't think—" he began, and realized the hopelessness of his position.

Sam had turned the gas out and was already half out of the window. Rezaire followed him.

"You'll have to help me, Sam," he whispered.

"Just do as I do. Get out backward and stand in the gutter, leaning forward and supporting yourself as well on the slates with your hands. Then work along crab fashion."

Fearfully Rezaire obeyed him. The slight fog had drifted away and he could see right up the roof ahead of him to the ridge whence he had clung and then fallen. He stayed there motionless for a moment, feeling quite giddy with the fear that he might fall again, when there would be nothing to save him. He dared not look down between his legs. His heels projected over space. At his side Sam began to shuffle slowly along. He could hear the soft padding of his hands on the tiles and the scrape of his feet on the gutter which, old and rusted, bent perilously under the movement. But though the gutter, the only thing between them and the garden forty feet below, twisted and creaked, it did not break. The minutes seemed like hours, but at last they found themselves crouched at the side of the next attic window which was shut.

"We'll have to go on," whispered Sam. "I don't think we can get in."

"No, no, I can't," returned Rezaire, who had by now quite lost his nerve.

As if in support of his appeal they heard voices somewhere in between the two roofs and saw a head appear for a moment to the left silhouetted against the sky. They kept very still, and the head disappeared. But it was evident the police were still on the roof and were now doing what they might have done a short while before with more success—climbing up at intervals to look down the far slope of the roofs. And at that moment Rezaire's fingers on the window-panes stuck into something soft and clinging. It was a mass of cobwebs.

He at once whispered excitedly to Sam: "Sam, I believe this house is empty. I know there is an empty one in the street. We can force the window. There'll be no one inside. Quick!"

The moment Sam had grasped the significance of the statement, he took out his long thin knife and in a moment he carefully pressed back the hasp. The window creaked open. But even as they crawled in, Rezaire heard the scraping of feet on the roof and saw the head again peering over the crest of the roof, this time much nearer. He fell hurriedly into the room in a heap, not knowing whether he had been seen or not.

Inside was pitch blackness and the stale musty smell of a room that has not been lived in for a long tune. He could hear Sam moving somewhere to his right, though their feet trod light on the thick carpet of dust. He felt in his pockets for a match, but at that moment there was a little scrape and a glow appeared in Sam's shielding hands. It showed them a bare unfurnished attic, similar to the one they had left, with a door at the far side. Then the match went out, followed by Sam's whisper: "Can't see much, even with a light."

"Best move in the dark," suggested Rezaire. "We'll give the game away if we show lights in an empty house."

"Do you think they're after us?"

"Don't know." He told Sam about the head he had seen. "They may have seen us from the roof and passed the word down below."

They made their way over to the door and softly turning the handle, opened it. The thick dead silence of a house that has been empty for months met them. It seemed eerie, almost uncanny. There was no tick of a clock or creak of furniture, nothing but the dead silence. After a moment Rezaire stepped out onto the landing and with Sam close behind him began to search for the banisters of the staircase.

They reached the second floor without mishap. Then Sam muttered: "I wish we'd gotten a torch."

"Doesn't matter," answered Rezaire. "We can find our way down all right. Much better not to show a light."

"No, I was thinking that the bobbies have torches and if they get in here after us…"

Rezaire stopped suddenly. "What makes you think they could get in here? Have you heard anything?"

"Nothing," replied Sam, rather nervously, it seemed for him; "but I just thought they might have an idea. I don't feel comfortable about it."

"Oh, come on," returned Rezaire, and, feeling his way, set off down once more. But Sam's nervousness seemed to have communicated itself to him. He was not afraid, and yet there was something fear-inspiring about the dead empty house—without light or sound. Supposing Sam was right and the police were after them even here? They were at a great disadvantage without torches. He wondered again whether they had not been seen getting in and whether the police were not even now waiting for them downstairs.

They finished the last flight of stairs to the ground floor. The hall was not so dark as the rest of the house, being vaguely lit from outside by a fan light through which the rays of a street lamp fell in a patch high up on the wall, but this only seemed to intensify the darkness of the rest. Suddenly Rezaire clutched Sam's arm. He could have sworn he heard a sound. Both stayed immovable for several seconds, hearing nothing save the hum of the darkness in their ears. Then it came again—a distinct noise, which might have been anything from a child's voice outside to the opening of a window at the back. Next he heard a rustle and a chink at his side and realized that the noise had reached Sam too, for Sam had drawn his knife or revolver. Rezaire felt a quick resentment against Sam. Using a weapon would probably not help them very much to get away and would only result in the detectives using their revolvers, and a longer term of imprisonment—or worse, if they were caught.

Very cautiously, with every sense alert, he moved from the foot of the staircase to the wall. The darkness pressed in on him; almost it seemed that it had to be pushed aside.

At last he got his hand against the wall and stayed there facing in the direction from which the sound had come—somewhere at the back of the hall. For a brief instant he heard it again. This tune it was a faint low noise—something like the purring of a cat, a noise he could not place by any means. The darkness hemmed him in all round. He did not know where Sam was, but was certain that he too was on the alert.

It seemed an hour that he waited. The silence that had been so dead before now seemed to be alive, creepingly, malignantly alive. He had the feeling that he was surrounded by people who could see him and whom he could not see. The tension of waiting and watching was beginning to tell upon him, and he began to get jumpy. At any moment he began to expect the flash of a torch in his eyes. At last he decided that his imagination was beginning to run away with him and softly began to move forward once more. He had gone but three paces when his left hand, which was keeping touch with the wall, encountered a door—that of a back room. At the same moment he heard the mysterious sound again—a low rasping purring sound. It seemed all around him; he could not tell where it was. The sweat was beading on his face now and in his desperation he clutched the butt of the revolver which he had put in his pocket as a last resource.

Suddenly, definitely, something touched him on the leg, and was gone again. His heart gave a wild leap and then paused for several seconds, while the blood ran slowly back. His forehead was wet, his lips were dry with fear. With an effort he collected himself and flung out his arm, snatching wildly all round him. He hit a doorpost, but nothing else. At the same instant the thing touched him again on the leg, accompanied by the same noise... He made a quick grasp at his ankles and it dawned on him what it was...

It was only a cat. In his overwhelming relief, unthinking, he gave a little half laugh out loud. It hardly seemed like his own voice, and the sound echoed eerily in the emptiness, followed by a low frightened exclamation from Sam somewhere behind.

He bent down and stroked the animal, purring and rubbing itself against him. He smiled to himself as he thought what a fright it had given him.

Then he stiffened again into immobility as a new thought struck him. The house was empty and untenanted; what was a cat doing there? It was well fed and not frightened or hungry. It must have got in somehow and surely recently, since empty houses are not left open. Of course, it might have got in by the attic window after he and Sam had done so—or it might, he considered slowly, have got in at some other window—after others had got in. The police might even now be in the lower part of the house—waiting. The cat which had frightened him so much at first now appeared to him to be a warning. He stole forward a few paces till he came to what, as far as he could feel, seemed to be the top of the kitchen stairs where he paused to listen again. Vague indeterminate sounds came up to him that might have been real noises or might have been imagination. The cat purred round his feet at intervals, just when he was trying to listen.

He waited several minutes. He had to get down because that was the only way out—through the back garden. The street and the front door would be watched, the other windows were too far off the ground. He wondered whether Sam was following. He had heard nothing of him since that exclamation at his laugh.

He set a foot on the first step. As he did so, he could have sworn he saw right down at the bottom a faint reflected glow, as of a torch somewhere round the corner and shrouded by the hand. He stopped where he was and a board creaked under him at the change of weight. The glow disappeared—and the moment it had gone he could not have told whether he had imagined it or not.

Then his attention was again arrested by a sound. This time without doubt it was a sound of human agency. It was not the cat and it was not his imagination. He knew now that there were men in the house at the bottom of those stairs, men too who also knew that he was somewhere in the house and were watching for him. He stood still, listening further. Once the certainty had come to his mind, his fear left him. He was back at his old game again—his wits against theirs, and despite the odds, he was backing his own. But he had a handicap in Sam. Had it not been for Sam he would have long ago walked out in safety as Mr. Carlyle, and would have been calmly sleeping the sleep of the just at some hotel preparatory to driving down to Beaulieu in his car the next day. Now, thanks to Sam, it was nearly ten o'clock and he was only a short distance from where he started and with the police on his trail. He wondered whether he could not give Sam the slip, and then he thought of Sam's vindictive words—of Sam's thin cruel knife. He knew Sam would have no mercy on him. He thought again of Sam's knife. He would rather give himself up and take his imprisonment than find himself at Sam's mercy, having betrayed him.

Of course, the thought slipped into his mind for the first time, he might betray Sam and get away, but if he did so he would have to be absolutely certain that Sam would be definitely caught by the police. If Sam got away after that, he would not rest till he had revenged himself. He thought, a third time, of Sam's knife and shuddered…

Then he stiffened to attention. His thoughts had wandered. A sense of danger descended on him. There was movement in the darkness below him. Without knowing how, he became aware that the police had left the floor below and were on the stairs. They were beginning to advance— he could almost hear restrained breathing—and in another minute they would meet. He must get back, and must get back in absolute silence, or the torch would flash out. He had no torch and would be helpless. The torches were the key to the situation. If only he could get possession of them or destroy them…

Cautiously he began again to back up the stairs, setting his feet down silently in the dust. He fervently hoped that Sam had not been following him up, to collide with him or speak to him at the top of the stairs.

He reached the top and backed round behind a thin wooden panel that cut off the kitchen stairs from the hall. There was a small lavatory at the end of the hall, and the door of this stood open, so that the window showed up a faint oblong of dark sky a little lighter than the surrounding blackness. By crouching down he could get the doorway to the kitchen stairs between himself and this window, so that anyone coming up would pass across the square of light. He took his revolver out of his pocket, holding it club fashion by the barrel and waited. He had a plan—desperate enough, it was true—but he had to do something. His position was indeed hopeless, as long as his opponents had the only torches.

On the other side of the panel he could now distinctly hear the guarded breathing of the first man. Soon he would leave the last step and be in the hall a foot or so away—and between Rezaire and the lavatory window.

He crouched there in absolute silence, his eyes glued to the oblong of night sky.

Slowly it began to darken; something was crossing it. He made out the vague profile of a face with a moustache, and below it the outline of a hand holding a torch, ready to switch on. The other hand he knew—after the interchange of shots with Harrap on the roof—would be holding a revolver.

He took silent aim, and then struck out with his revolver butt. There was a sudden sharp cry, a crash, and a tinkle of broken glass as the torch fell. Almost at the same instant a shot went off, as if a startled finger had pressed too heavily on the trigger. The shadow had drawn back and was no longer between him and the window. A voice cried out: "Come on! Hands up! You haven't got a chance." Another torch went on on the kitchen stairs, but Rezaire stayed still on the ground, and the light, cut off by the panel against which he crouched, did not reach the hall. He heard a hoarse whisper—"Put it out, you fool!" and the light went off again.

Silence descended. He knew his opponents were on the stairs, debating what they should do. They did not care, without preparation, to rush the hall with the top of the stairs held by, as far as they knew, three armed and desperate men. Rezaire crouched there waiting. He could hear nothing of Sam and wondered again where he was. The tense expectant silence lay heavy upon the house once more.

CHAPTER VII

HIDE AND SEEK

As Rezaire crouched there, he swiftly began to form some plan of action. As usual, he attacked the problem from his opponents' point of view, by trying to guess what they would expect him to do next, and then doing the opposite. He now believed that after a moment they would rush the stairs, with their torches held in front of them from the moment they started, so that they would have the full advantage of the light. They would do this thinking he was still at the top of the stairs to catch them against the window. Against this attack he would not have much chance, unless, as just now, he were to be near enough at hand when the torch was actually switched on to knock it out. But by this time they had guessed that he was crouched at the top of the stairs.

All this reasoning took but a few seconds, for to put himself in his opponents' place was by now almost an instinct with him. Pausing only to grope for the dropped torch which he put in his pocket, he retreated as silently as possible to the doorway he had felt previously. This, he surmised, led into a room off the hall facing the back of the house, and he proposed to hide there and, if possible, get past the police when, as he calculated they were sure to do, they made a rush along the hall from the kitchen stairs.

As he felt his way into the open doorway, he wondered again where Sam was and wished he knew. He wanted very strongly to impress on Sam the fact that he was not to shoot. Though he was involved in the game as well as Sam, he did not want the stakes higher than they were already.

He waited but a minute before the anticipated rush came. In the brief second between his hearing the preparatory noise and seeing the bright gleam of a torch, he felt a quick pride in the fact that he had foreseen so accurately.

The police rushed up the last stairs and along the passage—the beam of light before them. Rezaire, just behind the door, gripped his revolver tightly. He hoped to be able to repeat his trick from the back room and then get past in the darkness and confusion. The whole scene momentarily impressed itself on his mind in the reflected light—the dirty house, bare walls with marks of vanished pictures, the banisters showing up white against the shadow behind—and peeping through them, right up at the top, Sam's face, with leveled revolver.

He had barely time to take in the significance of this last when there was a sudden report, a cry, and the place was once again plunged in darkness. Something that must have been the torch smashed against the doorway in which Rezaire was standing. Sam had fired at the light.

Rezaire, strung up to tense excitement, could have cried out aloud. Despite his relief at the fact that the rush had been stopped, the very thing he had dreaded had come to pass. Sam had fallen back on his gun. Now the police would shoot without hesitation.

The next moment the air seemed full of bullets. Sam had fired again in the darkness and they were firing back at him. Evidently they had only had the two torches as no other light appeared. Rezaire, thoroughly frightened, drew well back into the room and crouched behind the door. His first thought was to get away; and the next moment he decided quite definitely that he must part with Sam despite the other's threats of what he would do if he were "double-crossed." But he dared not do it unless he could be certain that Sam were not in a position to take revenge.

The firing stopped. An idea struck him and he crawled over to the window and raising himself peered out. But as far as he could make out he could not get out that way; there was too big a drop into an area beneath. He would have to get down into the basement. He turned away, and as he did so, there was a hum past his head and a crash behind him. Someone creeping into the room had fired at his silhouette before the window. He dropped to the ground quaking with fear and crawled silently to a corner. A momentary panic descended on him. There was someone else in the darkness of the room with him—someone who had fired. Outside there was silence; inside there was even deeper silence, the stillness that reigns when two men are close to one another in the dark seeking to kill.

Suddenly there came a breaking sound and a crash outside in the hall, as of a heavy body falling from a height. Vaguely Rezaire wondered whether Sam had fallen through the banisters or had jumped, but his thoughts were mainly concentrated on the enemy in the room with him. A single shot followed the crash, and then another unaccountable watchful silence. He thanked Heaven that the police appeared to have no more torches, or he would have been completely cornered, and then suddenly he remembered the torch he had picked up himself. He had a light and they had not. He might turn that fact to advantage.

He drew it quickly from his pocket and held it in his left hand. He could feel that he was shaking badly. This was not the sort of work he was accustomed to. The pitting of wits and words and nimble brain against those of others, was what he excelled in—not this, what Sam had called "Sydney Street business." He pulled himself together and ran over in his mind what he was going to do. Present the torch and the revolver in the direction in which he believed his foe was; switch on the torch, shouting "Hands up!" fire, if necessary, at his opponent's leg or revolver arm; then make a rush for it. Of course he would have to be prepared to shoot once or twice; for at the moment he was badly cornered. He gripped the torch more firmly and nerved himself to what he was going to do.

A very slight noise came from the opposite corner of the room, giving him an idea of his enemy's whereabouts. Slowly and quietly he leveled the torch and the revolver and took a deep breath. At the last moment he remembered to hold the torch away from him at arm's length in case the other should fire at the light.

Then he pressed the switch.

"Hands up!" he called in a voice that woke the tense silence of the house.

But no beam of light leaped from the torch as he touched the switch. It had of course been broken in its fall and like a fool he had not thought. Before hardly his mind could realize that he had given his position away, he saw a quick stab of flame on the darkness opposite and something hit the wall with a crack just by his ear. His opponent had fired at the sound of his voice and had nearly got him too.

Whether it was fear or excitement or whether he intentionally pressed the trigger he could not be certain, but close on the heels of the first came that of his own revolver, and almost immediately after that another answer came from his opponent. Rezaire crouched down, fear-stricken, in his corner. He could not compete with this at all. It was not his game—this firing in the dark at the sound or sight of an enemy. These men had been brought up to it—to deal with desperate criminals; but he was not a desperate criminal. Sam, he felt almost sure, playing the same game of cat and mouse outside, was enjoying it.

An overwhelming desire came to him to get out of this room where death was watching for him and right out of the house. He thought longingly for a moment of his car in the Jermyn Street Garage and of his launch waiting for him at Beaulieu. Why could he not just get up and walk out? It all suddenly seemed to him to be like some monstrous dream. Barely two hours ago he was just Mr. Carlyle, the author, without a care in the world and without a policeman on his track, yet with every-thing ready and planned to the last item in case he should have to take to flight, owing to his activities as James Robinson. Now he was hemmed in in a dark house with police all round him ready to fire at his slightest movement, and a probable murderer for companion.

At length he collected his courage and began to crawl as quietly as he could to the door on his hands and knees, making each move with infinite caution. After what seemed like several hours he at length reached the doorway and put his head round into the hall. Here too he experienced that same feeling of tenseness all about him, of men strung up to the highest pitch—listening. He could hear a very vague movement along the hall in the direction of the front door and something that might have been restrained breathing somewhere close at hand. From outside in the street came a confused murmur; probably that of a crowd attracted by the chase over the roofs and the shooting.

In the hall there had now been silence for some time. The police did not like to fire because they did not want to hit one of their own men, while Sam with so many against him would probably not fire unless he was certain. The whole tense silence was leading up, he felt, to some climax.

Rezaire wondered where Sam was. From the noise he had heard some time previously he guessed that he was no longer on the staircase.

With infinite caution he crawled slowly round the doorpost and out into the hall in the direction of the back stairs, keeping as close to the wall as possible. His whole mind was concentrated on silence. Every breath, every step he took was a business in itself. With slow cautious movement, each hand went in front like a feeler before he definitely put it down.

He worked his way about six feet along and then his gently-groping hand just brushed something. His heart almost stopped beating and he drew his hand back as if it had been stung, crouching into himself and expecting any moment to hear the report of a pistol in his ears. But nothing happened. Imperceptibly almost, so slowly did he move, he advanced his hand, till the very tips of his fingers just touched the obstacle again. It did not move. Like a breath of air his fingers wandered over it and recoiled once more as he realized what it was. It was part of a man's clothes—some tweed material. But still it had not moved, and emboldened he touched it again. It was a man's leg, and instead of being upright it was lying along the ground.

A fresh shock came to him as, after a minute, he realized that it was indeed a man, lying motionless on the floor. It was a body. Not Sam, for he knew the clothes Sam was wearing, so it must be one of the detectives or police. Sam had hit someone then, and the man was either dead or unconscious. Again the horror of Sam, the desire to be rid of him, came over him, swamping for a moment his memory of Sam's threats.

He crawled slowly over the inert body. He was now approaching the end of the hall and crossed over to the side from which the kitchen stairs started.

The same silence still hung about the whole place. The detectives, it seemed, knew Sam could not escape and that they only had to wait till he gave himself away by attempting to get past them. In the meantime they had probably sent out for more men and torches.

He came at last without hindrance to his original position, where he had first knocked the torch from the man's hand and here he waited for some time, trying to see by means of the lavatory window whether there was anyone there. The police, however, experienced in this sort of work, had pulled the door to, so that the light was cut off, and he could see nothing. But he was certain that one man at least was guarding the head of the stairs and he set himself hurriedly to devise a means of getting him out of the way.

About thirty seconds only had elapsed when suddenly he found himself in the midst of a hand-to-hand struggle. He could only vaguely tell how it had all happened. Someone advancing swiftly and silently from behind had collided with him and the next moment they were struggling together on the floor. He heard a voice call out somewhere down the hall. His opponent struck viciously at his head with some weapon, missed and hit him heavily on the shoulder. He heard the man grunt as he drew his arm back for another stroke and recognized the grunt. It was Sam's voice. He was fighting with Sam.

"Sam," he whispered despairingly in the other's ear, overcome with terror lest Sam in his desperation should kill him. The grip relaxed for an instant, but the next moment another man had blundered into them, and the three of them were fighting together once more. The tense silence was all shattered. The climax had come.

They rolled this way and that, fell heavily against another man coming up somewhere in the darkness and then, locked in each other's arms, crashed against the partition that divided the hall from the kitchen stairs.

There was a rending of wood; an instant while they poised on the edge, during which Rezaire clung desperately to the man he was fighting with; and then they had crashed through the partition and fallen direct to half-way down the stairs whence they bumped heavily to the bottom.

For a moment Rezaire lay half unconscious from a blow on the back of the head. Dimly he realized that someone at his side was groaning. A revolver had gone off at some point during the fall, and the echo of it was still in his ears.

Then a hand seized him by the collar and he struck out feebly. A voice hissed in his ear: "Be quiet, you fool!"

He realized it was Sam and scrambled dizzily to his feet. Someone else was coming quickly down the stairs. A man was getting to his feet close by him, and he stepped clear just in time. Guided by Sam's hand he rounded the corner at the bottom of the stairs and was in the passage that, as in the other house, presumably led to a scullery and a back door.

They went several paces along, then suddenly drew into the side. The door was open into the back yard and silhouetted against it they could see another figure advancing toward them from outside.

"Let him pass," whispered Rezaire as he felt Sam let go his arm and thought he was going to shoot, and they drew back against the opposite wall. At the same moment he had an idea, and pulling the useless torch once more from his pocket pitched it lightly down the passage away from the back door. It fell with a clatter at the far end just as though someone up at that end had stumbled.

Instantly the detective ran forward, passing so close that he almost touched their bodies pressed against the wall. Another man too made a rush from the stairs and apparently fell over the body of the one that lay unconscious at the bottom.

The next moment Sam and Rezaire had stepped out noiselessly into the scullery. The way was clear to the back garden and safety amid the crowds of London; and they had a definite start, for none had heard them go.

As they reached the outer door, Rezaire tripped slightly. The next moment a piercing wail, as of some disembodied spirit, echoed eerily through the empty house.

CHAPTER VIII

VIEW HALLOA

The wail died away into silence. There followed for a moment the stillness of complete surprise. Then Rezaire plucked at the astonished Sam's sleeve.

"Come along quickly. It's only the cat."

Sam cursed under his breath, as they ran out into the garden.

But the unfortunate accident had given away their escape sooner than would otherwise have happened. The men in the house, warned by the sound, almost immediately began to run after them to the door.

Sam and Rezaire dashed quickly into the shadow of the wall, and made for the end of the garden. Despite that piece of ill-fortune Rezaire began once again to congratulate himself on his luck. When the police had entered the house they had apparently only left one man on guard outside, never thinking that their quarry would get past. Yet that man had been drawn into the house too, and was now behind them. Rezaire felt inclined to shout aloud with joy as they ran noiselessly along on the soft soil. After all the narrow escapes they had had, the fact that there was now nothing actually between them and the open spaces of London seemed almost like freedom. But there were half a dozen pursuers not a score of paces behind—and they were armed. His new found sense of freedom vanished like mist as he remembered this latter. After all, matters were now on a different footing. Before, the police would not have fired, but now they would fire on sight. For both Harrap and Sam had fired on them and had hit. He was now quite decided in his mind to get away from Sam at the first opportunity—provided he could be certain Sam would not be free to follow him. Sam had shot one, if not more, of his pursuers, and thus had gone very near to putting the rope round both their necks.

He found himself climbing the wall at the end of the garden. The detectives, by the sound, were at the door they had left. Looking back he saw lights in the windows of all the near-by houses and excited heads craning forth. The chase over the roofs and the shooting had aroused the neighborhood.

He jumped down the other side and discovered that he was in the garden of the house opposite. The alley way which ran at the back of Mrs. Gibson's garden did not reach as far as this. Then he heard a sudden cry from Sam, still on the top of the wall, and saw him strike out with his fist at someone on the other side. One of their pursuers, quicker than the rest, had caught them up and got hold of Sam's foot. For a moment Rezaire felt a strong impulse to run on himself and leave Sam to his fate. This was his opportunity. Then fear of Sam overcame the impulse. If he were to betray Sam like that—and he had now decided that he must—he must be certain that Sam was definitely caught, and would not be free to take his vengeance. No, the time had not yet come. He turned back a pace and catching hold of Sam's arms, pulled with all his force, Sam also kicking out with his feet. There was a muffled exclamation from the other side and Sam almost fell on top of him. They picked themselves up, Rezaire thankful that Sam had not used his revolver again, although it was too late now.

Turning sharp to the right, Rezaire led the way over the wall into the next garden, and so into the next. His plan was to work back toward Mrs. Gibson's house till he came to the alley he knew of which led out into an unfrequented back street. The detectives were shouting somewhere behind, but owing to the darkness, it was difficult to pursue by sight, and they had to go by the unavoidable noise he made in getting over the garden walls.

He came to the next wall and then an idea struck him. Instead of getting down into the garden on the far side, he continued on the top running along the flat bricks with Sam behind him. Doing this he could make much more distance, could go more quietly, and avoided the necessity of scaling a wall every twenty yards. Suddenly a shot rang out and a bullet whistled past his ear. The police had caught sight of him against the sky and had fired. At the same time, owing to the shock, or misjudgment, he caught his foot in a strand of tough ivy and fell right off the wall.

For a moment he lay there, the breath knocked out of his body. A cold sweat broke out over him at the narrowness of his escape. He had forgotten for the moment that in the eyes of the guardians of the law he was now a desperate criminal who had already probably killed one policeman, and was to be fired at on sight. And despite his warning and counsel, this was Sam's fault.

Sam's urgent whisper floated down to him. He was crouching on the wall: "Good God, man, are you hit?"

"No," stammered Rezaire.

"Then get up and come on," snapped his companion, "instead of lying there. This isn't a game."

Another shot rang out. This time nearer and Sam crouching yet closer to the wall fired back. There was a cry, and muttering: "That'll stop you for a bit," he jumped down into the garden beside Rezaire. The next moment they were scaling the wall at the side.

"Where the hell are you going?" asked Sam, as they dropped over into yet another garden.

"Trying to find that alley," panted Rezaire. "Once we get into it we can run dead straight out into a street."

They went on a short distance. Sam was panting loudly with the exertion of climbing over the walls and the running. Rezaire, the more fit of the two, was not very distressed. The police were about two gardens behind.

They came to the next wall, and as they scaled it, Rezaire gave a short exclamation of relief. To his right he could see, vague in the darkness, the thick shadow of the alley he was seeking, with its doors into the back gardens. He made for it and dropped thankfully down between the walls. In a moment Sam was beside him.

"I can't go much further," he gasped. "I'm done."

"Come on, man," urged Rezaire, as again the impulse seized him to run on by himself. "They'll shoot you on sight," he added, and Sam pulled himself together.

They ran on about thirty paces down the alley, gaining rapidly on their pursuers, who were still hemmed in among the garden walls. There was, in fact, now a chance that they might get so far ahead that the police would lose them altogether. But just at that moment a man stepped out of one of the doors from the gardens. He was obviously not a detective; apparently he was only one of the many who had been drawn by curiosity to the scene and was looking about to see if he could see anything of what was happening. He certainly saw all that he wanted to. Rezaire, in full flight, ran straight into him, so that he staggered in a dazed fashion in the middle of the alley. Sam, cruder in his methods, hit him with his fist under the ear, the full force of his arm and the impetus of his speed behind the blow. The man gave a gasp and sank to the ground. A moment after, as they sped on, they heard his frantic shouts behind them, dispelling their hopes of shaking off pursuit.

The alley took a sharp turn to the left. They ran on some distance and then emerged into a street. No one was in sight. Rezaire turned to the right and Sam, laboring heavily, followed him.

"For God's sake," panted Sam, "let's hide somewhere, or walk. I can't run any more."

Rezaire slowed down for a space. It was essential that they should get out of sight as soon as they could, yet if Sam could not run… He looked swiftly about and a brilliant idea came quickly to him. Just ten yards ahead, drawn up by the curb, was a small car, which was empty. It was standing outside a house with lighted windows, whence issued the sound of a gramophone, and was evidently the property of some young gentleman who was footing it inside.

"He'll have to foot it back home as well," thought Rezaire grimly, as they came up alongside.

He gave a swift glance round, but there was hardly anyone in the street, though a hundred yards or so away the night life of 9:30 p. M. London was roaring past in the Strand.

"Get in, Sam" he ordered, and Sam, gasping loudly, without sign of surprise or protest, sank wearily into the seat. He was bleeding badly from a wound across the face. Rezaire working hastily but methodically, with one eye behind him on the entrance to the alley, opened the throttle slightly and switched on the spark. He did not know much about cars, but luckily it was of a type that he had once driven—a small two-seated Rover. He went round to the front and rapidly jerked up the starting handle. The car did not start, and Rezaire cursed. The noise was very loud in the silence of the street, but seemed to pass unnoticed. Sam, in the passenger's seat, sat up and looked anxiously at him. He rapidly jerked the handle twice more without result. Then a curtain in the house was suddenly drawn aside as a man looked out for a moment. A shout came vaguely to them through the closed window, and the face disappeared.

"Quick!" urged Sam. "He's coming out…

Rezaire worked furiously at the handle and with a sudden clatter the engine sprang into life. Running round, he scrambled wildly in over the side into the driver's seat. As he let the clutch in, the door of the house was flung wide, and two young men raced down the steps.

"Hi! Let that car alone," called out one of them angrily, as the car moved slowly forward. A third man came down the steps after them. A cluster of figures was at the open front door and the windows. The car began to accelerate, as the two young men ran out of the gate onto the pavement. At the same moment a shrill whistle from somewhere further behind told that the police had come out of the alley into the street, and were also on their track.

"Quickly! Quickly!" snapped Sam in excitement. "They're after us." He looked over the back and drew his revolver.

"Be careful!" flashed Rezaire over his shoulder. "Don't shoot."

"I shall if I have to," retorted Sam between his teeth. "I am not going to be caught."

The two young men, running hard, were gaining on them and were now only five yards behind. A small body of police and detectives could be seen in pursuit a short distance behind that.

Rezaire, swearing at its slowness, threw the car into second gear. But the change necessitated a slight slowing down, and, before they could pick up their speed once more, one of their pursuers got his hands on the hood and sprang onto the footboard on the driver's side. The car quickly accelerated just before the other could catch up.

Instantly their assailant, cursing them vigorously, tried to switch off the engine, but Rezaire fought him off by holding his hand over the switch. All the while he kept his foot firmly pressed upon the accelerator, and the car was gaining speed the whole way. Losing his head, the other then began to wrest his hands from the steering wheel, while Sam leaned across from the other side and tried to push him off. They could hear his companions encouraging him with shouts from a short way behind.

The car swerved madly from side to side as the two pairs of hands struggled for the wheel. At last Sam succeeded in dealing their opponent a blow on the head with the butt of his revolver, which he more skillfully followed up by another on the fingers that grasped the steering wheel. The young man reeled under the shock and Sam, who was now standing up in the seat, pushed him in the chest as hard as he could.

He gave a cry and fell, rolling along the muddy road for a little distance. They heard his companion shouting "Stop thief!" and behind him the shrill police whistles. The wheel, suddenly freed from the strain to which it had been subjected, swung over to one side. Rezaire made a desperate clutch at it and with a swerve got the car right, Sam nearly falling out at the suddenness of the movement. But before he could get the car properly under control again, the turning into the brilliantly lighted Strand with its flow of traffic, and its busy evening crowds, was upon them.

Rezaire slowed down as much as he was able in the short space, for he had been accelerating all the way up to throw his pursuers off. Then he wrenched the wheel round to the left. A knot of people, who had been attracted by the police whistles and were standing at the corners, scattered like chaff. The car went round, lifting at the abruptness of the turn, and sped in a half curve across the road. Rezaire could not get her round completely for fear of a complete overturn, and so took the curb of a refuge in the middle of the street. With a sickening jolt to the springs they ran up onto it, grazing a lamp-post. A man who was standing on the refuge with his back to them was struck by the off fender of the car and knocked into the road. A taxi just behind, going the same way, pulled up with a whirr and a screech. A bus driver swerved out of his way, cursing him vigorously and nearly ran down a cyclist. Everything in an instant was thrown into confusion.

As Rezaire got the car under control once more, picking it out by a hair's-breadth from a dozen accidents, he saw a policeman running at him from the side, hand uplifted, angrily shouting something. He accelerated, passing round on the wrong side of a bus and the policeman was cut off from view. The police whistle again shrilled out in his ears above the roar of traffic, as their original pursuers emerged into the Strand. People were standing on the pavements staring about them and wondering what was the matter. A man yelled a sentence at him as he passed. Rezaire accelerated further, thankful that it was too early for the theater crowds, and that the road was comparatively clear.

Sam, who had pocketed his revolver again, wiped the blood from his face and, looking over the back, began to tell Rezaire what was happening.

"The police can still see us," he muttered. "Some of 'em are running this way. There are a couple more in the chase now. Damn! A bunch of 'em have got in that taxi that nearly ran into us. Knock as much as you can out of her, for Heaven's sake."

"I can beat a taxi all right," returned Rezaire through set teeth, "if only I can get a clear road." He charged at the Waterloo Bridge crossing, hooting wildly. The car swayed and bounced from side to side. Something loose in the off-side, where they had graced the lamp-post, was rattling loudly.

"The taxi is out of sight now, behind a bus," resumed Sam. "There it is again."

They whizzed through the crossing, people scattering to right and left, and narrowly missed another collision with a private car. The chauffeur and the policeman on point duty both shouted at them to stop as they flashed past.

"He's taking the number," chuckled Sam. "If that's all they can do, they have my permission to go right ahead."

The traffic problem became more complicated as they sped on westward. Though the streets were not crowded, there were quite enough vehicles and pedestrians about to make fast driving really difficult, if not at times almost impossible. Rezaire saw that his only chance was to get as far ahead of his pursuers as possible. By so doing he was outdistancing the hue and cry, and would not be held up, since the various policemen on point duty he was passing did not realize that he was a fugitive from justice till after he had passed. Also, he was bound to be caught in a traffic block sooner or later and the more distance he could gain before then the better chance would they have of escaping in the crowd. The traffic became thicker as they approached Trafalgar Square, and they were forced to slow down. The taxi from behind, which Sam could pick out because of a policeman standing on the step, began to gain slightly.

"They're coming up a bit," he said.

"How far are they?"

"A good way still… Curse! I believe some of them have got another car—a private one. Yes, there's a 'tec in it. They're coming up fast."

In a few seconds a powerful two-seater car was at their heels, driven by a young man in an opera hat. At his side, door held open, ready to jump out, was, as Sam had said, two detectives, who had evidently commandeered the car from somewhere outside the Savoy. The car hung behind them a moment, then seizing its opportunity, dashed forward, overtook them, cut in, and applied all brakes just in front.

Rezaire's brain, however, had not been idle. He had guessed that, if overtaken, this would be the means adopted to bring them to a standstill. As the car cut in, he also applied both brakes and swung the wheel over to the right. Their near front mudguard scraped past the rear mudguard of the two-seater, and then they had shot across the road to the right even as the detectives sprang to the ground. Rezaire passed at a good speed just in front of a bus coming in the opposite direction, and shot up a side turning on the north side of the Strand. Before the detectives had time to look round, the Rover was out of the street going northward.

"Gee!" muttered Sam. "You certainly are a wonder. That was quick work." He looked back over his shoulder. "They haven't even turned again yet… Ah! There comes the taxi! They're waving it up here."

But Rezaire did not answer. His eyes were fixed on the road ahead. He was wondering what would be best to do when they had to abandon the car. For though he had turned aside from Trafalgar Square, all the crowded thoroughfares of St. Martin's Lane, and Charing Cross Road, lay ahead of him.

He swept on past St. Martin's Lane and managed to turn into Cranbourn Street without mishap just before the policeman's hand went up.

"Just through in time," muttered Sam with satisfaction. "He's holding up the traffic now. There comes the taxi. Damn! Of course, they've got through on the nod…"

At that moment a bus in front of them signaled and slowed down rapidly. There was a block at the turn of Charing Cross Road. Rezaire applied his brakes, but they had been going too fast. At a considerable speed they charged into the end of the bus, buckling up the front of the car. A woman who was about to get out screamed and fainted. They saw the conductor for a brief instant, mouth open in angry remonstration. A man on the pavement shouted something indistinguishable as the Rover came to an abrupt standstill. They were caught at last.

Without hesitation they both leaped from the car and began to run. Some little way behind them the pursuing taxi drew up with a grinding of brakes and discharged its load of policemen and detectives.

CHAPTER IX

AT THE PICTURES

They were in the crowd and dodging in and out before anyone had quite realized what had happened. The natural instinct of the onlookers was to surge round the actual scene of the accident, so that Rezaire and Sam were ten yards away before anyone who had not definitely seen the crash connected them with it.

Then the ubiquitous small boy piped up: "There they go!" and another: "Wot they runnin' away for?" and in less than a minute two or three men were running after them and calling out to them to stop.

Rezaire ran on swiftly without looking behind him. He did not know whether Sam was with him and he did not really care. In fact he hoped he was not; for Sam with his conspicuous cut across his face which their pursuers must have seen, was now more of a handicap than ever. By now their description must have been flashed to every police station in London, but, while that of Sam would be fairly accurate, there was every chance that he himself was still described as James Robinson. It would really be very much to his advantage to lose touch with Sam now, and his mind reiterated his decision to get rid of him, if only he could do it in such a way that he would be safely caught and unable to execute his threats of vengeance. For that was the one big hitch to trying to get rid of Sam,—the chance that he might escape and come after him with his knife.

He swung round a corner almost knocking over a girl. Behind him he heard the clatter of hurried footsteps, but did not know whether it was Sam or his pursuers. He knocked into someone else. Despite the fact that the theaters had not emptied themselves yet, the street seemed very crowded. He was looking for some place where it would be darker and where he would have some chance of hiding and throwing his pursuers definitely off his track.

He reached another corner and as he turned it cast a swift glance behind him. The man close at his heels was Sam after all. Trust Sam to stick to him when he alone had the secret of their destination. About twenty yards further behind he glimpsed the short man with the square cut moustache leading the chase, and noticed with a shiver the bright gleam of a revolver in his hand. Even while his head was turned, a young man standing in the corner doorway of a tobacconist, quicker witted than the rest, put out a hand to grasp him. He dodged it easily and heard a sharp cry and the clatter of a stick as Sam following up hit out at their adversary.

He ran on down the street not quite knowing where he was. In that wild swerving rush amongst the crowds, he had rather lost his bearings. He knew that he must get away from the more crowded thoroughfares, for even without the hue and cry at his heels he realized that he and Sam must be very conspicuous without hats, and with hands and faces dirty and clothing torn from the scramble over the roofs, apart from the cut across Sam's face. Already a considerable number of people were following them, judging by the sound, though this must have been more of a hindrance to the police in keeping the quarry in sight than a help.

They ran to the next corner and stopped abruptly. Not looking where they were going they had run right into another part of the first street again. As they paused, already people were looking curiously at them. Behind them the chase was coming up. The situation was critical. As soon as those who were now regarding them with amused or interested eyes realized that they were escaping from justice, then capture would be a matter of seconds.

Rezaire twitched Sam suddenly by the sleeve and with as unconcerned an appearance as possible, so as to disarm the growing suspicion of the passers-by, walked straight into the entrance hall of a cinema which stood just round the corner.

"Here, where the hell..." began Sam, but Rezaire silenced him at once.

"It's our only chance," he returned in a fierce undertone. "I know it's not good, but..."

With a furtive glance over his shoulder he went further into the shelter of the hall. He could still be seen from outside; for the place was brilliantly lighted. Would he have been observed to have gone in? Yes, almost certainly; they had been for a moment the center of attraction and people were still staring after them; still, there was just the chance that all those who had seen them enter would have passed on by the tune the police arrived.

The Commissionaire was at his elbow, his eyes on the cut on Sam's face, slightly dubious of their ability to buy a seat.

Rezaire made his mind up instantly, before the official could speak. Quickly he went to the box office and hearing again Sam's smothered protest as he did so, ordered two seats, paid for them without waiting for change, and the next moment was at the dark entrance to the theater itself, with Sam slinking at his heels. It was rather like walking into a trap, but it was the only possible thing to do that he could think of. As the curtains, held open by an attendant, dropped behind him, he heard the girl in the box office make some amused remark to the Commissionaire. He had staved off capture—but, he feared, only for a short while.

The roar of the hostile street outside was cut off, to be replaced by the notes of a piano and violins. He stood still for a moment in the friendly darkness and drew two or three deep breaths. The strain of trying to appear normal, when in reality his lungs were bursting for air after the chase through the streets, had been very great. The gloom of the cinema, lit vaguely at the exits by red lamps and by the flickering screen at the end, enveloped them in protecting fashion. Even Sam felt the sense of sudden change from danger to comparative though momentary safety, for he whispered nervously: "Seems a better idea than I thought. Do you think they'll find us in here?…"

"This way, please," interrupted the attendant, flashing a torch at their tickets. "Follow me, please."

"Couldn't say," answered Rezaire as they stumbled along after her. "The 'busy's' won't know we've gone in here, but the trouble is that someone may tell them. We were so blamed conspicuous without hats, and looking like a pair of scarecrows. But we can't do anything else now, and there's a chance we haven't been seen."

Their seats were indicated, and they sank thankfully into them, every bone aching and sore. It was the first minute's rest they had had since Rezaire had led the way out of Carlyle's room. For several moments they reveled in the luxury that even a cinema seat could bring to strained and bruised limbs. Then Rezaire sat upright and looked round; finally he bent down and appeared to grope under the seat.

"What's up?" muttered Sam, but the other did not answer for a moment. At length he suddenly got to his feet, saying in an undertone that could be overheard by the people next them: "There are some better seats over there. Come along!"

Sam surprised, but obedient, got up and followed him out of the row again, across the gangway, and into two seats some distance away.

"What's the point?" asked Sam in astonishment. "Why did you change about—making yourself conspicuous like that?"

"We weren't conspicuous," retorted Rezaire sharply. "They may have noticed us leave those seats, but I bet they didn't notice us come to these. The point is that now that girl who showed us to the seats doesn't know *where* we are."

"I don't see what good that…"

"No, but perhaps you will," snapped the other, exasperated at Sam's slow wit.

"Now look here," began Sam in an angry whisper, but Rezaire not giving him a chance, cut in: "And instead of criticizing so much what I do, you might do something yourself. You might have thought of providing yourself with a hat, like I have." He displayed a felt hat upon his knee. "And for Heaven's sake wipe that blood off your face."

Sam stared at the hat in surprise, looked round for a moment as if he were about to make an angry reply, and then subsided, furtively mopping his face which was still bleeding. Rezaire, the leader by virtue of his brains, was on his own ground once more, and, as in the past five months, Sam had to follow his lead.

"Where did you get it?" he said meekly at last.

"Under the seat of the man next me when we were over there. You'd better get one from here. None of 'em'll notice."

Then quickly he nudged Sam for silence. Already one or two people were looking round at the noise of their whispering and they sat very quiet for several minutes. Rezaire looked at the pictures on the screen and after a little while discovered with satisfaction that they were somewhere in the first half of a six reel picture, which meant that the show had still some time to run.

Then he began to consider his present situation. His next line of action depended a lot on the course that his opponents took and that in turn depended on whether they received reliable information, if any at all, as to their presence in the cinema, and also upon whether they were considered desperate criminals. Of course, Sam might not have hit anyone when he had fired, but he rather feared…

"Sam," he whispered quietly, his head very close to the other's. "You fired when in the empty house, didn't you?"

Sam nodded.

"Hit anyone?"

"Two, I think; and I knifed one. I couldn't help it," he added. "I shouldn't have got away at all. One of their bullets nearly got me too. And someone slashed my face."

Rezaire sucked in his breath. "It's a hanging job then," he said at last, "—for you."

"Yes," muttered Sam fiercely, "and I'll see that it stays one. I'm not going to be taken like a rabbit."

Rezaire sat back in his chair. The old repulsion that he had for Sam swept over him. His terror was now pulling him two ways. His fear of being dragged into another fight with the police, of being even associated with Sam who was now a murderer, was urging him to give him the slip; his fear of what Sam would do to him, if he did betray him, impelled him the other way. Unless, again the thought insinuated itself into his brain, unless he could betray him in such fashion that he could not escape at all, could not exact the vengeance he had sworn. He turned the matter over and over in his brain. It was typical of his self-reliance and confidence in his own wits that, despite the present position, he still envisaged ultimate escape for himself, if only he could rid himself of his companion.

As he weighed the pros and cons of the affair, his mind, always on the *qui vive*, became aware of a slight disturbance at the back of the theater. People in front of him were looking back over their shoulder. He touched Sam to attract his attention and warily looked round.

At the curtained entrance by which they had come, framed against the lighted hall outside, he saw a policeman in uniform and a plain-clothes man with him. One was peering into the darkness, the other was talking to the attendant and evidently asking questions. They had found out. Further behind still, Rezaire saw the short man with the square-cut moustache. The light fell upon his face, and it was set and stern. No wonder, too, if Sam had killed one of the policemen. He wondered whether they would say what they had come for; whether they would stop the performance.

He turned his head slowly back to the screen.

Sam was whispering to him, almost breathing the words in his ears, so anxious was he to avoid being overheard.

"Cops are at the front. Why not step out at one of those exits down there by the orchestra?"

Rezaire nodded. He felt he ought to have thought of it before. He should have done that, the moment he came into the cinema. They could have slipped out while the police were at the front. Then he remembered that the reason he had not carried this plan out at the time was that he was at the back of his mind hoping against hope that the police would not find out they were inside, and that it would have been foolish to reappear conspicuously in the street within a minute of their disappearance. A futile hope he saw now, with all those people about outside to tell them where they had gone. He and Sam hatless and disheveled, running round a corner, breaking into a sudden walk and diving into a picture palace, could not have appeared anything but unusual.

He half rose in his chair, looking toward the exit which Sam had pointed out. If they got up and went quickly now while the police were still at the entrance hall, they could do it. Then he sank back suddenly into his seat once more. He realized that the police were not quite such fools as he was going to take them for.

At the very moment he had looked toward the exit, two girls had been going out. Beyond them, as they drew the curtain aside, under the rays of the red exit lamp, he caught a glimpse of another obviously waiting figure. He had been stupid to think that the detectives, knowing that the men they were after had gone into the cinema, would come in by one entrance only, without immediately posting men at the others.

Sam had also seen the man and was sitting back in his seat. Despite the darkness, they both felt that the eyes of the detectives stationed at the different exits were upon them.

A rustle spread slowly over the audience. Its attention was gradually being distracted from the screen. Something was on foot. Heads were turned and inquiring whispers arose. The center of interest appeared to be somewhere just behind and to the right.

Sunk in the comparative security of their seats Sam and Rezaire turned their heads slightly and peered out of the corners of their eyes. Down the gangway along which they had just been conducted, a little procession was coming, headed by the attendant with the electric torch. The rest was made up by a policeman in uniform and two plain-clothes men. The girl when questioned had obviously remembered Sam and Rezaire and was now leading the police toward the seats into which she had shown them.

The excitement round about grew greater. All the rear part of the audience was now watching the uniformed figures. This was a thrill equal, if not superior, to those depicted on the screen. The murmur of excited whispering rose almost above the noise of the small orchestra down at the lower end. Questions were passed from row to row. Those at the end nearest the gangway, where the invading newcomers were, leaped almost at once into the light of publicity. They were the favored ones; they were of the inner circle, so close that they might almost ask the policeman what he was after. One of them in fact did, a little man with spectacles that glinted in the half light, but apparently received no answer. The police were taking no chances, were not going to let their attention be distracted when they were dealing with armed and desperate criminals, even in a crowded cinema. Under cover of the general perturbation Rezaire could not help whispering to Sam: "Do you see now why I changed seats? No one knows where we are now, and that attendant only remembers where she originally showed us."

It was quite true. The girl paused when she came to the seats to which she had conducted Sam and Rezaire and flashed her torch onto the ones they had occupied. Then she flashed it in a wider circle to the front and back and further along the row.

The detectives too were stooping forward scrutinizing the persons who sat nearby. The attendant turned to them after a moment with a puzzled look. Then she questioned the people who sat there.

A young man, proud at thus finding himself suddenly in the public eye, answered volubly but apparently to little purpose. Evidently he had remembered the two getting up again but did not know where they had gone. One of the plain-clothes men stepped forward and asked him something. He pointed to one of the exits, then changed his mind, and pointed to another, and his questioner shrugged his shoulders and turned away. Evidently he was not being helpful. From his position of momentary safety Rezaire almost smiled despite the danger. It pleased him in a small way to think too that the youth, who was so eager to impress the police with his observance of the two men who had sat next him and then gone away, had evidently not yet even noticed that his hat had disappeared at the same time.

Nearly the whole audience by now was watching the drama. Many were standing up and those behind them did not object, for no one was looking at the screen. Only the violins and the piano continued unheeding. The policeman conferred with one of the detectives, who shook his head. They looked round over the sea of indistinguishable pale faces turned toward them in the gloom, but could evidently make out nothing in the half light. Then they turned and went back to the entrance hall again, followed by scores of curious eyes.

Rezaire sat back in his chair revolving the new situation in his mind. As was his invariable custom he put his opponent's case before him. For the moment the police were baffled. They had tracked their quarry into the cinema and had traced them to the very seats into which they had been shown. But they were not there. Unless they had walked straight through the theater before the men were posted at the exits they must be there still; but the young man who had sat next them would have told them that they occupied the seats for a certain while and had not passed straight through. Hence it was certain that they were still in the cinema— somewhere among four or five hundred others. Thus far, Rezaire argued, would the police reason. From there, two courses were open, and he did not know which they would take. They could, on the one hand, see the manager, have the show stopped and the lights turned up, and then either conduct a search of every row of seats, or close all doors except one, and tell the audience to file out. That could only be done in the case of great emergency, because both the management and the audience would have to be compensated. The other course open to them would be to set a guard on every exit in order to see that their prey did not escape them and wait till the end of the performance.

Rezaire glanced over his shoulder again. He could see nothing, but he did not doubt that somewhere in the entrance hall the detectives were talking it over. They knew there was no great hurry for them; for the birds were almost certainly in the net, although they did not know exactly where.

He turned back again. At the exits he occasionally caught a glimpse of the men on guard. The audience had by now somewhat settled down once more. With the departure of the police from the auditorium, interest had re-centered on the screen. Sam, who had asked once or twice what they were going to do and had been told to keep quiet, was now silent and anxious. His sudden dependence on Rezaire's brain was in almost ludicrous contrast to his periodic outbursts of arrogance.

Rezaire, weighing the matter up, and noting that nothing had yet been done, was of opinion that the police were waiting to the end of the performance. It was now nearing the hour when the cinema would close, they were certain their quarry was in the net, and the wait would give them time to collect any help they needed.

Realizing this, he next turned the full power of his brain onto the solution of the problem. It had a two-armed solution, as he saw it; either how to get out without being captured, or, better still, how to get out without being seen. A moment's thought showed him that the future plans of his would-be captors depended very largely on the docility of the general public. The crowd would have to submit to scrutiny and regulation at each exit, or else be made to file out slowly by one exit only. This would only be possible if they behaved well. If they were aroused, amazed, or frightened the police would not be able to control them... His brain catching at the last word "frightened" suddenly leaped across the intervening space of reasoning to a possible solution of his problem. If the crowd was frightened, could be made to panic, then he and Sam, secure in their midst, possibly even unrecognized, could laugh at the police.

Rezaire smiled to himself. At last an idea, a wild one indeed, but perhaps feasible, had come into his head.

He turned to Sam and began to whisper.

CHAPTER X

ESCAPE

Sam, frankly incredulous at first, at last began to nod in dubious approbation as Rezaire's plan unfolded itself. After all he saw that beggars could not be choosers, that any plan was better than no plan at all, and that he could not think of a better.

"Can we do it by ourselves, do you think?" he asked.

"I don't know. We've got to try. Luckily there are several girls just in front of us. Once we start it well amongst them, it'll spread all right."

"I wonder whether…"

"Well, you've got to *make* it go, Sam. Think what depends on it. Your neck'll certainly be stretched if this last hope doesn't come off, and it'll be over the Alps to the awful place for me."

Sam grunted at the obviousness of this, and Rezaire resumed his rapid whispering.

Then slowly and stealthily they began the preparations for their desperate coup.

Reaching out underneath the seat, Rezaire secured a discarded newspaper and Sam a couple of programs which, with care and silence, they crumpled up and placed under the seat just in front of them. A scarf belonging to one of the three girls who sat in front was added to the pile, also the lining of Rezaire's new hat and some paper Sam had in his pockets. Finally they added the contents of all the boxes of matches they had on them and over this pile and over the plush of the seat in front, Rezaire poured the small amount of petrol from a cigarette lighter he had in his possession. They had to work very slowly and stealthily to avoid attracting their neighbors' attention, but they were helped by the fact that, at the moment, the interest of the film was nearing its climax. Unobserved by Rezaire, Sam, the more unscrupulous, to whom escape was a matter of life and death, adjusted the heap of material so that it lay against the flimsy dress of the girl just in front. On her and her two companions the brunt of the success depended. The fire itself would be nothing; the panic that they hoped to start was the main thing, for panic was more contagious and spread faster than fire itself.

Despite all their preparations it seemed, when done, even to Robinson, to be a very slender chance of escape. So little depended on what they could actually do themselves, and so much on good fortune, on what would happen when the matter was out of their hands. The more Rezaire considered it, the more it seemed that only colossal luck would help him, luck and the workings of those strange emotions latent in that science—crowd psychology—of which he knew so little. If once only he could start a real panic, no reason could quell it; it would burn of itself without further fuel, feeding, as all crowd panics feed, on suggestion, contagion, and imitation.

He bent over to Sam again and said: "Are you ready?"

"Yes."

"Mind you keep the scare going and stop anyone putting the fire out at the beginning."

"Right."

"Well," resumed Rezaire coolly, "here's luck to us!"

He nonchalantly took a cigarette out of a case, produced a match-box with one match in it, which he had kept in reserve, and lighted the tobacco. Pausing a moment to see that the wood was burning well he deliberately dropped the match, as though intending to put his foot on it.

For a bare moment the little stick lay burning on the pile of material they had collected; for a bare moment Sam thought that it had failed and would go out. Then it ignited another unused match that lay next it, which went up with a flare and a sputter. The next second the petrol on the pile leaped into sudden life under the heat, the newspaper caught and next the cotton stuff of the girl's scarf. In the midst of it all, like miniature fireworks, the loose matches ignited in little spurts of flame.

At the same moment Rezaire and Sam jumped to their feet and shouted "Fire!" as loudly as they could. The voices rose above the orchestra; everyone's attention was snatched away from the screen by the one word which has such a magic power over the crowd mind. A man near Sam jumped up and shouted "Look out!" and a girl screamed.

The flames leaped up, but they were not very big. In the big hall of the cinema the fire looked very tiny. It seemed that one should warm one's hands at it rather than run away. Rezaire felt a sudden sense of unreality as he continued to shout "Fire!" and backed away from the blaze. He felt that no one was with him; that people were merely curious, startled, apprehensive,—anything but frightened. He did not experience the emotion of fear in himself and therefore it was doubly hard to communicate it to others. A man on his right, quick-witted, made a rush to put it out, but Rezaire got in his way, just as the man, cursing him for a fool, made to pass. Simultaneously the three girls just in front shrieked and jumped to their feet.

All this had taken but a few seconds. Hardly any had yet realized what had really happened. Nearly all were balanced on the knife edge of apprehension between fear and common sense. It was the psychological moment at which many a man with presence of mind has averted a panic. And in that moment the flames licked suddenly up to the petrol in the plush seat of the chair, and thence in a flash to the girl's dress, n ear which Sam had surreptitiously pushed the pile of material.

In that, second, what looked like being a farce, turned to real tragedy. The hungry flames enveloped the girl suddenly, and her screams rang out into the crowded cinema, screams of real terror and pain. Her two companions lost their heads and scrambled over the seats in front in a wild rush to get to the door. Many others took up Sam's and Rezaire's cries of "Fire!" and several women began to shriek. Someone turned the lights on at the back. Smoke drifted about the part of the auditorium where the fire had started. Individual movement to get away from the flames suddenly merged into general movement, helped by Rezaire and Sam. Several people near the exit ran out and an attendant, meaning well, suddenly flung wide the doors with a clatter. This sudden suggestive sound was the last straw. There was a sudden rush for all the exits; the screaming of women was heard above the noise. Sam and Rezaire keeping together pushed hard away from the fire, urging the crowd on. Rezaire, whose eyes were everywhere, saw one of the doorkeepers hurrying up with a fire extinguisher, and in the rush jostled it out of his hand. It fell on the floor where someone kicked the plunger so that it began to discharge a vicious stream of fluid among the ankles of the crowd, thus increasing the confusion.

Sam, callous and powerful, fought his way to one of the lower exits, eager to get out while the panic lasted, Rezaire following in his wake. The screams of the girl whose clothing was burning rang in their ears, and Rezaire felt a twinge of remorse. He had not intended that that should have happened, but—it had saved them. He realized in a flash how futile the results of his plan would have been, had it not been for that touch of real tragedy. Glancing over his shoulder as he pushed along behind Sam's bent shoulders, he saw through the drifting smoke a man trying to smother her burning dress with his coat.

Then for the next few minutes his individuality was swallowed up by the monster he had created. The real panic of the crowd communicated itself to him and he fought wildly with the rest, hoarsely shouting "Fire!" at intervals. The noise of screaming and shouting rose above all else.

The pianist in an attempt to quell the tumult, was playing the National Anthem, but the chords could hardly be heard in the uproar. The film had stopped, suspended in mid-air. They were very near the door now. Would they get out before the panic died away as suddenly as it had begun?

They came to the doorway, close wedged in a struggling throng. Rezaire, getting control of himself once more, looked about for the police, but could see no sign of them. They had doubtless long ago been swept aside in the rush.

Somewhere behind he could hear a man shouting out: "It's all right; it's out," and another "Pass out gently, please." He raised his own voice in an attempt to prolong the panic: "The films have caught fire," he heard himself shouting and then: "Celluloid! Celluloid!" The crowd struggled, paused, swayed, and struggled once more.

The night air struck cool upon his sweating forehead. He was outside. He was past the police. Still clutching the remains of his hat he disengaged himself from the crowd and ran directly across the road into the friendly obscurity of a shop doorway.

Here Sam joined him, and hidden in the gloom they watched the mingling of the two crowds, that which had collected in curiosity round the entrance, and that which was pouring out in terror—a fear, which turned quickly into a somewhat sheepish shame, as self-control returned on the heels of departing panic. Several women were sitting down outside the theater being attended to by friends; men were adjusting their clothing torn in the rush; an ambulance had rushed up; two reporters, note-books in hand, were questioning a group of men. Several policemen were in evidence, and an obvious plain-clothes man had already forced his way back to the door. Despite the panic they had been very lucky to have escaped observation.

Sam turned to Rezaire.

"Phew!" was all he said. "Of all the luck!"

"It might never have succeeded," Rezaire found himself saying in a voice hoarse from shouting.

"It wouldn't have done, if I hadn't set that girl alight."

"You set that…"

"Now, look here, Rezaire, less of this! It's all very well for you, but I've a noose round my neck. I'm not going to dance at the end of a rope just to save a girl's garters from being scorched."

Rezaire looked at him in disgust, and then looked away. He had had enough of him. His only thought—and by now it was more of a burning desire—was how soon he could get rid of him, get him securely in the hands of the policemen and will his own safety. He looked at Sam again and said: "You haven't got a hat yet, Sam, you damn fool, and your face is bleeding again."

"I got that in the empty house fighting to get you away!" retorted Sam.

"I don't care how you got it, but it'll give you away as sure as God made little apples. They've seen that cut, and every policeman in London I should think by now is looking for a man of your description, with a scar across his mug."

Sam mopped the blood away from his face.

"Well, this is a damn silly place to start scrapping," he said. "That 'busy' over the road'll have us. What's our move now?"

"Jermyn Street. To my car—if I can rouse out the chauffeur. I wish to hell you'd got a hat." Rezaire was tired and his nerves were frayed by all he had been through.

"Well, I haven't, so you can shut your bloody mouth! Now I want something to eat. What's the time?"

"Nearly ten-thirty. Theater crowds will be out now. May make it better for us or may make it worse. For God's sake, man," he resumed querulously, "do something to that blood on your face."

A man strolling past suddenly stopped in the doorway near them and in another moment entered into conversation. He was full of information and told them there had been a fire in the cinema opposite, also that there was some funny business on with the police.

"They're after someone, they say. Too late for it to be in the evening papers, but I was speaking to a constable and he tells me there's been a motor accident or somebody shot or something down the Strand. They're after the chaps that did it."

Sam and Rezaire nodded unenthusiastically.

"Hope they get them," went on the man sententiously, and Rezaire, a little of his old spirit returning, agreed vigorously.

"This sort of thing ought to be stopped," he said in determined fashion.

"In London, too, of all places," went on the other. "That's all right for Paris and them foreign parts, but here no! Hullo! Hurt yourself, Mister?"

"Just a cut," said Sam sullenly.

"Ah, nasty things, cuts," he resumed volubly, "if they're not looked after. Get blood-poisoning."

He stayed talking for two or three minutes longer and then went off.

"What do you make of that?" asked Sam suspiciously.

"Oh, nothing behind it. But it just shows how conspicuous your face is. If a bobby sees you like that he'll stop you at once on suspicion."

"Well, I'm doing the best I can with it," growled Sam. "I can't help it."

"We'd better move on now. Things seem to have blown over."

The crowd had certainly drifted away. The side doors of the cinema were being bolted. A policeman or two still hovered round the entrance, and Rezaire guessed that the place had been thoroughly searched, despite the fact that it was fairly obvious the birds had got away in the first panic. He wondered whether they attributed the fire to him or to accident. If to him, it would make them realize, he thought proudly, that they were up against someone with brains for once. He felt very pleased with himself. He had outwitted them all so far—even with the handicap of Sam's companionship. Sam! He began to think about Sam again. The matter wanted a lot of thinking over. He was only waiting his opportunity now, and then—if it could be arranged—the police would lay their hands on Sam and not on him. But he must be very, very sure they got Sam.

With some trepidation he hailed a taxi and they got in without mishap.

"Down to Piccadilly Circus Tube and wait there," he ordered.

At Piccadilly he got out and, followed by Sam, handkerchief to face, was swallowed up in the crowds in an instant. He was making for the lavatory. A wash and a brush up were absolutely essential. His ragged clothes and general dirtiness made him very conspicuous.

A few moments later they emerged, but looking fairly respectable once more, despite the fact that Sam had not a hat.

They got into the taxi and drove off again, Rezaire telling the man to drive into St. James' Park. He wanted time to think out his next move. Despite the fact that he was once more free, he knew that he must go very carefully. The news would have long ago been circulated to the police centers, and also by them to the principal ports and stations, for he gave the police credit for guessing that criminals of his type would have made arrangements for a flight to the continent. But they did not know of his motor launch and, though they might watch the stations, they did not know of his car. He had laid his plans well, and even despite the handicap he had been forced to shoulder, he was slowly working his way to success.

After about half an hour he ordered the taxi to return to the neighborhood of Jermyn Street and in the obscurity of St. James' Square they got out and paid the driver. This man also remarked on Sam's cut in a friendly way, at which Sam flinched visibly; but Rezaire, more cool and collected, realized that the fact that a man with a cut was "wanted" could at the moment still only be known by the police. The general public, taxi drivers, railway officials, and so on, would not know that, till the morning papers were out. The taxi driver would remember; but by that time they would be safe at Beaulieu lying up till the evening when his launch would put in to the deserted quay.

They walked away and Rezaire said: "For Heaven's sake, man, pull yourself together. No one knows about your cut except the police. Don't jump like a schoolgirl every time anyone mentions it."

"I can't help it," said Sam, humbly enough for him. "I haven't got your nerve. I keep thinking that everyone's after me."

"So they will be if you go on like that. The bold way is the best way. The unexpected is the…" And at that moment the unexpected happened. They met a constable face to face under a lamp, Sam at the moment actually mopping the telltale cut in his face with his handkerchief. There was no time to bluff, to wonder how much the constable knew, no time to do anything. For a moment they stared incredulously at each other, then Rezaire saw sudden recognition come into the policeman's eyes. His hand went to his whistle. He took a step forward. Sam's nerve gave, and the next moment they were racing up the road toward Jermyn Street.

Behind them they heard once more the shrill whistle blast and the heavy clatter of pursuing feet.

CHAPTER XI

TWO FLATS

Rezaire felt furious with Sam, as he fled up the street. If only the fool had kept his head, they might conceivably have bluffed the matter out, despite the scar. Or even if they found they could not deceive the constable, they might have attacked him and tied him up before he could give the alarm. But to turn round and run like that... Rezaire cursed Sam heartily, as he found himself once again after all his escapes pursued through the streets of London.

For the moment too his brain was blank of ideas. It had been busy enough, just before, but only with plans for making good his escape by car and launch, not for dealing with following policemen. He had thought that he had done with that part.

He sped on, knowing well that in a very few seconds the whistle would bring them all upon his track again—almost certainly those very detectives who had been after him earlier in the evening and who were probably now searching everywhere for him after his escape from the cinema.

He turned, running lightly, into Jermyn Street, thankful that the crowds and the traffic were beginning to ease off for the night. If he could only hide for a couple of hours he felt no doubt of his ability to throw off his pursuers in the empty streets.

He heard a whistle in the distance ahead of him, saw other figures. Sam was close behind, but at the time the first constable had not yet turned the corner. He caught a glimpse on his left of the open doorway to a block of service flats and an empty lighted hall. In that same brief instant he saw also the bottom of a lift disappearing upward. The hall was deserted because the night porter was at the moment taking a tenant up in the lift to his flat. He made his mind up in a flash and almost instinctively turned in, Sam following him. They moved silently and swiftly across the hall and the next moment were ascending the carpeted stairs, the lift moving on ahead of them.

Sam was too upset at the sudden reversal of their fortunes to make any comment, also too used to Rezaire's sudden and daring moves which so often were successful.

"Where do we go?" he whispered, as they kept pace with the lift, holding themselves just out of sight of its occupants.

"Don't know. All I want is a place to lie low and rest in. I'm trusting to my luck now."

"They will have seen us turn in."

"Bound to; but it will take them a moment or two to discover exactly where, and if we can get inside one of these flats… Shh! The lift's stopping."

The lift hummed to a standstill, several stories up, the gate clashed open; someone was warned to mind the step. Rezaire and Sam waited in the staircase at the back of the lift, only half a flight below the floor at which it had stopped. They heard footsteps on the carpeted landing, heard a man's voice saying, "Good-night, Harris."

"Good-night, Mr. Challoner," returned the lift man, and the gates clanged to again.

As the lift started downward, Rezaire and Sam moved cautiously up, avoiding being seen by the lift-attendant. They arrived on the landing to find a young man in evening dress with an opera hat on the back of his head trying to fit his key in the lock.

As they approached him noiselessly on the thick carpet, he achieved success at last, and the door of the flat swung open.

He straightened himself with an effort. He was not exactly drunk, but at the same time had evidently been having one or two. Then catching sight of their reflection in the glass of the door, he turned round with surprise.

Rezaire surveyed him quickly, a swift stream of impressions running through his brain. Fair hair, pale face with incipient fluff of a moustache, weak mouth and chin, and rather watery goggle eyes. An absolute type— the Piccadilly lounger. Very little brain; might easily be bluffed.

"Good evening, Mr. Challoner," he remarked suavely and Sam though visibly surprised for a moment, twisted his cut features into a smile and also echoed the greeting.

"Good evenin'," returned the youth, his eyes goggling from one to the other. Where the devil had he met these chappies before, he was asking himself.

"You don't remember us?" went on Rezaire, still feeling tentatively for a handle to the situation. Far down on the ground floor he heard the lift come to a standstill and knew their voices could not be heard.

"Er, no, 'fraid I don't, and all that, don't you know."

Rezaire turned to Sam with affected heartiness.

"There, Dick, I told you when we saw him down in the street that he wouldn't remember us."

The youth, puzzled and slightly incredulous, was beginning to edge back into his flat. His brain, never very good at any time, was certainly not working well after the drink he had had. He put his hand against the doorpost to steady himself, and this suddenly gave Rezaire an idea.

He resumed with a knowing smile: "As a matter of fact, it's a wonder any of us remembered the other after that night."

"We'd certainly had one or two," chuckled Sam, taking the cue.

The youth's face cleared a bit. Evidently he had been a trifle sprung when he had met them, or else they had. That would account for it. One met a lot of people when one was like that. But still, dash it all, fellows oughtn't to go bearding other fellows at midnight when they were trotting home to bye-bye, just because one had happened to have a drink with them at one time or another.

"Do you know the Premier Lounge?" suddenly asked Rezaire in playful fashion, but in reality drawing a bow at venture.

The arrow struck. The goggle-eyed young man beamed. Of course he knew the Premier.

"Well, that was where we met. We had a heavy night there one evening…"

"Er, by Jove, so we did." He couldn't remember it at all, but still— there it was. After all, the heavier the night, the less one remembered it. He had been like that before. Life was very full of chappies he had met during a heavy night at the Premier Lounge and couldn't remember. But still at midnight; and to pursue him up to the door of his own flat!

He looked at them suddenly in a flash of sobriety. Sam was staring at him with a fixed grin that made him feel as if he were being hypnotized. Rezaire also was smiling. There seemed to be something behind it. Ought he to ask them in? Perhaps they wanted to touch him for something. Dash it all, had he promised them anything that night in the Premier? They looked as though he had borrowed money from them, but with his stray bar acquaintances the matter was usually the other way about. He cleared his throat nervously.

"Er, awfully jolly of you to look me up, and all that sort of thing," he began. Hang it all though—midnight! "Er, did I, er…"

"There!" said Rezaire triumphantly. "That's wonderful." He put his hand in his pocket. "I never met anyone before from whom I'd borrowed money who hadn't remembered it." His eyes, laughing and friendly, were yet narrowly watching the effect of this upon the other. The situation needed delicate handling. He took his hand from his pocket and held out five £1 notes.

Sam slapped his thigh and laughed loudly. "He doesn't remember," he began in that cheery fashion of his. "Well, I'm damned! Say, Fred,"—this to Rezaire,—"we might have got away with it."

"No," said Rezaire sententiously. "I always pay my debts. When I saw the gentleman coming in here down below, I said: 'Why, if that isn't that nice young chap…' pardon me, of course, Mr. Challoner, but those were my words"—Mr. Challoner, flushing upward from his Adam's apple, emitted a deprecating sound—"young fellow who lent me a fiver and I've lost the card he gave me."

"Oh, I say, really, it doesn't matter, you know… Between friends…" This was positively an unprecedented event in Mr. Challoner's young life. Most of his acquaintances treated him as a kind of perpetual and inexhaustible overdraft. He made as if to decline the proffered notes.

"Those were your very words, Fred," Sam corroborated. "As a matter of fact, you went on: 'And I know Mr. Challoner will excuse us for running up the stairs after him like this just when he wanted to go to bed, but debts between gentlemen…'"

Sam was in his element. Slightly muzzy youths with a lot of money, no brains, and a taste for drink, dope, cards or bets, he considered his legitimate prey.

"Come on," urged Rezaire, thrusting the money into the other's hand. "You must take it, and then we must be off." He turned airily as if to go, though he had no such intention, but was merely pulling out this his biggest bluff of all.

It succeeded.

"Oh, I say, really, don't go. Come in and have a drink or something." All suspicions had now vanished. Chappies who came galloping after you at midnight to pay debts must be all right.

"Well, I don't mind," said Sam dubiously.

"It's awfully good of you, but we ought to be going," resumed Rezaire, playing his fish. His quick ears had caught the faint sounds floating up the lift well—without doubt the arrival of the police.

"Oh, you must. You really must. It's all ready."

"We shall disturb your household."

"Oh, there's only my man, and he's asleep; but it doesn't matter if we do wake him up."

Rezaire, smiling to himself, thought otherwise. Down beneath he heard the lift gate clang. He allowed himself to be persuaded at last.

"Well, it's really awfully good of you," he said, and with Sam stepped over the threshold.

"Oh, not at all," murmured the youth, who had not yet got over his surprise at being paid back.

Rezaire himself closed the door, taking care to do so without noise. The outside world was suddenly shut off, as Challoner led the way somewhat unsteadily to the dining-room.

"Cheap at the price," murmured Rezaire to Sam, who winked in answer.

"Put him to sleep for a bit?" he queried, and touched his waistcoat pocket.

Rezaire nodded.

The unconscious Mr. Challoner led the way to the dining-room, where a decanter of whisky and a siphon with glasses were evidently awaiting his parched arrival home. He took the decanter after waving Rezaire and Sam to armchairs and began to pour out. The glass rattled against the rim and he apologized.

"To tell you fellows the truth," he explained affably, "I had a bit of a binge tonight. Met a lot of the lads and what not."

"Well, we should hardly have noticed it."

"You look as fit as hell," added Sam.

"Awfully good of you to pay back that fiver. Say when! Help yourself to soda! You know, I'm hanged if I can remember it at all."

Rezaire looked inquiringly at Sam who, finger to waistcoat pocket, secretly nodded affirmation. Rezaire thereupon called their host's attention with much delight to a Jacobean oak cabinet standing strangely enough somewhere directly behind him.

The young man turned round to explain further and as he turned his back Sam's long arm shot out from his pocket and for a moment hung over the third glass. A white powder dropped and effervesced into nothingness in a second. A short while later the unsuspecting youth was drinking the doctored whisky and soda and Rezaire and Sam were chatting amiably to him, ears stretched to catch any noise from outside.

They finished their drinks and began to make slow preparations for departure. Mr. Challoner swayed suddenly as he got up.

"Tell you the truth, you fellows," he began again. "I had a bit of binge tonight. I don't feel quite as well as I did."

"Never mind, old man," said Sam sympathetically. "We all get like that at times."

"A drop of drink doesn't hurt anyone," added Rezaire, as the young man abruptly sat down again and half closed his eyes.

"Infernally sleepy," he muttered. "Must have been those liqueurs." He opened his eyes very wide for a moment more and gazed mistily round, then suddenly shut them.

The other two waited a moment. Then: "O. K.?" queried Rezaire.

"Yes. He's good for eight hours. What'll we do now?"

"Put him in his bedroom quietly."

"Why the hell do we want to do that? We haven't got time to go tucking up half London and kissing it good-night."

"No. I know. But the cops may come here yet. If he's in bed and obviously tight, they'll push off again…"

"Humph!" grunted Sam unconvinced, but obediently helped to carry the inert form of Mr. Challoner out of the dining-room.

"Quietly!" ordered Rezaire. "We don't want to wake the blooming valet."

A brief search revealed the bedroom and the young man was taken in; his boots, coat and collar were removed, and he was laid on the bed. While doing so, Rezaire seized the opportunity to retransfer the five pounds that had served as bait to his own pocket. He strewed the clothes about the room and left the light switched on.

"See," he added with the pride of an artist, "he was too tight to undress properly."

They went back to the sitting-room where Rezaire dried and replaced upside down on the tray two out of the three used glasses, Sam watching in admiring wonder.

"You've got a head on you and no mistake," he whispered at length, but Rezaire went quietly on without replying. The head that Sam admired was at that very moment occupied with schemes for definitely betraying Sam to the police in order to ensure his own escape.

Rezaire finished what he was doing and peeped into the hall. Sam came to his side and had just finished reloading and adjusting his revolver when faint voices came to their ears. Through the outer door of the flat they could hear men talking together in the landing outside. They paused motionless. The voices grew louder and suddenly the whirr of an electric bell shattered the silence, followed by a peremptory knocking on the front door.

"My God!" muttered Sam wildly. "How the hell have they…"

Without a word Rezaire grasped him by the sleeve and pulled him rapidly over the hall to where a tall alcove, curtained off, hid a row of pegs for coats and hats.

In a minute they had settled themselves in concealment, awaiting apprehensively the next turn of the wheel of fate. The curtain had barely swung to behind them to the accompaniment of the knocking and the insistent bell, when a door further back in the flat opened and Mr. Challoner's valet, grumbling to himself, in trousers, nightshirt, and overcoat, came out and made his way to the front door.

CHAPTER XII

TRAPPED AGAIN

He opened the door. Almost at once the little hall became full of policemen above whose voices rose the valet's querulous tone of remonstrance.

"'Ere, 'ere, what is it?"

Then the night porter's voice, questioning: "Mr. Challoner's in, isn't he? These gentlemen would like…"

"I suppose so. I don't know."

He moved away to the bedroom door, opened it, looked in and came back. "Yes," he added, "but he's asleep."

Another voice, evidently a detective, suddenly took up the running: "Never mind that at present. Just listen to me for a moment, my man. I am a detective and we want your help. The facts are these. There are two men, whom the police want, somewhere in this block."

"Gumme!" ejaculated the valet.

"They were chased into the building, and the only time they could have got through the hall without being noticed was when the porter was taking a resident up to his flat. They haven't gone out since and if they haven't made a get-away at the top or hidden in the box rooms, which we are now searching, it is just possible that they got by some trick into the flat to which the porter…"

"Mr. Challoner's flat?"

"Exactly. Now just answer a few questions, please. The porter said he was alone when he came up. He did not actually see him enter, so it is possible that they might have either forced a way in or got in under some pretext. Did you see anyone or hear voices when he came in?"

In the darkness Sam and Rezaire held their breath. If he had been awake and heard them, instant search would follow, for the porter knew the young man had been alone when he was brought up in the lift.

"No, I didn't hear anything."

"Are you certain? The porter says he thought he heard conversation as the lift went down."

"Yes, certain. I was asleep."

"Don't you usually wait up?"

"No. Sometimes he brings in friends to have a drink and sometimes he's very late, and sometimes…"

"Sometimes," interpolated the night porter, "he's just a bit…" He broke off and winked.

"Was he tonight?" continued the detective.

"Just slightly," replied the other glancing across at the valet for confirmation.

"How do you know these men didn't take advantage of his condition to force their way in as friends?"

Again Rezaire held his breath. This man was too quick witted. At this rate, they would soon be discovered.

"I dunno!" The valet scratched his head. Then an idea seemed to strike him and he went to the dining-room.

"There's only one glass been used," he said from the door. "He'd have had a drink with them for certain if he'd thought they were friends."

The two detectives conferred together for a moment. Evidently they were arguing that on the one hand, if Rezaire and Sam had got in under guise of friendship, they would have had a drink when Challoner did; on the other hand, if they had made their way in by force, Challoner would not have had a drink at all.

Then the other detective spoke: "Is your master still asleep?"

"He was when I looked in just now."

"Why hasn't he come out at all this talking?"

"Yes," went on the first man quickly, "and why was the hall light on and the dining-room light? That shows there's something unusual. Wouldn't he have turned them off?"

"No," interposed the valet scornfully. "You don't know 'is nibs. His lordship's bedroom light's on too." He walked to the bedroom door and peeped in again. Then he flung it open. "He sometimes forgets," he went on with meaning, "to turn 'em out, and to take his trousers off—and," he added, "me to get a decent crease in 'em again."

Through the open door, Mr. Challoner in shirt and trousers was displayed sprawling across the bed—mouth open, breathing stertorously. The night porter laughed.

"Does he look as though he were in a state to remember to clean his teeth, and blow out the candle?" began the valet again sarcastically, urged on by the laugh he had received, but the detective silenced his attempts at humor with a few curt words.

Then they walked into the bedroom and looked at the young man's inert figure. The reek of whisky came up to them and they returned to the hall.

"I don't think they're in here," one of them said t at last.

"Don't see how they can be," returned the other.

"If they had been, for instance, the first thing they would have done is to have put the lights out when they heard us coming. He, being tight, left 'em on."

"If they didn't come here, is there a door or window outside in the building anywhere else, where they…"

"None, except the box rooms, and Harrison's doing that now."

"Still, I don't know. There's one thing we didn't think of. They might have got in here without the young fellow knowing at all."

"Oh, I don't know, that's rather…"

"Not at all…"

Their voices dropped. Rezaire heard one of them say something about a "search warrant" and the other replied that they'd have to "chance that."

After a while they went to the door, and one of them said to the valet: "All right, you can go back to bed again; but we may come back later on…"

Then they filed out.

The door banged behind him, leaving the valet standing in the empty hall with a dazed look.

Behind the curtain Rezaire and Sam drew silent breaths of relief. Those had been tense moments. Rezaire smiled as he remembered how his forethought in laying Challoner on the bed, in putting away the two glasses they had used, and in leaving the light on had misled the police. It was always the little things which counted more than the big ones, because it was always in the little things that the less clever men made mistakes. Rezaire had so trained himself that it had almost become second nature to him to think of these small items, even though at the moment he had not really anticipated that the police would enter the flat.

The valet moved about in the hall for a bit, and then snapped out the light. They heard him doing something rather strenuous in the bedroom; probably undressing his master or at least taking the trousers off that he might crease them. Fortune had certainly aided Rezaire in that it was apparently not an unusual occurrence for Mr. Challoner to go to bed with his clothes on. After a while the man came out again and went back along the little passage. A door banged and silence fell in the flat once more.

Sam at length ventured to move, stretching his legs.

"Gee, but I'm cramped," he whispered.

"So'm I. We had a bit of luck."

"Yes. Why didn't they have a look round while they were about it?"

"I suppose the arguments didn't seem in favor of our being here. Besides, they're still doing the box rooms up top. Perhaps they can't legally search the place on spec, unless they actually saw us go in."

"What shall we do now?"

"Well, personally," returned Rezaire, "I think I shall go to sleep."

"Go to what?"

"Go to sleep! I'm dead beat; it's about half past eleven; and Heaven knows how much more chivying about we shall have to do. It's the first opportunity I've had, and I'd be a fool not to take it."

"But where…"

"Here! I don't want to move for fear of bringing that valet fellow out on us. His suspicions are now unconsciously aroused, so we'd better let him get to sleep. Also, if we sleep for a couple of hours, the police may have given up and we may have a chance of getting out. It's no good trying to get out now."

"The streets will be quieter too," added Sam, a trifle dubiously. "I must say I'm sick of running about in crowds and having to hit someone every few minutes."

"Well, there you are then! Let's sleep!"

"What about keeping watch?"

"That'll be all right. I can wake up at any time or at any noise."

Sam grunted and settled himself more comfortably.

There had been but a few minutes' silence when Sam suddenly nudged Rezaire.

"Say," his fierce whisper came out of the darkness, "I don't deny you're clever enough, and you've saved me two or three times. But don't you go getting too clever. If you think you're going to steal off while I'm asleep and leave me you're bloody well mistaken. I'll get you for it, if it takes me a week, and the way I'll cut you up will make you long for prison or even the rope. You won't tell me where your get-away is, but I'm going to stick to you till you show me. You've got to take me safe there or you'll…"

"Oh, stow it! I won't give you away," lied Rezaire, but the cold fear of Sam suddenly settled about his heart once more. When he did cast Sam off, he would have to be very careful that someone was waiting to snap him up quick.

Silence fell again. Rezaire, utterly exhausted by all he had gone through, wondered for a moment what the police were doing and how he would get out. He was fairly certain that, when they found nothing upstairs they would have the house watched until dawn. Then weary in body and mind he fell asleep.

Some while later he awoke with a sudden jerk and looked at his watch. It was one o'clock. He had been asleep about an hour and a half. Some indefinable sense of something not quite right had roused him and he listened intently without moving. He could just hear voices outside on the landing—evidently the police still on the trail.

He leaned across with his hand and touched Sam gently so as to rouse him without making him speak. In a moment Sam had come to and both sat up in the confined space, cramped and stiff.

Rezaire crawled outside the curtain, turned round and put his ear close to Sam's.

"One o'clock," he whispered. "The streets'll be empty enough now. But the police are still outside on the landings and stairs. I don't think they're yet certain that we're not in this flat."

"Any other way out?" asked Sam.

"We'll have a look round and see."

They got to their feet and stealthily set off on their tour of inspection. The flat was not a big one; a small hall, dining-room, sitting-room, two bedrooms, and at the back a tiny kitchen, and a room where obviously the valet slept. The windows, as far as they could see, gave either onto Jermyn Street or else on to a small well or courtyard at the back, but the flat was far too high up from these to be of any use. There was no fire escape or other means of getting out save by the main stairway and the hall, where the detectives were. They stood in the dark kitchen, their cursory search over, and Sam scratched his head.

"Damn it!" he muttered. "Isn't there any way out of the back?"

"Evidently not."

"There ought to be a back door."

"Well, there isn't."

"How do the tradesmen bring the meat and so on? These toffs surely don't have a bloke walking in at the front door with two or three pounds of fresh beef!"

"No, they..." Rezaire broke off suddenly and half turned to the window. He had had an idea. Almost at the same moment another thought apparently supervened in his mind and he checked himself.

"What?" asked Sam sharply.

"Nothing," replied Rezaire, gradually turning his back on the window. "I'm as much at sea as you are."

But he had not been quick enough. Sam was suspicious. He knew as surely as he stood there that his companion had thought of something and then had instantly decided not to tell him.

"Look here," he demanded, "what were you going to say?"

"Nothing, I tell you"

"You—well will tell me," Sam blustered, "you little—or I'll—well cut you up!"

"Stop your fool mouth, Sam," returned Rezaire undaunted. He was not afraid of Sam's threats at the moment because he knew Sam had nothing to go upon. Also Sam could not put them into effect as long as he held the secret of escape. He was calling Sam's bluff and Sam wavered.

"If I'd got any plan worth telling you," he went on, "I'd spit it out, but I thought of something and decided it wasn't possible."

At his matter-of-fact statement and calm tones Sam subsided, muttering: "I thought you'd got hold of a way out of here and then determined to keep it for yourself."

"You're a fool, Sam," returned the other. "How many plans have I thought of this evening and kept to myself?"

"I'm—I'm sorry," said Sam, completely mollified, and Rezaire breathed again. For Sam had been right. He had just thought of something and in the same instant had decided not to tell it to Sam. He had remembered suddenly that in nearly every one of these service flats the kitchen window had an outside lift to the courtyard below for the use of tradesmen, a small platform running on a cable, and a pulley, on which groceries and meat were placed and drawn up. If there was one in this flat it would provide a possible means of escape.

Nonchalantly he made his way to the window and under some pretext peered out into the darkness. Yes, he had been right. There against the sky beyond he could just see two thin black lines that were the cables stretching up to the pulley above. Where the lift itself was he could not make out. If he were to get away by it, it would have to be first pulled up level with the window. And Heaven only knew how once in it he could be able to regulate the descent. But one thing was certain: there would only be room for one at a time.

He turned away as Sam came to his side.

"Nothing there," he lied. He certainly was not going to tell Sam. There was only a way of escape for one, and he had found it. They could not both use it, and he would not let Sam go first because he did not trust him to send it up again. Once Sam found himself clear of the place, he might decide to go off on his own. Sam, on the other hand, suspicious, overbearing, and yet dependent on him, would never let him go first for fear of the same thing. And he would be quite right, for it seemed to Rezaire the ideal way of escaping from Sam at last. His brain began to evolve schemes for getting a chance at it by himself.

"Come back into the hall," he whispered at last and in the darkness they began to move back. Keeping strict silence, Rezaire let Sam lead. Halfway he himself stopped and noiselessly returned to the kitchen. Working swiftly, before Sam should discover his absence, he opened the window and began to haul up the lift. It worked very easily, there being a counterweight, but every now and then the pulley above squeaked loudly, echoing in the darkness between the high walls of the block of flats.

He pulled downward on one cable, while the other with the lift slowly moved up. It seemed ages before he could make out the lift, a darker mass just below the window-sill. He had just made it fast, when he heard a noise behind him. Sam had returned. Quick as thought he whipped away from the window into the shadow, moving swiftly and silently round till he stood close to the dark form at the door. Sam had paused without a sound on the threshold, and was peering in evidently hoping to catch him. He had only been just in time, he thought, as he formulated a story in his mind which would deceive his companion.

"Hallo, Sam," he whispered easily at last. "Did you hear..."

There was a sudden startled exclamation and then the light was switched on. Facing him at only a few feet was the surprised face of the valet.

CHAPTER XVIII

EXIT SAM

Rezaire had barely time to realize that the valet, awakened by some sound, had arrived to take a hand in the game, when the light was switched off again, and a loud shout of "Police" echoed through the silence of the flat. At the same time the newcomer, fear dispelled by the presence of a tangible foe and evidently reassured by the fact that he was not a big one, grappled him with vigor. They swayed this way and that for a moment, then Rezaire's leg was hooked from under him and he was swung off his feet. The next moment they had fallen heavily through the kitchen doorway and were struggling on the floor of the passage outside.

In a very few minutes Rezaire realized that his opponent was much stronger than he was. His arms had been pinioned to his side in the first onslaught; now, however, the grip slackened and then abruptly changed. Two hands gripped his throat; two thumbs began to squeeze his windpipe. He threw his own up and pulled at them with all his force, but the man was too powerful for him. It was like pulling at an iron clamp. The cruel thumbs pressed into his throat, and stars began to swim in front of his eyes. A sickly tickling sensation settled in his gorge; the blood started to throb in his ears and behind his eyeballs. He realized in a sudden flash that this was more serious than a mere struggle. He was being choked to death. The mad fear of physical pain and death that was the guiding influence in his life settled on him. He thought wildly for a moment of Viv, wished he had behaved better to her. He tore ferociously at the fingers that were choking him; but without avail. The revolver that was in his pocket he could not get at, for it was right underneath his body.

Relentlessly the thumbs constricted his throat, squeezing the very life out of his body. In an excess of terror he kicked out at his opponent, at anything. Something crashed heavily at his side and broke to pieces. Surging in his ears came the reiterated shouting of the valet for the police and a loud hammering on the door of the flat.

Then someone fell heavily over both of them. It was Sam at last, come to his help. For a moment or two the three of them struggled together, then suddenly disintegrated. The cruel hands were gone from his windpipe and he took several gasping breaths, while his head swam madly in a whirl of sickness. At his side he heard Sam's voice: "Quick! Quick! Stop his opening the door to them."

Then Sam was off and he heard him stumbling in pursuit.

He got unsteadily to hands and knees. The flat was full of noise, the valet's shouts, Sam's curses, the hammering on the door. There was still a loud drumming in his ears, a retching in his gorge. He crawled weakly into the kitchen and collapsed, thoroughly frightened, sick with fear and pain, feeling half dead. Out in the hall he could hear the sounds of Sam and the valet fighting, the one to open the front door, the other to prevent him. Everything seemed to him at the moment unreal, something which did not really interest or concern him.

There came a crash of glass outside, then a bang, and the voices of the police suddenly closer. A sharp cry followed, then two shots, and the sound of running feet. The next moment someone had rushed into the kitchen.

A door banged; a key turned in the lock. The light was switched on revealing Sam, disheveled and bleeding again from his old cut, standing to one side of the locked kitchen door. One hand was on the light switch; the other held a revolver.

Looking round Sam saw Rezaire.

"Oh, there you are," he snapped in hurried sentences. "Why didn't you come and help me? Stand clear of the door in case they fire through it. I've done your friend in for you, but not till after he'd let them in. They'll shoot me on sight—if they get a chance."

Rezaire did not move, but with closed eyes sat tenderly fingering his throat, and Sam picked him up and dumped him in a corner, still only semiconscious. A paper had fallen from a pocket torn in the struggle and Sam unobserved picked it up. For a moment he held it in his hand; then he smiled, for he recognized what it was. It was the all-important letter, the secret of Rezaire's launch, and of his way of escape. Hurriedly he slipped it out of the envelope and took possession of it, a grin of triumph on his lips; then with a flash of cunning he returned the empty envelope to Rezaire's pocket while he still sprawled in the corner in dazed fashion. The next moment a voice was heard outside telling them that they were caught and might as well give themselves up, and a heavy battering began on the door of the kitchen.

"Hell!" muttered Sam. "What'll we do now?" He waited a moment and then fired suddenly through the door. There was a shout outside and the hammering stopped for a few moments. An answering shot crashed in and through the room, shattering a plate on the dresser. Sam, sheltered by the wall, laughed aloud. Rezaire, still cowering in his corner, stared at him in amazement tinged with repulsion. Sam, face streaming with blood, revolver in hand, actually seemed to be enjoying this. He looked at that moment every inch a fighter. He appeared capable almost of fighting his way out single-handed.

The hammering at the door recommenced and continued despite Sam's shots. Evidently they were working at it sideways from cover. Judging by the splintering sound also they were using some sort of axe or chopper.

"Come on," said Sam suddenly to Rezaire. "Get your gun and join in. This is our last stand. We can't get out, so we'll have to make a good end. I'm—if I let them take me off to jug and the rope. Don't know that I shan't jump out of the window." He looked across the room in that direction.

Rezaire, slowly pulling himself together, went quite white at the last words. He must keep Sam away from the window. If Sam saw that lift waiting ready just below the sill, he would take it and Rezaire would not have a look in. Sam would have a chance of getting away and he would be left, whereas he intended that it should be the other way round.

"Wonder if it's a big drop," mused Sam.

"Look out!" warned Rezaire quickly to distract his attention. "There's a panel giving."

Sam, waiting, revolver in hand for the first sign of their adversaries, let the matter of the window slide and watched the door.

Rezaire got to his feet in the corner and licking his dry lips nerved himself for what he knew he must do. He must make a rush for the lift without letting Sam see. He dared not try and hold Sam up, for Sam was dangerous. He knew that he would be shot like a dog if he were caught in his attempted treachery.

One side of his brain kept saying: "Now! Now, before it is too late!"; the other: "Wait! Wait, till it is certain he will be captured." He dared not risk Sam's escaping, impossible as that event now seemed. He dared not risk the chance of Sam's vengeance. And Sam was capable enough and brave enough in his way to escape in spite of the terrible odds. He crouched there, torn between fear of Sam and fear of the bullets, an abject figure, very different from the cool resourceful leader and shaper of plans of a few hours before.

With a sudden crash a panel fell inward and Sam's revolver came to the ready. But the police were cautious. Nothing showed. Instead, the onslaught was shifted to another panel.

"Come on," snarled Sam to Rezaire. "Get your gun out. You've got to fight for it. Your brain's no good now."

Trembling with fear, Rezaire produced his revolver. His brain, that Sam now despised, was busy even at that moment with schemes for outwitting him. A new thought flashed into his mind. Dared he shoot Sam suddenly before he made his dash? It would be safest. Almost immediately he recoiled at the thought. He was not brave enough; he had not yet shot a man; and besides he might miss and then Sam's wild vengeful fury...

Then three things suddenly happened at once. Another panel fell inward with a crash, Sam threw his revolver up and fired twice, and Rezaire, nerving himself up to the pitch of action, ran for the open window.

Half across the sill he saw Sam turn suddenly, heard his exclamation: "You blasted little rat! By God, I'll get you for this!" He saw the little round mouth of Sam's revolver jump up to cover him, saw it disappear in a little red spurt, felt a bullet whistle past his ear.

With a sharp cry of absolute terror, he flung the revolver he was clutching straight at Sam's face, working with maniacal fury, and leaped from the sill on to the outside lift, flinging his arms, as he did so, round the other cable. The weapon, wildly flung, missed Sam, and struck the electric light globe. There was a sharp report and the place was flung into sudden darkness, on the background of which another spurt of red flame from Sam's gun again stood out for an instant as the lift suddenly began to descend.

Crouched on the lift, Rezaire plunged downward at an increasing speed; and the dark room with its echoing report of revolvers, its smell of powder, and, above all, Sam's face, the eyes blazing hatred and vengeance, suddenly seemed miles away. Sick with terror, he was yet conscious enough to tighten the grasp of his arm round the upward flying cable, and heard the whirr of the pulley far above drop to a slow creaking as his speed was reduced. The cable running between his arm and chest began to burn like a rod of hot iron through his clothes, but he tightened his grip still further until he had his motion under control.

There was a slight bump, which shook him off the lift; then he found himself standing on earth once more. Around him the tall blocks of flats soared up to the night sky. Somewhere above, where the quivering pulley-ropes reached upward, he heard the sound of shots, and realized that Sam was still making a fight for it. Lights were snapping up in several windows round about.

He drew a deep breath. Incredible as it seemed he was out of it all. His life was no longer in danger; he was free at last of Sam, and if Sam was taken, as he assuredly must be, he need fear him no more. The last ten minutes began to seem to him like some impossible dream, and his old daring and resource, refreshed by the sleep he had had not so long ago, began to come back to him.

He shook himself, and adjusting his clothing, began quickly to move away. As he did so, he heard the sound of footsteps, and shrank suddenly into the dark shadow. Two figures came up, passing close by him—policemen. They stood for a moment a few paces away looking up at the window. As he had anticipated, the flats had been surrounded, but this he did not mind, for he was not cornered now; he had all the deserted streets of night London before him.

He edged along the shadow till he found the entrance to the courtyard, where he slipped out. But as luck would have it, just as he rounded the corner, one of the policemen turned and saw his furtive movements under the light of a street lamp.

There was a shout, a whistle, and the next minute he was again running through the streets, though even as he ran, he thanked his stars that this time he had not Sam with him.

He ran a few paces up the street and found himself in Jermyn Street once more, where he turned. With any luck he should be able to shake off his pursuers quite easily in the streets. There were only two or three policemen after him at most, for the rest and the detectives were up in the flat where Sam was making his stand.

A small paved alley way presented itself at his side, leading up northward past a church into Piccadilly. He took it and for a moment was out of sight. As they came into the place behind him he emerged into Piccadilly at the far end.

He ran straight across Piccadilly, looking neither to right nor left. The street stretched away on either side of him, deserted in his vicinity, save for two people returning from a dance, and a taxicab. In another moment he had plunged into a similar passage, called Piccadilly Place, on the far side and slightly to the left. Running to the end of this—it was only a short distance—he gave another swift glance backward and saw that he was again out of sight for the moment. He turned sharp to the right and stopped dead in amazement.

It was a cul-de-sac. He should have turned to the left. He turned about and then suddenly realized that he had already lost ground and that his best plan was now to hide in a doorway and let them go past. They had not seen him turn and emerging into this street, they would never think that he had taken the cul-de-sac end.

He went on a few paces, and concealed himself in a deep shadowed doorway, panting heavily. The sound of running drew nearer, came to the end of the passage, paused a moment, and then resumed to the left. They had not thought it worthwhile to look in the cul-de-sac. He peeped cautiously out. There were three of them. He realized suddenly that the street he was in was Vine Street and that exactly opposite him was the famous police station. He could not help chuckling at the fact that he had actually dodged them within a few yards of a police station. But he must be quick, for when they had traversed the other street and saw no sign of him, they might turn back.

He stepped out, intending to turn down Piccadilly Place once more while his pursuers were in Sackville Street.

But as he reached the corner he ran bang into a figure coming the opposite way—a figure in blue uniform—a policeman.

Both were surprised at the impact, but Rezaire, the quicker, realized two things. First, that this constable, from his manner and walk, did not know him, or even of him, being apparently one of the ordinary night duty men returning from his beat. Secondly, that, in spite of this, his suspicion had already been to a certain extent aroused by his strange behavior, which suspicion he must quell at once. In addition, he had not much time to do this, for the others might at any minute be back. A brilliant inspiration came to him in a flash, one after his own heart, which had been given birth by the strange and irrelevant picture, coming suddenly unbidden into his mind, of the young fool Challoner lying drunk on his bed.

With an air of portentous solemnity and unsteady gait Rezaire advanced a forefinger and poked the constable hard in the region of the middle button.

"Tag! You're it! Now you cash me, ol' fren'," he announced, and zigzagged back again across Vine Street.

The constable, torn between amused tolerance and ruffled dignity, followed him, whereupon Rezaire turned round and exclaiming: "Thash ri…" knocked his helmet off, and promptly collapsed in the very doorway of the entrance to the cells.

"'Ere. 'Ere," began the constable sternly. "You can't do that. You cummer longer me." He turned to pick him up, and at first, to ensure capture, Rezaire resisted vigorously. But a large hand twined itself in his collar and another seized his arm. He just had time, unobserved, to slip his hand to his pocket and throw away the important letter which would incriminate him, before he was being slowly but surely propelled into the police station.

Within a quarter of an hour Jimmie Rezaire had had his finger prints taken, and minus boots and the contents of his pockets found himself sitting in a police cell for what was left of the night, on a charge of being drunk and disorderly in Vine Street at about one-fifteen A.M. He had given a fictitious name, for he knew his clothing was safely unmarked and from long experience he had nothing else dangerous on him, now that he had got rid of the one thing that would have given him away. Outside, half the detective and police force of London were searching for him. His bold ruse had succeeded beyond hope, and for the moment he was safe.

He lay down and composed himself for slumber. His way to safety now seemed absolutely clear. Though a description of himself and Sam was probably at the moment in the police station, it was almost certain that his was that of James Robinson, the agent. To the authorities he was just an ordinary drunk and disorderly. He would pay his fine next morning, walk out, take his car down to Beaulieu before that night, and then his launch to the Channel Islands, France, and safety. But he could not forget Sam's furious face, the light of hatred and vengeance in his eyes. Supposing Sam had not been taken after all, impossible as it seemed. Sam was a fighter and, where brute force and resolution were concerned, could get out of very tight corners. He thought again of Sam's words, of Sam's knife. Sam, he knew, would now think of nothing except to get even with him. He shivered at thought of what Sam would do to him if he got him in his power. The prison cell, even the cells of Dartmoor, seemed more attractive than finding himself in Sam's hands after what had happened.

Then sleep came to claim him. But just before he dropped off, a low chuckle broke from his lips. True to his principles he had certainly this time taken the most unexpected course; for the very last place in the whole of London that the police would search for a fugitive from justice would be in a Vine Street police cell.

CHAPTER XIV

THE OPEN ROAD

A fine spring morning looked down on Jimmie Rezaire sauntering along Jermyn Street. An hour previously, after an excellent breakfast, sent in from a neighboring restaurant, he had been taken before the magistrate. Here he had played the proper part, that of a gentleman, who, having misjudged his capacity at a dinner with some old college friends, was by then deeply ashamed of himself. He had, he admitted, hardly been able to remember the incidents of the previous night and he was hardly more surprised than shocked to find the walls of a cell round him when he woke. Could it be arranged that his name did not appear in the papers? He sincerely hoped he had not committed any other crime save that of being drunk and disorderly. Yes, certainly, he pleaded guilty. His family... The magistrate thought it could, and Rezaire was not bothered with any demand for details or to make any disclosures. He disbursed a fine, gave the policeman who arrested him half-a-crown, another to the man who gave him back the contents of his pockets, and was let out by a side door amid a general atmosphere of good-will. He had chuckled to himself. His identity was undisclosed and not a single one of the police knew that they had had through their hands the very man whose description was being circulated to them. After all, how should they? Even had the description tallied exactly, which it did not, they would have thought twice before they fitted it to the inmate of one of their own cells.

Rezaire next had bought a map of South England, a portmanteau with a few clothes for travelling, and a new suit to replace his damaged garments. Seen in the light of day, they told an eloquent tale of his adventures of the night before, though of course in the police court he had described it as a result of his sad downfall from the paths of sobriety. He also purchased an automatic from an obliging dealer in Soho, who asked no questions about licenses and a small amount of ammunition. He was taking no chances.

In Jermyn Street he gave the block of flats a wide berth. Despite his nerve he did not wish to go any nearer the place where he had spent such a terrible time. It all seemed like a far-away dream to him now. That young fool Challoner, the drugged whisky, the struggle with the valet—he shivered at that memory—Sam and he in the kitchen, and his wild plunge to safety on the service lift. He wondered where Sam was now—either dead or in jail he hoped.

Well, the break-up of the gang, as he had always thought, had been sudden and complete. Sam and Harrap both either killed or taken; Joe taken; Viv—he wondered where Viv was. He hoped she had gotten away. Viv was a good sort. They had been great friends—in fact more— once, and then he had chucked her and yet she had not hated him for it. Rather she had always stuck up for him against Sam, almost as if she… He owed Viv a lot, and if she had gotten safely away, he vowed that he would do everything in his power to help her further.

He whistled cheerily to himself, as he made for the garage. Before him was the open road; the sun was shining; there was no Sam to bother him; he had had a good breakfast; what more could he want? He turned into a side yard off Jermyn Street where there was a big garage and went into a little office.

"Morning, Mr. Harding," he said to a man he found there.

"Good-morning, Mr. Carlyle. Lovely day for a spin. Going out?"

"Yes. Is the car all right?"

"I think so. Your man's just greasing her up in the yard somewhere."

He stepped to the door and spoke to a garage hand: "Joe, tell Dixon Mr. Carlyle's here."

In a minute or two a short squat man with a dark face and black brows that met in a straight line across his forehead appeared in his shirt sleeves. He jerked a hand to his head.

"Morning, sir."

"The Mercedes ready to go out, Dixon?"

"In about a quarter of an hour."

"I want to go out for a longish run today. Newmarket," he added for the benefit of Harding. "Get her ready and fill up with everything."

"Very good, sir."

The man turned and went back to his job. Rezaire stayed watching his back for a moment, a little smile on his face. A good fellow Dixon, and just the man for him. A fellow who would not balk at anything he was asked to do, however strange, and who would keep his mouth shut while doing it. It was to his advantage to do so too, for he would not want to risk his master's displeasure. For Rezaire knew a thing or two about him which Dixon did not wish others—particularly the police—to find out. Rezaire always chose his tools with a certain amount of care. Following Polonius' famous advice to his son: "The friends thou hast, and their adoption tried, grapple them to thy soul with hoops of steel." Rezaire had found that there was no steel hoop so strong as the knowledge, for instance, that the police wanted a man for a little affair of an accident in which an old lady was killed, and a certain car driver had not stopped, and had not been traced. Yes, Dixon would do anything he wanted without question, because Dixon knew well enough which side his bread was buttered. Rezaire turned back into the office and went and picked up a paper.

"Extraordinary affair, this of last night," remarked Mr. Harding.

"I haven't seen the paper yet," replied Rezaire coolly. "What was it? Jewel robbery?"

"No, more than that. It's got big headlines in all the papers. Police chasing fellows all over London and shooting at 'em. More like New York than London."

"Have they caught them?"

"They've got one or two. Not the ringleader, apparently."

"I must read it. D'you mind my waiting here?"

"Not in the least, Mr. Carlyle. Sit down."

He offered him a chair and then went out on some business. Rezaire sat down and, with a smile on his face, glanced through the paper. Glaring headlines hit him straightway:

"AMAZING SCENES IN STRAND."

"POLICE CHASE DOPE RUNNER ACROSS ROOFS."

"DETECTIVE KILLED IN MIDNIGHT ROUND-UP."

All the usual phrases stood out across the page. Rezaire began to read. There were one or two things he wanted to know.

"At about seven P.M. last night Detective Inspector Harrison, together with other members of The Criminal Investigation Department, Scotland Yard, commenced the round-up of a gang of illicit traffickers in cocaine who have been troubling the police for the last four months. This gang, Scotland Yard have good reason to believe, has been behind nearly all the recent smuggling of cocaine from the continent, and last night, by a clever capture, the secret of their headquarters was at last…"

Rezaire read on with interest. The whole roundup was described in detail. He learned how Joe had been bluffed and had lost his nerve, he learned of the nefarious operations of James Robinson, Agent (the police had certainly found out a good bit from their search of his office), of the collusion between Robinson and Carlyle in the next house (they had not found out the whole truth about that yet, as apparently *both* Carlyle and Robinson were "wanted"), the chase across the roofs and the search under the night sky. Nothing was mentioned about Vivienne; it looked as though she might have gotten away.

He whistled as he read; he was learning a lot which he had not known before. Harrap, it appeared, hiding behind a chimney-stack, had only wounded a man on the arm despite all the shooting. Eventually he had been himself shot in the head, captured, and taken to the hospital, where he now lay unconscious in a precarious condition.

The girl whom they had tied up had been extensively interviewed, and the paper was by way of making her a heroine. Rezaire smiled in pleased fashion as he read of her ruse in locking the door, under pretense of unlocking it, and thus preventing them from getting away through the house. He appreciated brains and on that occasion he had certainly been outwitted.

Then he came to another flare up of headlines, as the reporter began upon the fight in the empty house:

"DEATH DEALING IN THE DARK."

"SYDNEY STREET SCENES"

Here he whistled as he read. From the point of view of the police, who had evidently only issued a very guarded statement, it was all very vague, but apparently one detective had been killed and two plain-clothes men wounded, one with a knife. It was obvious too, as he read on, that they were not certain how many of their opponents had been there. They were evidently counting on three men, Sam, Robinson and Carlyle, and in all probability were considering Viv as still with them.

He skimmed over the motor car chase, which was told in detail; he knew as much about that as they did. The reporter evidently arriving late on the scene and pressed for time to get his copy in, had only a brief description of the fire in the cinema, but Rezaire was gratified to see it was rightly attributed to him. But there the tale stopped. There was nothing more. The rest of the story had been too late for the morning papers.

He dropped the sheet in disgust. Despite his interest there had been one thing, and one thing only, that he had really wanted to read, and that was that Sam had been captured.

He was almost certain of it—but still he wanted to see it in black and white. He knew that Sam's reckless bravery, coupled to the fact that he was fighting for his neck, was enough to get him out of any situation, even one as hopeless as that in which he had been left in the flat. He had let many other chances go by in order to secure a really good one and it would be terrible to know that it had failed. Terrible in more senses than one, for Sam would then be after him. Now that he had betrayed Sam and

Sam knew it, he feared Sam and his keen long bladed knife more than anything else in the world. He knew enough of Sam to realize that he was now perfectly capable of tying him up and torturing him slowly to death—if he got him in his power. He would have been happy despite all the police in London, if he could only have known for certain that Sam was safely under lock and key.

He put the paper away at last. It told him nothing about Sam. Doubtless the midday papers would have it all in. He rose and went to the private locker in the garage which was one of his many hiding places for keeping things too important or dangerous to carry on him. From this he took a passport made out for France in his own name, another revolver, some French money, and a few papers. Then he drew from his pocket the map he had bought and for some while studied the road from London to Beaulieu—the Southampton Road.

A minute or two later Dixon came up once more, looking very smart in green livery.

"She's all ready now, sir," he said, and Rezaire got up.

In a few minutes' time, with his suitcase beside him, and Dixon in front at the wheel, he was gliding in his big car westward down Piccadilly, having countermanded the order for Newmarket as soon as they were out of the garage. Behind him, he thought, as he leaned luxuriously against the cushions, he was leaving all his life of the past five months with its breathless and hectic climax, its policemen, revolvers, chases and danger, and above all, behind him he was leaving Sam and his knife. Before him stretched the open road which led to Beaulieu, his motor launch, and the spoil of his last months' work, in short, freedom—until—he smiled grimly—until the game that he loved, the game of crime and revenge—of pitting his wits against those of law, order and government—tempted him again.

They passed Hammersmith, Brentford, Isleworth, and got on the road to Staines and Egham. He was now quite safe. No one knew his car; no one knew his launch; and he did not think any of the police would know him by sight, for they had after all not seen his face properly as yet. He sighed, stretched himself, laughed as he thought of his last night's lodging in the police station, and opened his map once more.

By Basingstoke and Chichester was what he had told Dixon, in short, the Southampton Road, till he was told to turn off, which would be somewhere about a place called Bassett. More than this he had not told him, despite the fact that the man was far more to be trusted than Sam.

They threaded their way through Staines with its perpetual smell of oilcloth, crossed the river, climbed the hill out of Egham. The day was bright and crisp—a regular early spring day, with a lift in the air and a promise under foot. Rezaire almost wished he could stay in England, now that spring was coming. Then he thought of Paris, the green and white boulevards, the little tables under the trees—Paris in spring was even better than England in spring. He loved Paris.

The car glided down the long slope at Virginia Water, past the famous Wheatsheaf Hotel at the bottom, up again for Bagshot.

The hum of the wheels grew higher and higher; they were travelling at a good forty miles per hour now. They flashed past an A.A. scout on a cycle. Rezaire looked idly out of the window as they passed. Suddenly he saw in the hedge, only visible as they drew level, a man with a note-book. Now Rezaire was skilled enough to know a plain-clothes man when he saw him and for a moment his heart leaped into his mouth. Then he drew breath again, laughing at his guilty conscience. Of course everyone was not awaiting him on the road. He realized what the man was doing. It was nothing more nor less than an ordinary police trap to catch motorists exceeding the limit; it was nothing to do with him. It dawned suddenly on him that it was something to do with him, for he was exceeding the limit. He picked up the voice tube and spoke to Dixon: "Gently. I believe that was a 'trap.'"

He saw Dixon nod his head in answer and slow down to a crawl; then suddenly they reached a slight bend. Ahead of them on the road were two uniformed figures.

"Look out!" called Rezaire, snatching up the tube again. He realized with chagrin that the man he had seen in the hedge was the second man of the trap, not the first, and that therefore the slowing down had been too late. He half laughed to himself at the sudden change of his luck. After all the escapes he had had within the last twelve hours—to get caught by an ordinary police trap. It did not really matter; he was, of course, quite safe from recognition, since they could not know who he was and were probably not yet on the lookout for him here; but still it was annoying.

To his amazement, however, Dixon suddenly put on speed instead of slackening down at the constable's signal. The car leaped forward at the two figures in the roadway with upheld hands. As it bore down on them they jumped aside. Rezaire caught a glimpse of the mingled surprise and indignation on their faces, and then they were past. Out of the back window he saw them taking down the number. The police trap suddenly assumed more threatening proportions; for they had broken the law a second time by charging it, which was a much more serious crime.

CHAPTER XV

FALSE COLORS

For a moment Rezaire was too amazed and angry to do anything, then he snatched the voice pipe again and waiting till they were some distance away and out of sight brought the car to a standstill.

"You damn fool," he began, head out of the window. "What did you charge through like that for?" He was really angry, for Dixon had nearly spoiled everything. It would have meant nothing to Rezaire really to have stopped, apologized courteously, shown his license—made out incidentally in the name of Carruthers—given a name and address, and gone on. When he was in Paris, a summons in the name of Carruthers at a fictitious address would really hardly have affected him.

"If you get caught in a trap," he went on furiously, "it's much better to stop. Surely you of all people ought to have learned that by now."

"I'm very sorry," said Dixon sullenly, "but you told me to do it."

"I didn't. I shouted "Look out!""

"You said 'Go hard!'"

"Good Lord, I didn't. What should I say 'Go hard!' for?"

"I thought perhaps you didn't want to have anything to do with the police."

"You mean you didn't want to yourself," retorted Rezaire. He sat back in the car and reflected. It was really extraordinarily annoying. A short while ago he had been as free as the air, now the police were after him again. They had got the number of his car and what was worse they would now probably detain him or make inquiries. He would not be at all surprised if this did not give away the whole show. Suspicion would be aroused, for people do not generally run through police traps without stopping unless they have some good motive for avoiding the police. He sat biting his fingers and thinking it over.

Dixon's face suddenly appeared again at the window. He had been rummaging in the tool box at the back.

"Anyway, we've done it now, sir. Better be getting on or they may send after us."

"That's not much good," snapped Rezaire. "We'll be stopped at the next village."

Dixon grinned. He seemed to know that his master was anxious to avoid the police. Insensibly they seemed to be drifting into mutual conspiracy.

"'Ow will they stop us?" he asked with the air of a man who has a point to make.

"By the number, you fool."

"Ho! Will they?" Dixon grinned again. "Look 'ere." He produced and held up two number plates which he had taken from the tool box. Then he said triumphantly: "They may have got our number, but they haven't got this one."

"BK3140," Rezaire read out in surprise. "Is it a registered number?"

"I suppose so," admitted Dixon. "It isn't registered by us though. Anyone might have it."

"Well, it's safer than our other is." Rezaire began to see the possibilities of the scheme. "We can get through on this."

"Shall I put 'em on then, sir?"

"Yes, but be careful none of these passing cars sees you doing it. And be quick! They may come on after us in a car, though they're more likely to phone to the next village."

Only two cars passed while Dixon was working and in a very short space of time Rezaire's car bore the registered number BK3140. The old number plates were put in the bottom of the box, the car purred into life again, and they were once more on the road heading southward.

As Rezaire had guessed, though they saw no one at Sunningdale a mile or two further on, at Bagshot two constables stood on the roadway examining the passing cars. As Dixon approached, one of them stepped forward, glancing at a paper in his hand. The car evidently answered to the description. Then he saw the number and paused. He spoke to his companion, who shook his head, and in that moment the car glided past. They were through; thanks to Dixon's foresight, they would not now be held up. Rezaire wiped his forehead. He had really been very nervous about the affair. For though he knew no one yet guessed who he was, this was only true as long as he behaved normally; the moment he began to run through police traps without stopping, there was every chance of bringing last night's pack down on him again, for they would not have been idle during the latter half of last night. Doubtless all the main roads round London, as well as all termini and ports were being watched and anything suspicious would be at once reported direct to Scotland Yard.

He laughed as he thought of the policemen in Bagshot, waiting for the car with his number that never came. They would phone back in the end and probably the circumstances would be reported, but by that time he would be well on the way to freedom.

The long sweep of road unrolled before the purring bonnet, villages swept up to them and passed in a confused impression of little houses, village greens, sign posts, and war memorials. Dixon was driving very carefully now and taking no risks of coming under police notice once more. Soon after twelve-thirty they arrived on the outskirts of Basingstoke. Here Rezaire told Dixon to drive to a hotel for lunch and in a minute or two the big car was being backed into the courtyard of the Black Boar Hotel.

Rezaire got out and stretched himself.

"So far so good," he said to Dixon.

"I'm sorry, sir," replied the man, "about that trap. I thought you wanted to blind through it and to hell with the boys in blue."

"No, no, always treat them properly—unless there is no other way. We may have to 'blind' through them before we're finished."

"Well, you can trust me to do that." He put his face close to Rezaire's and added confidentially, "I 'ate the blighters!"

"I know you do," Rezaire laughed. "That was a very good scheme of yours," he added, "having those number plates ready. Now go and get yourself something to eat and be ready in about three-quarters of an hour."

Dixon nodded and grinned and disappeared into the saloon bar for a pint of food.

Rezaire in the coffee room of the Black Boar sent out for a paper and eagerly looked it through. His story was all there again in big headlines. It was, without doubt, the news of the day. There was a little more than had been in the London morning papers, but not much. He would not be able to learn what had happened in Mr. Challoner's flat till the first of the evening papers' midday edition arrived from town. The only item of interest was that the detectives had now discovered his ruse of disguising himself as Robinson and Carlyle alternately and were looking for one man only instead of the two. Here followed a smudgy photograph and a description (in which he recognized Mrs. Gibson's touch).

Three of the gang he saw were definitely reported to be still at large, so Viv had not been captured on the roof, but like Sam and himself was still free at about midnight. There was nothing more of any interest except that Scotland Yard was offering a reward. Rezaire felt rather annoyed at the latter. He had never in his career had a price on him before, for generally he had covered up his tracks so well. That resulted from having Sam as a companion, Sam who apparently only made himself conspicuous by killing policemen.

He folded the newspaper up and looked round. The people at the next table were discussing the affair. It was certainly making a stir, while common enough perhaps in say Paris or Chicago, that sort of thing did not often happen in staid respectable London. An old gentleman was holding forth with some asperity on the inefficiency of the police and Rezaire felt almost inclined to get up and correct him. The detective force was by no means inefficient; in fact they had displayed almost too great an efficiency. The real facts of the matter were that for once, as did not often happen, they were up against a criminal of their own mental caliber, who knew the ropes; and at the moment it was still anybody's game.

Rezaire finished his lunch and strolled to the doorway into the court-yard. The hotel had been one of the ancient coaching inns with a big gateway from the street, while the old yard was now used for parking motor cars. Several cars had come in while he was at lunch and were drawn up on the far side of the yard. Round the Mercedes Dixon was hovering with an oil can and a rag.

Rezaire, cigar in mouth, felt at peace once more with all the world, but underlying it all was a vague sense of discontent. During the last sixteen hours whenever he had most felt that things were going well and smoothly and that no obstacle lay before him, something had cropped up unexpectedly and all but laid him by the heels. He did not at all like that happening; in fact he almost preferred the moments when there were definite difficulties ahead of him and he knew what they were. Then he could set to work with his brain, which was his best weapon, to devise a way out. But with these sudden setbacks, he started, so to speak, level with everyone else and was just as likely as not to be beaten on the start. Despite his cigar and the atmosphere of well-being that a full stomach and a spring afternoon had brought, Rezaire mistrusted the moment.

He watched Dixon for a minute longer and then began to walk across the yard to him. It was about time they were moving on. Two small boys were dodging about with little note-books, engaged on the pastime, always attractive to boys of a certain age, in collecting the numbers of motor cars. Rezaire was half-way across the court when a maid came out after him with his bill and he returned to settle up.

He waited a short time, getting some loose silver, and when he came out again the whole atmosphere of the courtyard had undergone a subtle change. There was a little crowd round his car and the one near to it. Dixon wore a worried look and was arguing with another chauffeur. An officious looking man was trying to intervene. One of the small boys with his book was also there, and evidently in a position of some importance. The others, loafers, garage hands, and so on, were offering gratuitous advice which no one listened to. Rezaire walked quickly across. As he did so, he heard Dixon's voice, indignant and angry: "I tell you that's my number."

"I tell you it ain't," retorted the other chauffeur. "I've had this one for years."

"So've I."

"Well, where the 'ell did you get it then?" He paused and added triumphantly: "I don't believe you know. What district is it?"

"Yes," added an onlooker with the air of one bringing home a point. "Where is 'BK'?"

"What the bloody'ell does that matter to you?" retorted Dixon heatedly.

"It matters a bloody lot!" said the chauffeur equally heated. "You p'raps get run in for something and my bloke gets the blame."

"Let the police settle it," put in the officious man trying to soothe the combatants. "Someone's gone for them."

"Yes, let 'em," said the other chauffeur, thrusting his face up against Dixon's. "Wouldn't suit your book that, would it?"

"'Course I don't mind," retorted Dixon, evidently taken aback. "I'm not going…"

"Now then, what's all this, Dixon?" asked Rezaire, arriving in the crowd with a feeling of apprehension. He had known in his heart just now when he felt so content that something would go wrong, and evidently it had.

Several voices tried to answer him, the small boy's note-book was waved in his face, but as the crowd stood back he saw the answer himself. Side by side with his car was a large red Rolls-Royce limousine. His own car was a Mercedes and painted green—quite a different car,—but the trouble was obvious. On the front of each was the number BK3140. The luck, both good and bad, which had been so consistently attending him was still with him. Of all cars to run into the yard of the Black Boar at Basingstoke, the one car that mattered most had arrived, that which in reality bore the number that Dixon had substituted for his own to avoid the police at Bagshot.

It had been a thousand to one, even a million to one chance, but Fortune, feeling that she had perhaps favored Rezaire too much already, had laughed and brought the two cars side by side.

CHAPTER XVI

EXCHANGE NO ROBBERY

For a moment Rezaire hesitated, appalled by this stroke of bad fortune. Then he realized that this was one thing he could not bluff out, because the real owner of the number would have incontrovertible proofs of his ownership and he would have none. The only thing therefore to do was to make his getaway as soon as possible. Since he did not think he would do it unobtrusively, it would have to be quick, though it would, of course, raise that infernal hue and cry against him once more…

A policeman entered the gate, preceded by the other small boy and attended by three or four loafers. At the same moment from the hotel appeared a stout gentleman, evidently the owner of the Rolls-Royce, accompanied by the manager of the hotel, a man of middle age and of the ex-officer type.

"Now then, Parkins," began the stout man, evidently angry at having to leave his lunch. "What's all this?"

The other began to pour his tale into his ear. The manager chased the loafers out of the yard. The policeman took out a note-book. Rezaire managed to get near Dixon and whisper: "Get her going and wait for my signal."

Dixon replied by the merest flicker of an eyelid and the next moment they were both swept up into the controversy, Rezaire hoping desperately that the policeman had not heard of the car that had run through the police trap near Sunningdale.

"Now then, what's all the trouble?" began the representative of the law.

Rezaire let the other man pour out his grievance, which he did very angrily, and then himself said: "I don't know anything about the numbers, except that I only got this one a short while ago. It had another before, which I had transferred to my other car." He spoke with an air of finality and good temper, hoping to point the difference between himself and the Rolls-Royce owner in his favor.

"Is that all?" said the policeman in surprise, looking round on the crowd. "Well, there's one way of settling it! Have any of you looked at the licenses?"

No one had thought of it, Rezaire realizing that he himself had not either. There was a general move to the cars again. Dixon, Rezaire noticed, got into the driving seat as if to show the license better.

"Well," said the policeman to the big man after inspection, "you're all right, but yours"—he turned to Rezaire—"has got another number."

"That's my old number," said Rezaire glibly, edging imperceptibly to the gateway. "I told you I just changed it and got a new one."

"Where's your new license?"

"I haven't received it yet. Probably they've made some mistake at the office." He felt almost ashamed of the tale he was telling. It was so feeble and third rate, not worthy of his other bluffs. It would not deceive a child. But it was achieving its object in that it had given him time to set up a gradual movement of the crowd, always swayed by imperceptible suggestion, toward the gateway as if to discuss the matter in the street.

By the time the policeman had decided that the whole matter wanted looking into and was demanding his name and address, he had attained his objective, and the whole group were standing in the gateway, where outside already another small crowd was forming.

He took a deep breath and first looking to see that there was no traffic outside, glanced back with meaning in his eyes toward his own car where Dixon sat ready at the wheel. The moment their eyes met, there was a sudden plunging whirr as the self starter woke to life, then a roar and a crash, as Dixon accelerated and let gear and clutch in almost simultaneously. The big car leaped forward straight at the gateway.

There was a shout and an instant stampede, everyone flying for safety to the side. The Mercedes leaped through the gateway, narrowly missing one of the small boys. As it swung out, Rezaire jumped for the footboard, caught it, scrambled over the door, and into the seat beside Dixon. The next moment they were racing down the street.

The scattered crowd at the entrance to the hotel stood still for a moment in dazed silence. For the first few seconds none knew that Rezaire had gone; they were indignantly wondering why the car had charged them. The chauffeur of the Rolls-Royce was the first to realize that he had been, as it were, snatched out of their midst.

"'Ere, stop 'em. He's off," he cried wildly, and ran out into the street, followed by the policeman, angry and indignant.

Other members of the crowd streamed out and took up the cry. But their shouts grew faint and disappeared as Dixon wheeled the green car sharp round at a turning. They had escaped but only for the moment, for soon the wires would be humming with their number and description, and all the police in the towns and villages round would be on the lookout for them.

They threaded their way quickly out of Basingstoke on the Winchester Road. In answer to Dixon's query, Rezaire had replied: "Carry straight on for Southampton. They don't know where we are bound for, and it is as safe as any road is."

"We'll be 'eld up, sir, somewhere."

"Well, we'll have to chance getting through." There was silence for a while as the long grey road unfolded before them. Then Rezaire, who had been sunk in thought, suddenly said: "You did that very well, Dixon."

"Thank you, sir."

"How far are you prepared to go?"

"In what way, sir?"

"In this way. I've got to get to a certain place on the coast tonight at all costs. Are you prepared to help me?"

"Yes, I am."

"I repeat," he said with meaning, "'at all costs.' Whatever it may involve."

Dixon thought a moment, then he said: "Of course you know that I don't like the police and want to keep clear of them, but still"—he hesitated—"I don't want to take on anything dangerous just for amusement like, if you understand my meaning."

Rezaire smiled. "Quite so. Now look here. This is what I'll offer you. I'll give you £50 down later tonight, when I've got where I want on the coast. If there's been trouble of any kind, I'll double it. You see," he added softly, "there might be shooting…"

"Shooting?"

"Yes. You notice I'm telling you quite a lot. But by now you're in it as much as I am."

"Oh, I'm not afraid of shooting," returned Dixon airily. "Besides, for a hundred quid, I'd…"

"And further, if by any chance after it's over you find it inconvenient, shall we say, to stay in England—you follow me?"

"Yes."

"I'll take charge of you and get you away to the continent and leave you in France with your hundred pounds. Is that a deal?"

Dixon barely hesitated. "Right, it's a go."

Rezaire sat back again satisfied. He had sized up the man at his side fairly well from the very first day he had engaged him, and he knew that he was honest after his lights. He was fairly certain that even without the hold he had on him he would not give him away. Dixon was certainly not clever but that was an asset. It would not dawn on him to do anything else but that which he was told.

They passed through one village—North Waltham, Rezaire thought—without mishap. No attempt was made to stop them, no one appeared to notice them any more than any other car.

At the next village, however, a mile or two further on, the two village constables were out in the center of the street. One, about one hundred yards in advance of the other, was waving incoming cars to slow down so that he might see their numbers and, if necessary, signal to his colleague to hold them up.

Dixon, however, simply put on speed. The first man got the number, as the car flashed past, and signaled frantically to the other. This man stepped out into their path with hand uplifted.

Dixon's reply was to lift the car from thirty m.p.h. to thirty-five. The constable just had time to jump clear. They heard his shout as they flashed past.

"He moved all right," chuckled Dixon, as they went through the quiet village like a tornado. A pony and trap outside a shop started as they passed, and began to bolt. A knot of laborers returning to work dispersed like chaff. They ran over a dog. Looking back through the dust, Rezaire saw one of the policemen had just stopped the pony and cart; the other was running for a building in the main street, evidently the post-office.

Further on they passed an A.A. scout at a crossroads. He also had had warning and on reading their number signaled them to stop, but they merely laughed at him. He stood looking at them for a moment and then ran back into the roadside telephone box.

"We'll have to do something different," said Rezaire at last, who had been thinking over the situation. "They all know we're on this road now and though so far they haven't stopped us, they're reporting our progress pretty accurately. They know we're making for the coast somewhere. They'll concentrate a big force of police somewhere and put up a barricade. Also, they'll soon have someone on our track in another car."

"Let's turn off the road and go somewhere else," suggested Dixon, as they overtook another car.

"H'm! But I want to get to a particular place." He glanced back at the car they had passed. Ahead of them was another one: for there were lots of cars on the road. An idea came into his mind. These cars would get through without difficulty. The obvious thing was to change cars, if possible. His own car had become too dangerous. He pulled a map out of his pocket and studied it.

"Take the next turning to the left," he ordered at length, "before we come to King's Worthy."

"Right," said Dixon, and as the turning came in sight, at the bottom of a long dip, slowed down and wheeled round. Rezaire noted with satisfaction that there was no other traffic in sight at the moment of turning to see which way they had gone.

They went on for about a mile, passed one turning, and eventually took a road to the right, which, while only a third class road, yet showed signs of being fairly regularly used. A little way along this road they came to rest, drew in to the side, and waited.

"Now," said Rezaire, "pay attention, Dixon. This is what I am going to do. I'm going to hold up the first car that comes along, and take it instead of this. This car is too dangerous for us."

"Hold 'em up?" exclaimed the other.

"Yes, with guns."

Dixon was thrilled.

"Lumme, that's the stuff!"

"Then we'll be able to get back along the main road for some way without being stopped. I'm going to change my appearance as far as possible and you'll have to get out of that uniform. They've got our description at Basingstoke."

Dixon seemed to enter into the spirit of the thing at once with a zest that showed he was not averse to breaking the law. He was a man who perpetually hovered on the border line between honesty and dishonesty. If he got a good job, he kept it as long as he could; if he saw a chance of making a bit dishonestly, he turned his hand to it with equal facility.

In a few minutes his uniform lay in the ditch, he was wearing an old cap and coat of Rezaire's and Rezaire had also redressed himself from his purchases of that morning. One of the two revolvers had been given over into Dixon's keeping. Then they lifted the bonnet of the car to make it appear that they had had a breakdown, and settled down at the roadside to wait for a victim.

Rezaire had chosen his road with considerable skill. It was a road sufficiently used to make it probable that someone would turn up before long and yet unfrequented enough to ensure that there would not be much traffic to disturb them. There were no houses within sight, save a farmhouse just over the brow of the hill. The stage was set; they were only waiting for the other actors.

In about twenty minutes, during which a motor bike, whose offer of help they refused, and two farm carts were the only vehicles that had passed, a small car appeared round the corner. With satisfaction Rezaire noticed that its only occupants were two girls.

Dixon stood out in the road and waved them to stop.

They drew alongside and Rezaire advanced with uplifted hat.

"Are you broken down?" began one of the girls. "Can we take a message to a garage for you?"

"Yes, we are broken down," began Rezaire, "and we want you to help."

"Well, can we…"

"We would like to borrow your car, please."

There was something in his meaning smile that made the girl look uneasily at her companion. Was the man insane or what? She looked at him again; then made as if to put her car into gear again, but Dixon's hand suddenly shot over onto the dashboard and switched off the engine.

"How dare you! What do you mean?" she began and found herself looking at a revolver which Rezaire had produced.

"I'm very sorry to trouble you," he went on easily, "but, as I said, we must have your car. You can have that one of mine. No, it's no good looking surprised. I'm in earnest."

"If this is a joke… What do you want?" faltered the young driver. Both girls were now looking frightened. There was something very sinister in Rezaire's polite tones and menacing revolver, something very evil in Dixon's grinning face under the thick dark eyebrows.

"This is no joke. I'm afraid it doesn't often happen that you meet what you might call bandits on the English highways, but you have done so today. Now will you get out, please? I'm in a hurry." His voice took a steely ring that betokened he meant what he said.

White and frightened, the two girls got out. "You may get in my car. It won't be long before you get help. Please don't be frightened. I'm not going to hurt you."

Dixon, after a brief glance at the small car, started her up.

"Calthorpe two-seater," he muttered to Rezaire. "I can manage her easily."

The two girls were whispering together. Rezaire's quick ears caught a word or two and he interposed suavely: "I should advise you not to shout or try to make a noise. As I said before, I'm a desperate man, and I'm quite prepared to shoot, even girls—if they are silly."

The whispering stopped. The two girls clutching one another's hands stood by the roadside. They were still dazed at the unreality of it all.

"Now, quickly, Dixon," ordered Rezaire. "There'll be something along soon. Just hold your revolver pointed at these two young ladies. There's something I want to do."

While Dixon covered the girls with a grin, Rezaire transferred his suitcase to the new car, and then diving into the bonnet, he took off the top of the carburetor and removed the float, which he crushed under his foot.

Then the two got into the little car, Rezaire still leaning out of the back with his revolver. The Calthorpe moved slowly off leaving the Mercedes and the two frightened girls in the middle of the quiet country road.

"Poor old Mercedes," murmured Dixon, as he changed the gear with a grating sound. "This box of tricks isn't a patch on 'er. I've looked after her for a good while and I'm sorry to leave 'er."

"So am I, but we can get on some way now before those two get the word through."

"Made me laugh," suddenly announced Dixon a moment later, "the way you spoke to 'em. Something like a serial story I was reading in my paper the other day. Flash Eddie, the gentleman cracksman, the 'ero was. He spoke like that whenever he lifted anything off a bloke." A new respect seemed to have come into his voice, which was not the respect of a chauffeur for his employer but of the dealer in small crime for one whom he recognizes as a master of the art.

A few minutes later they turned back onto the Southampton Road and were once more speeding southward.

CHAPTER XVII

PURSUIT

They passed through King's Worthy without mishap. Though there were several police in evidence, they took no notice of the two men in the small Calthorpe when they were looking for a green Mercedes with a different registration number.

Thanks also to their disguise they passed in safety through Winchester itself where they sensed a certain air of expectation as though the news were already known that the mysterious green car they were looking out for contained the London criminals about whose doings the previous night the papers were so full.

"We've run through 'em once," murmured Dixon nervously, as they passed two groups of policemen about fifty yards apart. "I wonder they haven't built a barricade to stop our doing it again."

"They don't need to here," replied Rezaire. "You can't go more than ten miles an hour anywhere in this old town."

They threaded their way through the old capital of England, losing their direction once and being obliged to ask. Rezaire after his manner would have questioned a policeman but Dixon could not stand it. He had not the experienced coolness or nerve of the other; in fact it was all Rezaire could do to prevent his cowering down as they passed every uniformed figure.

At last they found themselves out on the Southampton Road.

"Push her along now, Dixon," ordered Rezaire with a sigh of relief. "We want all the time we can get."

"Why, we're all right in this car."

"We are for the moment. But it won't take long for those girls to walk to a farmhouse or get picked up by a car and it'll take even less time for the police to realize that we are the fellows who have pinched their Calthorpe."

"H'm!" grunted Dixon. "You're right. But I can't knock much out of this little bus compared to my Mercedes."

"Well, do what you can. They're not fools, these police. I should think by now every bobbie in England is watching out for us."

"What, for just running through a trap and having a wrong number?" queried the other innocently and Rezaire glanced sideways at him.

"That, and other things," he said shortly and looked at his watch.

It was about four o'clock. Thank Heaven it would be dark by about seven and his chance of escape would be doubled.

He hoped there was no hitch about the launch, but he knew the mechanic in charge was a reliable man and so was old Levy who had put the deal through. Besides he was paying well and, as Levy had hinted, the mechanic had done a queer job or two in his time.

They passed through Compton and Otterbourne, dipped down into Chandler's Ford over the railway and up the hill. They stopped once to replenish the petrol and oil, and a clock at the garage showed ten minutes past four. The little car was going well, but not very fast. Rezaire wondered how long it would be before the police on the roads leading south from Winchester were notified that the Mercedes had been abandoned. It was now getting on for an hour and a half since the change had been made. But he was getting nearer and nearer safety. They could not be more than about seven miles from Southampton; and he felt he could almost smell the sea. The sun was low on the horizon. The road dipped between dark woods on either hand and Rezaire became conscious at last that night was not so far off.

As they left the last houses of Chandler's Ford behind them a further group of houses came in sight ahead. Rezaire scanned his map anxiously, for he would soon be nearing Bassett where he would have to turn off to the right to avoid Southampton and to get to Totton and the side roads for Beaulieu.

Suddenly he sat up and touched Dixon on the arm. Ahead of them among the houses the road appeared to be blocked by something. As they drew closer, he could see that two farm wagons had been placed across the road at an interval, blocking first one side and then the other, so that any vehicle would have to slow down and go through in zigzag fashion. It was the first road barricade they had come across and it showed that the police were taking no further chances. It seemed to Rezaire that in all probability he had by now been identified with the man the London police were after. He had shown such desperation in eluding capture that they must have realized that he was no ordinary wrong-doer trying to evade conviction for exceeding the speed limit. By now, too, the news would be all over the country that he was out of London, though he thanked Heaven they could not know where he was going.

A car overtook them and hooting loudly approached the barricade ahead slowing down as it did so. It crept in and out between the two wagons at a crawling speed and then passed on. Beside the second wagon Rezaire could once more see the hated blue uniform.

"What are we going to do?" asked Dixon quickly in some trepidation. "Do they know we've got this car?"

"I'm afraid they do by now. Can you charge it?"

"I can try." He slammed his foot on the accelerator as he spoke. "She's small and got a good lock. I can probably twist in and out at speed where I couldn't with a big car."

The last words were muttered as they were almost on the barricade. Rezaire caught a glimpse—it seemed to him almost a familiar one by now—of policemen waiting expectantly, heard a shout of "That's 'im," felt the off wheel lurch into the ditch as Dixon took her well over to get a swing round...then he closed his eyes.

There was a wrench, another terrible lurch, and the crushing jolt of overstrained springs. The car swung to left and then to right. Rezaire felt himself bucketed about like a pea in an eggshell and had to hold on to the door to prevent himself being thrown out. He opened his eyes again and saw that they were past the wagons. Dixon had had to take the car right into the bank on the other side, but it was this that had saved them from overturning, for he had been able to bank the wheels on the slope. A policeman struck out at them with a truncheon as they passed but missed them and hit the side lamp which shattered to pieces. The car swerved and leaped violently like a live animal as Dixon took the ditch again and brought her back on to the road. Rezaire, rather frightened and peering over his shoulder, suddenly saw to his dismay a big red car drawn up behind the barricade facing the same way that they were going. Even as he looked he saw two men rushing for the door and another at the starting crank. The police had indeed left nothing to chance; they even had a car waiting to pursue should their quarry get past.

The next moment the barricade, the waiting car, the group of hurrying figures were veiled in the dust of their passage as they sped on and in another minute they were round a slight bend to the left.

"You all right?" grunted Dixon.

"Yes," panted Rezaire. "Thanks. You did well. But give her all you can. They'll be after us."

"Good God! Was that their car?"

"Fraid so."

"We can't distance that in this thing."

"Do your best. I'll try and think of something." The little car roared on down the smooth tarred road at all the speed that Dixon could get out of her. With set face and eyes glued to the road in front of him he drove like a madman and the car bounced about as if it were a tennis ball. From somewhere underneath came the harsh grating of a broken spring which had snapped when they had charged the bank. Hooting wildly, a minute later they overtook the car that had gone through the barricade ahead of them. Rezaire, looking over the back for the first sign of the pursuing police, saw the astonished faces of its occupants. Then they flashed past a fork off to Eastleigh on their left.

The road flew away from under the wheels, the dust eddying behind them. The car they had overtaken was now out of sight, and the road stretched behind them unoccupied. But only for a moment. Suddenly there appeared, to Rezaire's dismay, the big red car of the police, coming up at a terrible speed.

"Quicker! Quicker!" he shouted.

"Can't do it," cried Dixon as the Calthorpe jolted and bounced along the road. "Something'll go soon, as it is."

"They're coming up."

"They'll have to then…"

Rezaire, still looking over the back, saw the red car gaining on them slowly till it was only fifty yards behind. The two cars raced onward, passing, overtaking other cars. Rezaire began to curse to himself for at that speed he could never take the turning off to Totton which must be rapidly approaching and yet if they went straight on they would be in Southampton. A wild idea came as he realized the urgency of stopping the following car.

"Be ready to take the next fork to the right," he called to Dixon. "I think I may be able to stop them."

The big car drew on. Fifty yards closed to forty, forty to thirty. Rezaire could see the set face of the man at the wheel and the others leaning forward from the back. There was only one thing to do. Softly he drew his revolver, the revolver he had not yet used. Though his fingers trembled he was going to shoot in the hope of frightening them off. It was his only chance.

They overtook another car and passed it, right in the teeth of one coming from the opposite direction. The angry driver, applying his brakes to avoid collision as they took his road, shouted something at them as they went past.

They made a few yards by this since the red car was forced to give way to the oncoming vehicle, but in a few minutes it had also passed and was a bare fifteen yards behind.

Rezaire drew a deep breath and leaning over the back leveled the revolver. Dixon out of the corner of his eye saw him and shouted: "For God's sake be careful! I don't want to swing. Shoot at their tires."

"Neither do I," muttered Rezaire between set teeth and aimed at the big front wheels of the red car only ten yards behind and already drawing out to the side.

The revolver snapped; the report was caught up and swept away at once in the rush of their passage, so that he hardly heard it. He saw a momentary hick of dust rise on the road. He had missed. He took aim again. The big wheels bounced and sprang madly under the body, as if they knew they were being fired at. Once more he fired but could not see where the bullet went. The pursuing car was edging out to the right to overtake them, and he knew what his opponents would do. They would come up alongside and by crowding in on them would force them either to slow down or to run into the hedge. And the more they went over to the side, the more difficult it was to shoot at the tire. He did not think he would ever hit.

Slowly they crept up. It seemed incredible that a car could overtake so slowly and yet be travelling at such a speed. He took aim once more. The air seemed full of dirt and small stones. One of the policemen in the car was standing up and shouting at him, but he could not hear a word. They did not seem to realize what he was trying to do. Perhaps they thought he was firing at them. His arm, resting on the hood, jerked this way and that. He could hardly hold the revolver, much less aim carefully. He fired again and hit the number plate—he saw the sudden impact;—then again he hit, this time somewhere on the side of the disc wheel.

There was a sudden grating of brakes and the police car slowed down suddenly, pulling in behind them. Another car had appeared going in the opposite direction and a collision had only just been avoided. The red car was once more directly behind them. It was now or never. He must hit—he must hit. The dust was whirling into his eyes. The little Calthorpe jerked and bumped with the grating of the broken spring. The car behind him seemed to hypnotize him, a fierce red monster relentlessly pursuing to snatch him up in its jaws. With a little sob he took aim once more.

Several things suddenly seemed to happen at once. As he looked along the barrel, for a fraction of a second he was aware of the man by the side of the driver also leveling a pistol at him. Then he heard a whistle past his ear and a smash behind him. There was a cry from Dixon, a sudden sickening swerve of the car and at the same instant his own automatic, pointed at their front wheel, went off once more.

There was a loud report. One of the tires of the following car appeared to be stripped bodily from the wheel, as though a giant invisible hand had plucked it off. The big car lurched to one side, plunged into the ditch, half got into the road again, took the ditch heavily once more, and by a miracle of good driving was kept straight, ploughing along through the hedge parallel to the road. The whole picture, the bent and twisted mudguard, the tense face of the driver above the cracked windshield, the absurd metal rim of the wheel, became suddenly remote and dropped behind. Rezaire had a last glimpse through the dust of the big red car stranded in the hedge half on and half off the road and then it was out of sight.

He scrambled back into his seat to find the inside of the car full of slivers of broken glass and Dixon, with white face and hands covered with blood from great cuts, grimly holding to the steering wheel. The shot that the police had fired had missed him but broke the windshield. In the same instant Rezaire noticed that he himself was bleeding slightly from one of the fingers of his left hand. Before he could speak, Dixon suddenly put on the brake, bringing the car up to a standstill.

"Can't stick it," he muttered and instantly collapsed with a little gasp across the steering wheel, the blood from his cut hands dabbling his face and running down onto his knees.

CHAPTER XVIII

SOUTHWARD STILL

With a hurried exclamation Rezaire got out. His one thought was to get Dixon out of sight before a passing car should notice him and insist on stopping to get aid. Already they must be close to Southampton and there would be traffic up and down the roads. Besides, the police, despite their setback, which by wonderful luck for them had not been nearly as serious as it might, would soon be after them once more.

He dragged Dixon, who had evidently fainted from strain and loss of blood, out of the car and onto the side of the road. With a swift look round to make sure that he had not been observed he next pulled him through a gap in the hedge into a rough piece of fallow ground about thirty yards wide bordering on a wood, where he was out of sight from the road.

Crouching down beside him he rapidly reviewed the situation. Obviously he would have to abandon the car and get to Beaulieu some other way. But equally obviously he could not leave things just as they were. Anyone finding the car like that would instantly conclude there had been a smash and would start looking for the victims. He broke off hurriedly as a Ford van came up from the direction of Southampton and seeing the deserted car began to slow down. Rezaire just had time to emerge from the hedge and get between the Calthorpe and the Ford so that the man could not see the blood on the seat.

"Had a smash?" began the other.

"Yes, nothing much, though."

"Want any help?"

"Oh, Lord no," replied Rezaire airily, hoping the fellow would not notice anything else. "Just broke my windshield, that's all."

"Car all right?"

"Yes, thanks. I'm going on now."

With an air of determination he began to get into the car—the engine was still running—and the Ford van driver after another curious look at him moved on.

Rezaire sat in the car considering a little. After a while he put the car in gear. It had occurred to him that he must get it away from where it was, for it was a source of danger as long as he was hiding close by. An empty car with a broken windshield was sure to attract everyone who passed and other vehicles would stop even as the Ford had done.

He drove a hundred yards or so, eyed curiously by the occupants of two passing cars. The wheel was wet with Dixon's blood and Rezaire felt rather sick. There was a lot of blood in the car, on the seat and on the floor and over the dashboard. Dixon must have lost a lot. Certainly he had stuck it well. Rezaire shuddered to think what would have happened if he had not been able to hit the other car's tire when he did, if Dixon had fainted when they were going at full speed.

Selecting a moment when there was no one actually in sight, though he could see a crossroad not so very far ahead of him, he drew the car gently into the hedge on the right hand side and got out. If a crowd was going to collect at all round the Calthorpe, it should do so where he wished. Then he crossed the road unobserved and got through the hedge into the same stretch of rough ground in which Dixon lay further back. For a moment he was tempted to leave him and go on on his own. After all, he had had his share of helping others; why should he continue to do so? It was every man for himself in his line of life, and let the police take the hindmost.

But his hesitation was only momentary. After all, Dixon had served him well and Dixon was loyal according to his lights. Had it not been for Dixon's skill and endurance he would probably now have been lying dead on the road. Sam he had had no compunction in betraying, because he knew Sam would have done the same by him, and also because Sam had forced his company on him by threats of violence. But Dixon was a different man altogether. Bending down to avoid observation from the road, he doubled back behind the hedge to where he had left his unconscious companion.

On arrival he pulled him a little further into the ditch among the weeds and undergrowth, so as to be completely hidden and began to staunch the wounds.

They were not very deep, although numerous, and after a while Dixon opened his eyes. It took him a minute or two to realize he was in a ditch.

"'Ave we 'ad a smash?" he whispered.

"No, thanks to you. You pulled up."

"Oh, yes, I remember. Then we stopped 'em?"

"Yes, but not so very far away. They'll be after us still."

"What about the car?"

"I've chucked that. We'll have to go on foot to the nearest station and get on a train without being seen. How do you feel?"

"Oh, all right." He sat up. "Bit rocky."

"I'll finish tying up these cuts for you, or they'll begin to bleed again, and then we'll move on. And keep down as much as possible. I don't want people to see us. I've left the car in the hedge about a hundred yards away, so that anyone will think we've had a smash over there. That'll give us a bit of a start. Besides, it's getting on for sunset now."

"Well, I'm ready as soon as you are." He grinned feebly. "Those two young ladies ought to 'ave 'ad 'Triplex.' I should speak to them about it if I was you."

"Now look here," murmured Rezaire after a while, studying the map. "Here's a station called Swaythling not so far away. If we can get on a train there we can probably get through Southampton to where I want to go. Come on."

They got to their feet and moving off with caution soon gained the shelter of the wood. Once in amongst the trees they looked back. Some distance behind them they could see the road and at one point a little group round the deserted Calthorpe with the blood and the glass all over it. Probably, Rezaire thought with a grim chuckle, they were looking for the bodies. Then they went on again and in a few moments were out of sight. Once more they had thrown the police off their immediate track; but, Rezaire feared, it would not be for long. Their adversaries now had a very good idea whereabouts in the country they were and every station would be watched; every village constable warned to look for them. In all probability the same men from Scotland Yard that had been on his and Sam's heels in London were now on their way down to Southampton following on the reports they had received from the different towns on the main road.

After about a quarter of an hour they approached Swaythling. They had been seen by no one on their way, but had had to hide from farm laborers on two occasions. Dixon owing to his bandaged hands had had difficulty in scaling gates and hedges, but had stuck it well. He had realized how easy it would have been for Rezaire to have left him when he was unconscious and was pathetically grateful and anxious not to be a handicap. The contrast, Rezaire thought, between him and Sam was very marked.

A short distance away, they stopped and held a council which resulted in their approaching a solitary house on the outskirts of the village and asking for a wash. It was better, Rezaire decided, to risk a talkative or inquisitive villager than to go about so conspicuously, Dixon with blood-stained bandages, white face and torn clothes, himself hatless and also stained with blood. They found a laborer and his wife inside sitting down to their tea and explained that they had had a cycle accident. The woman was only too anxious to help, attended to Dixon's hands, binding them up afresh and supplied them with some clothes and a hat, for which Rezaire paid her well. They left the cottage feeling that they had been put on their feet once more. They might now pass people without exciting comment, while Rezaire was fairly hopeful that they would be well away from Swaythling before the laborer's wife mentioned their visit to anyone in the vicinity.

Avoiding the actual village as far as possible, though they had twice to cross roads, Rezaire led the way toward the station. They crossed at the level crossing and walking boldly across the open space in front of the station buildings waited their opportunity for a short while and then got, very circumspectly, into the freight yard. To be observed now would have been fatal and though it was about sunset there was still a lot of light. Several trucks and freight-cars stood about the yard and into one of these Rezaire cautiously climbed.

"What's your game?" asked Dixon. "I thought you said we were going to get beyond Southampton?"

"Yes, but we've got to wait till there's a train. It's no good waiting on the station platform and taking tickets. I'm going to wait here."

"Humph!" grunted Dixon, but got into the cattle car. "This is like travelling in France," he added a moment later. "During the war, I mean."

"Is it?"

"Yes. Weren't you there?"

"No."

Dixon's voice was a little surprised and hurt. "Why, weren't you in the army or navy?"

There was a pause. Then Rezaire answered with a smile: "No. I was in what they called the Secret Service. And then"—his face suddenly hardened and grew bitter—"I left it. Now, stop talking and keep a look-out for any train in the right direction—southward."

For some while they stayed there in the security of the old cattle car. Twice the signal went down for trains toward Southampton, but each time it was an express that roared through. From where they were they could, by peeping out with some caution, get a view of the station approach and part of the platforms, and about twenty minutes after their arrival Dixon nudged Rezaire and pointed. Two policemen on cycles were coming up to the station. They dismounted and went inside. Then they reappeared on the platform scrutinizing the people there. Once they came right up to the end and stood there, looking out toward the freight yard and arguing about something, but eventually they went back into the station once more.

Rezaire saw that the net was being drawn tight. On all the stations, on all the roads, everywhere round the spot where their pursuers in the big red car had lost touch with them police would now be watching. Southampton in particular would be well guarded as it was the nearest gateway to the continent and freedom. And he had to break this chain to get through the close-drawn barriers, pitting his brain against the brains and organization of the whole detective force. For a moment he almost felt despair, then his natural buoyancy reasserted itself. After all he had had good luck on the whole so far. That ought to pull him through this last bit; that and what Sam called "his infernal cheek," but which was nothing more nor less than his ability to put himself in his opponents' place, guessing what they thought he would do and doing the opposite… Dixon pulled his arm, interrupting his thoughts. "Another train signaled," he whispered, and in a few minutes it came in sight, passing slowly through the station—a freight train.

"Come on, quick!" suddenly snapped Rezaire, and began to crawl out. "This is the one for us."

"But it isn't stopping."

"All the better." He was clambering cautiously down as he spoke. "A passenger train will be no good with those bobbies here and this is going slow enough for us to board it."

The freight train clattered and puffed its way along at a reduced speed. Calculating his time Rezaire left the friendly cattle car and dodging behind the other cars so as to avoid observation from the platforms came up almost to the line on which the freight train was running.

For a moment he paused looking back at the station, from which at the moment he was partially hidden by the base of a foot-bridge, then snatching his opportunity he ran out. Drawing alongside a car he caught at a bar and swung himself up on to the clattering swaying vehicle. Two cars behind he saw Dixon also clamber on board, though with more difficulty. No sooner was he on, than he instantly crouched down as inconspicuously as he could, in case he had attracted the attention of anyone on the foot-bridge or the end of the platform.

At last they passed out of sight of the station and no shout or other sign that they were noticed had been given. Rezaire drew a deep breath and clambered over the top into the friendly shelter of the empty car. He did not think he had been seen. The train clattered on southward into the gathering dusk. He did not know where it was going, but it was at least southward toward the sea and safety.

The engine labored on in the glow of the sunset. Rezaire, lying on his back at the bottom of the car, for a moment was absolutely at peace, a peace that he only wished could last forever; for he was infernally tired. He longed for sleep and freedom from worry, and yet he must still hang on. He was near safety, but he could not afford now to make a single mistake. For several hours more he must work at high pressure, foreseeing, guessing, devising plans, putting them into effect, matching himself against those who were also straining every nerve to lay him by the heels.

He rapidly surveyed the past twenty-four hours. Why, only this time yesterday he had been in Carlyle's room cutting the heads off lead soldiers, absolutely unconscious that his activities were to be so soon ended. The gang had been in existence then with perfectly working organization; now where was it? One dead, two captured, himself hotly pursued, and Vivienne he knew not where. He wondered where Viv had got to. Probably, if she had had any luck, she had got down to the neighborhood of Beaulieu ready to join him in the boat that very night. It was funny to think that out of all England she was quite close. By now she might even be safely on board the launch if it had arrived, for she knew where to find it. It seemed ages since he had left her up there on the roofs, not knowing whether she would escape or not.

A slight change in the speed of the train recalled his thoughts to the moment. He sat up and sighed. His brief rest was over. He must come back to the things of earth again, if he were to get to Beaulieu in safety.

He peeped cautiously over the top of the car. They were passing a station; he could not see the name but from his map he decided it must be St. Deny's. The next was Northam, the last before Southampton West. They put on speed again, passed over water, clattered between houses, whose long shadows lay across the train. Rezaire crouched very still, afraid lest he should be observed from one of the windows.

Outside Northam they halted for some while. Rezaire tried to see whereabouts he was, whether the train was going on to the Bournemouth line on which was Beaulieu Road Station, or whether he would be carried down the docks, which he did not want at all. But two men, shunters probably, came and stood in conversation just by his car so that he dared not move.

Then the train went on again, clattering over points, still between houses, with the roar of Southampton's evening traffic all about it.

They had not turned off to the docks. Southampton West Station loomed up out of the oncoming night and as they passed slowly through it, Rezaire managed to look out. The lighted platform was crowded with people. He wondered whether any of them knew what was in the air.

Suddenly he gave a start and crouched down once more in the obscurity of the car. For there at the end of the platform standing in the center of a little group was the short square-shouldered man with the clipped moustache who had been the chief of those on his track in London, the man he knew as Detective Inspector Harrison. So they were in touch with him once more as he had feared. They had guessed—and it could not really have been difficult—that the mysterious and desperate car driver on the Southampton Road was the wanted man of the night before in London. Even as he looked the short man turned to the station-master at his elbow and spoke rapidly—indicating the passing freight train. Rezaire guessed quite well that they were now wondering whether he might not be concealed on it.

Just outside the station they came to a halt and ahead the engine whistled angrily. Rezaire sat on the floor of the car thinking. He did not consider that the train had been stopped on purpose, but there was no doubt that Harrison was suspicious. The question was: how suspicious and what would he do? He might have the train definitely held up at the next station, or now that it had stopped he might come along with men and search it. He got to his feet and peered over the top. He could see no one, but perhaps he had better be prepared to make a swift get-away if necessary. He swung quickly over the side and down on to the buffers. He was fairly well concealed there and could certainly, if he heard people coming, have a clear run into the darkness. For by now the dusk had definitely turned to night and with the departure of daylight Rezaire's spirits had once more risen. He sat on the buffers peering down the line at the lighted platforms of the station with its crowd of people. Directly ahead of him alongside the railway was the sea—or rather the mud-flats of Southampton Water—the sea which at the further edge lapped the shores of France.

A sudden whisper from somewhere below made him jump, and he gathered himself up instantly prepared to spring. But it was only Dixon who, getting out from his place of concealment a little way back, had crawled up under the train.

"You startled me," said Rezaire angrily.

"Sorry," returned Dixon. "But you startled me. I thought you were a porter or something sitting there on the buffers. I bin watching your legs some time."

"Has anyone seen you?"

"No one."

"Not even when we got on?"

"No. I got right inside a car straightway."

"Do you know the 'tecs are here?"

"Here? Where?"

"On that platform back yonder."

"Gummy! Have they spotted us?"

"We shouldn't be here if they had," retorted Rezaire tersely. "But they may come along, because I saw them talking about this train... We must stick to these cars because otherwise we've no way of getting where we want... What's that?" he broke off sharply.

They listened for a minute; then Rezaire quickly slipped to the ground. From the rear of the train voices were heard and the flashing of lanterns could be seen. It looked as though Harrison was taking advantage of the halt of the train to come up on either side and search it. Again the engine whistled somewhere ahead. If only it would go on, as it might quite well do any minute.

"Quick! Get underneath!" muttered Rezaire, and in a moment they had scrambled down between the buffers and under the car. He did not know who the men were, but he was taking no risks. Then he began to make his way on hands and knees along the track underneath the train, away from the direction in which the voices came.

They made a certain distance this way, but always the party gained on them. They could see the light flashing on the rims of the wheels. Then just as Rezaire had determined to get up and make a dash for it, there was another whistle from the front, and with a jerk and rattle the train started off once more.

With a sudden curse Dixon, who was a little to one side, flung himself clear over the rail and outside the train. Rezaire, who had hesitated for a moment, was too late, and the next minute he dared not attempt it. A cold sweat broke out on his forehead. The wheels were moving on slowly but inexorably on either side; he could not now get out that way; and yet he must not get left behind, for this train was his one hope of salvation. His only chance was to get up as he had come, in between two cars even while they moved—and his very soul shrank at the risk.

The wheels moved past less slowly; beyond them he saw Dixon get to his feet and jump into the car above him. One opening passed even as he crouched in fear-stricken hesitation. In another second it would be too late, for the train would be going too fast for him to attempt it, and he would be left behind on the line, unconcealed.

With a little gasp he gathered himself for the effort, beginning to crawl forward as fast as he could with the train. He saw the rear wheels of the truck pass, got half to his feet, head turned to side to look for the gap, saw it, and got upright, scrambling forward as he did so in order to keep within the opening; received a bang on the elbow from a trailing chain, a heavy blow on the back from the car behind; and the next moment was running along between the buffers as the train gathered speed, looking for a way to pull himself up. One hand grasped a brake connection, the other a chain; he gave a jump and a heave, missed his footing, was dragged for a short distance, pulled himself up with the strength of despair, just missing the grinding buffers, and the next moment was seated on the end of the car bruised but safe.

Before he had time to move further, a sudden shout rang out loud in his ears. He looked round, and for a brief instant found himself staring into the face of a man—a brakeman or signalman—standing by the track with a lantern.

The man waved, shouted again angrily, and then was swallowed up in the darkness.

The train rattled on westward.

CHAPTER XIX

DISCOVERY

For a moment longer Rezaire crouched there in doubt as to what was best to do. In the end, despite the fact that he had been seen, he determined to risk pursuit and stay where he was, as long as possible; for at any rate the train was bearing him in the right direction.

He climbed along the side of the car he was on and got inside the one in front, where he found Dixon. To him he explained what had happened and Dixon too agreed that the best course was to stay with the train.

They sat in the bottom of the car watching the night sky overhead, streaked with the rushing clouds of smoke. The rattle of the train was in their ears; the smell of the smoke mingling with that of the mud-flats along which the line ran filled their nostrils. Ahead lay Beaulieu and the motor launch. Rezaire glanced at his watch. It was only about half-past seven; he still had three and a half hours.

They went on without stopping. They had already passed two stations and were just leaving a third behind them—Totton and Eling had been the names on the platform—when once more the familiar jerking rattle of the buffers passed like rifle fire down the line of cars, as the train slowed down. This time Rezaire was instantly on the alert. Now that he had been seen, he was suspicious of everything. Even allowing a certain time for the man who had seen him to tell others about it, there were several things that Harrison could have already done, from telephoning down the line to stop the train to driving on himself along the road—for almost certainly the London detectives had a car.

With a warning whisper to Dixon he was over the edge and down in his familiar position on the buffers, where he was still on the train and could see what was going on, yet could leave it at an instant's notice.

After a minute, with a jerky bump the engine suddenly woke up to life again, but this time the long line of trucks ran slowly backward.

"What are they doing that for?" asked Dixon at his side.

"Don't know," replied Rezaire apprehensively, eyes on the station they had passed, to which they now seemed about to return.

The cars curved off to one side, rattled over switches.

"Why, we're back on a side line now."

"It's the 'tecs. They've got onto us. They've had this train side-tracked in order to search it. Look!"

Against the lights of the station could be seen a little cluster of men emerging from the near end of the platform, coming toward them.

"How've they got here?"

"Motor car. We've been going slowly." Rezaire spoke absently, for his brain was busy with other matters. The train was backing into some sort of a yard on the up side of the track under the shadow of a ware-house. He had the feeling that there were other men concealed about him somewhere in the darkness. He was certain that Harrison would have laid his plans well, would not have run the risk of their getting off at one end, while he searched the other. He lowered himself to a sitting position on the buffers.

"Come on," he whispered to Dixon and dropped off to one side into the darkness. "We've got to get away from here. They're backing it into a siding where they've got men posted."

They stood for a moment, undecided, on the rail, watching the dark mass of the train slide past. Then suddenly they heard footsteps close by them in the darkness. Someone on the track was coming up in their direction. They could not see who it was; for the party that had come from the station had split up and the night seemed full of questing hostile figures. To leave the friendly shelter of the train now seemed to mean instant discovery, yet the long line of care was slipping past. The pulsing mass of the engine came nearer with its plume of smoke, red from the fire box, the driver and fire-man leaning out of their cab. There was only one thing to do as Rezaire saw it. He swung himself up again into a car, followed by Dixon. They could not as yet leave the train without being discovered,—and yet to stay on… Rezaire suddenly felt very like a rat in a trap. Every way of escape seemed barred and the best thing to do was to wait and take the first chance that came. Inside the car they crouched down. It had held coal and there were still several fragments lying about on the bottom.

Even as they clambered in, the train came to a standstill on the siding. The engine let out a blast of steam and was silent. There was a silence all about them as though the whole world were watching and yet the silence was alive. A stone crunched somewhere under foot, a whisper came to their ears, something clanged against a car, they heard a man talking in low tones to the driver of the engine a little way ahead. Rezaire and Dixon crouched there amongst the loose coal not daring to move or speak for fear of discovery.

Then slowly out of the night there crept a new noise far away beyond the station in the direction of Southampton. For a moment they listened uncomprehendingly; then suddenly Rezaire sat up. It was the roar of an approaching train and to his quick wits it spelt a possible way out. Should it be a passenger train, it would stop at this station; and if only they could get on undetected, as it started up again, they might yet get to Beaulieu Road Station in safety.

The roar grew louder in the still evening air and then he heard the steam shut off as it slowed down.

It was going to stop after all. At the same time another noise much nearer crept into Rezaire's consciousness. Someone was just outside their car, attempting to climb silently up the side. His brain became suddenly abnormally alert, judging the two sounds which to him meant danger or safety, the stealthy enemy and the passenger train which was coming to a standstill, the engine not twenty yards away. He felt for his automatic, grasped it, then relinquished it in favor of a big lump of coal on which his fingers had closed. Dimly against the light he saw a hand come up over the top and grip the side of the car, heard the faintest of whispers from the men outside. At the same moment his brain was subconsciously listening to the shout of porters, the opening and shutting of doors in the station along the line. In another moment the other train would be off again and his chance would have come. It would pass them quite slowly. Could he board it, it would mean safety.

There was a pause that seemed like eternity—then the guard's whistle blew. The puffing of the engine recommenced, drowning the other faint but nearer sounds. Suddenly against the light he saw the silhouette of a face over the edge of the car. Raising the lump of coal which he held in his hand, with all his force he flung it at the head. There was a crash, a smothered cry, a shout from below; he had a momentary impression of a hand clutching wildly against the sky.

Disregarding further concealment he leaped to his feet, with a shout to Dixon, and flung himself over the side nearest the passing train, even as men swarmed into the car from the other side. He heard a scuffle behind, someone fired a shot, but he was over. He fell hard on top of a man, struggled for a moment, broke away and ran for the passing train.

The lighted carriages were sliding past and with an effort he jumped, catching at a door handle. The train was not going very fast and he found himself safely on the footboard. Around him whistles shrilled and he saw the engine driver peering back. Glancing behind he saw a dim figure struggle for a moment on the edge of the car, then leap to the ground. It was Dixon, and now he too was running hard for the train, jumped up also, fell, was dragged a little, scrambled up desperately once more, and got into a carriage. In the light from the door, as he got in, Rezaire could see blood running from his head.

Rezaire, wiser, did not get into a carriage, but crouched where he was watching the shadowy figures of the detectives also running for the train. He counted one, two get on board and heard their shouts. The next moment the train, which had barely got under way, came to a jerky standstill. They had pulled the signal cord. Rezaire, doubled up on his footboard, peered back into the night. Figures seemed on all sides, some with light from the windows occasionally falling on them; some keeping to the shadow. Further behind him he heard shouts and unexpectedly ringing through the dark a woman's cry of "Help!" Dixon, he thought to himself. Heads were out of windows and he kept still, hoping the train would go on.

Someone was signaling from the platform with a hand lamp and in another moment the train began to back to the station it had just left. Rezaire knew he must act instantly if he were to win through. Already a man at a level crossing they were passing noticed him and called out. Quickly he opened the nearest door, scrambled into the compartment, where two elderly ladies were sitting in open-mouthed terror and amazement at this apparition from the night. Without a word he ran through the carriage, opened the door at the far side and so out into the other footboard. With a quick glance round he dropped off on the opposite side.

He stumbled and fell, picked himself up and began to run. As he sped, he saw the engineer and fireman of the passing train looking at him in astonishment. The next moment he was in the darkness of a timber yard, with its huge piles and stacks of timber. Instead of running further, he dodged behind one of these and crouched down out of sight.

Lying there in the poor concealment, he hoped he had thrown his pursuers off the track for the moment. He could not, as far as he could see, get out of the yard, but he did not want to; houses, gardens, streets, were all around and besides it was not part of his plan, which was bolder and cleverer than that—if it should succeed.

He could hear men on the track round the moving train which soon came to a standstill in the station once more. Rising half to his feet he peered out over the top of the timber and could look back on the whole scene spread out before him—the lighted station platform and the moving figures hurrying this way and that like a hive disturbed. He could see the engineer of the passenger train still peering out into the night in his direction and trying to make out what had become of him. A little way to his left was the signal box, within which he could see the signalman, pipe in mouth, moving about.

Then he became aware of a scuffle on the platform and a crowd gathering round one of the carriage doors and strained his eyes to see what it was. He could make out policemen and busy-looking men in felt hats and the station-master with gold lace on his cap. They were searching the carnages one by one under the impression he was hidden inside.

Suddenly the crowd parted and he saw what in the excitement of his own escape he had forgotten—Dixon. Dixon with a face and head covered with blood, handcuffs on his wrists, and a policeman at either shoulder. Dixon had not been so quick-witted as he had, or more likely had been half-stunned by the blow on the head he had received when jumping into the train. Dixon, battered and manacled, looked very dejected—a tiny figure amongst all the others on the lighted platform. Rezaire was sorry for him, but it was his own fault.

It had been every man for himself and Dixon had lost. Then the crowd closed round once more. Dixon, swaying slightly, as if he had been badly hurt, was hustled out of the station to where, as far as he could see, the police had their car waiting.

The scene on the platform redoubled in activity. Doors were being banged open and shut every few minutes. The guard and the station-master were speaking with one of the detectives and Rezaire thought he could see one of the old ladies whom he had frightened talking to a policeman. Then the bustle seemed to be temporarily arrested as though a further development were on foot. A new issue of some kind was arising. The engineer had got down and was shouting something to a porter. He was pointing along the line and Rezaire suddenly realized what all this sudden change portended. Both the old ladies and the engineer were persons who knew he was not in the train and had run off on into the darkness, and in another minute this would be realized by the detectives. For a moment the picture stayed as it was; then on a sudden it had changed. The guard was waving his lantern as he signaled the delayed train onward, and police, detectives, men of every sort, were running along the platform and down the line out in the direction he had been seen to take into the timber yard.

At sight of the sudden advance upon him Rezaire almost lost, his nerve and took to his heels, but he mastered himself in a moment. He had made his plan and he must stick to it, although it seemed it would be a near thing.

The engine started to move heavily forward. Slowly it gathered speed, passing out of Totton Station, leaving the excited chattering groups on the platform. At an increasing rate it approached—but so did the little crowd of his pursuers with their lanterns and torches. They were level with the engine now and spreading out. Down the side of the train appeared rows of curious heads, craning forth eager to see who was being pursued. It was a sensation indeed.

The engine overtook them and drew level with his hiding place. Rezaire shrank back yet further as the bright glow from the driver's cab passed over him. The fireman was leaning out scanning the ground at the side. Then came the carriages with their excited inmates moving slowly past. He heard scraps of conversation floating from the windows, curious, incredulous, fearful, sensational, pleased... The next minute he heard close at his ear the voices of his pursuers among the timber stacks, saw the searching beams of their torches.

"Quick there, Jameson, straight ahead! He's made for the level crossing. Two of you down to the left there to the main road..."

All around him were figures, detectives and police with torches, voluntary helpers, porters, curious idlers, plunging through the yard in every direction. He lay absolutely still, frozen to the ground. Discovery was imminent. In another minute one of them would stumble on him and the game would be up.

But the moment for putting his plan into execution had arrived. The last carriages of the train were going past now at an increasing speed, fairly fast, but not so fast that a determined man might not catch them.

He took a deep breath, rose to his feet, and ran straight for the train, leaping wildly over the logs that lay scattered about. He passed just behind a policeman who had his back to him, heard his exclamation, caught a shout from someone further away, then he was running for the last carriage as it slipped past him.

"Stop him!" came in a bull-like roar in Harrison's voice a short distance away, then a confused medley of shouts and orders. A man ran at him, tripped over the rail and fell. Someone else caught at his coat, but he struck out wildly and the man dropped away. Then he was on the track running after the train.

Thank Heaven it was not yet going too fast. The red tail lamp, a foot in front of him, glowed and beckoned, offering him safety, and he strained every sinew to get it, running awkwardly over the ties and stones of the track. A horrible fear came to him that he might trip and fall. He heard a murmur from a little group of people as he re-passed the level crossing.

The next moment he caught it up at his maximum speed and, catching hold of the brake connection, with a superhuman effort leaped up and forward and pulled himself onto a buffer. A moment later and the train would have been going too fast for him; he would not have been able to catch it.

A few feet behind a man, more active than the others, was straining every nerve to draw up. But he could not do it. His tense face, red in the glow of the tail lamp, dropped slowly behind as the train put on speed. Rezaire, sitting panting on the butler, felt his old spirit returning and to the accompaniment of the cheery rattle of the wheels, he grinned in a friendly fashion at the face of his pursuer before it slipped back into the darkness.

CHAPTER XX

A PERILOUS RIDE

Rezaire sat there for a little while trying to regain his breath, and looking back at the receding lights of Totton Station. He could just make out the figures of his pursuers. Some were still dotted about the line where they had given up the chase, but others were running back purposefully to the station. Hurriedly Rezaire ran over in his mind what their next move would be. Could they have the train stopped? That would not be much good if no one was there when it was stopped. He was now considered a desperate man and they would not rely on the station-master or porters at the next stop arresting him. Yet they must know that he would in all probability choose the first opportunity to leave the train on which he was known to be.

Then suddenly the solution jumped into his mind. The car! They had a car, the one by which they had come to Totton Station and into which he had seen Dixon being taken. That was what they would use. If the road was at all straight they would get to the next station almost as soon as the train. The train rattled over a small level crossing and bore off to the right. Before the station vanished from sight, he almost thought he could see the powerful headlights of the police car outside.

He clung to his perilous seat on the end of the rocking carriage. He must leave the train before they could get to him, but it did not look hopeful. He would not after all be able to go on to Beaulieu Road Station. He would have to make his way to Beaulieu from the next stop which would be Lyndhurst Road, about seven miles across country as far as he remembered. And almost certainly they would be at Lyndhurst Road before he was. The situation did not look hopeful. The only point in his favor, as far as he could see, was that owing to his having got on to the train from directly behind, none of the people on it, not even the guard, could know that he was there.

The car rocked and swayed, almost throwing him from his precarious hold. He wondered whether he could get to a safer position, into a compartment perhaps—if he could find an empty one and could reach it without being seen. It was worth trying at all events if he could screw up his courage.

Clinging desperately to the poor handholds that the back of the car gave, he pulled himself upright on to the buffers and held himself there a moment to accustom himself to the motion and balance. Then with infinite difficulty and trembling with a genuine fear, he worked round on to the footboard of the car on the off side.

Ahead of him the train curved away into the night like a snake, its lighted windows like gleaming scales on its sides and the pulsated glowing head far away at the front. The glow of the open furnace door lay on the flowing smoke above the engine; the reflection from the windows ran along the rails at the side.

The last half of the car was the guard and baggage section and along this he made his way without much difficulty. There was no window in it, and so he could stand upright. Then he came to the window of the guard's compartment itself and crouched down to pass it. Inside, above the rattle of the train, he could hear an occasional noise as the guard apparently moved some luggage about. Then he was past without being seen and was able to stand upright once more. He had chosen the off side of the train because passengers were less liable to look out on the side on which other trains passed.

He came to the front end of the car and crept round on to his old position on the buffers once more; thence across and finally on to the footboard of the car in front. Here came the most difficult part of his journey. He had to pass along the footboard, crouched down below the level of the windows, and yet had to obtain a glimpse of the inside so as to discover the empty compartment which he sought.

He bent down, hands upraised to grip the door handles, and crept past the first. From where he was he could see luggage on the rack and knew the compartment was occupied. He reached the next and suddenly, for a brief moment, his hand slipped. He gasped and clutched again, but at that moment all his old fear that he had been fighting off rushed back on him, the fear that had mastered him when he had clung to the roof edge the previous evening with Sam. He stopped there hardly daring to breathe, weak and sick with fear. His imagination pictured his body flung off the train, slipping downward with wildly clutching fingers, lying helpless on the track, mangled by the cruel inexorable wheels.

What was the use of all this struggling and striving, these constant dangers? Better by far surely to give himself up to the safety of a prison cell than risk all these terrible forms of death. He had not shot anyone, his hands were clean, and so they could not hang him; they could only imprison him for so many years. Safety for a term in Dartmoor seemed far preferable to this life of hairbreadth escapes, of playing with Death in all his most terrible forms. He knew he was not brave; he was afraid always and utterly of dying and physical pain. He thought of all the terrible, fearful things he had risked in the last twenty-four hours—the fall from the roof, the fight with the valet, and last but not least, Sam's cruel knife that, as its owner had threatened, would slowly cut him up rather than kill him outright, torture rather than death.

As if to complete his discomfort, at that moment there was a roar and a rattle and an express train passed on the other line, a whirling pulsating death within a few feet. He had an impression of heat and steam, of rushing wind and lighted windows streaming past—and then it had gone. His nerveless fingers almost lost their hold as he clung there. Crouched on the footboard, he became desperately, physically sick...

The spasm passed. He must nerve himself to do something. After all, the sooner he found an empty compartment the safer he would be. He pulled himself together and crept onward to the next. Raising himself by his hands ever so slightly, till his eyes were on a level with the top of the door, he looked in, and instantly sank down again. A man was inside reading a book. He moved on again. Two more occupied compartments he thus passed, knowing that he must look in, afraid lest he should be seen while doing so, and then he came to one that was empty, a first-class. With a sob of relief his fingers sought the handle and opened the door. More dead than alive from sheer physical fear, he crawled in, closed the door behind him, and sank onto the floor. He was safe for a while.

In a moment or two he pulled himself together. He had lost count of the passage of time, but he knew that they would be at Lyndhurst Road Station very shortly. He was terribly hungry and also, he saw from the glass, very dirty. He went into the lavatory to tidy himself up, then returned and looked out of the window. He was wondering whether he could see the main road from Totton, for along that he knew that his pursuers would come. If by chance they did not reach the station before him perhaps the best thing for him would be to go straight on to Beaulieu Road...

His eye fell upon a discarded newspaper and he instantly picked it up. He had not seen a paper since the hotel at Basingstoke and he fluttered the pages open with eagerness.

The headlines were there as before: "DESPERATE CRIMINAL," "MIDNIGHT CHASE," all the usual clichés that had been in the other papers. But the last news he had seen in the others was the report of the fire in the cinema. This one, an afternoon London edition, would have something later than that. He ran his eye down the stories, the eye-witnesses—the official statements. Ah! Challoner! The name leaped at him and he read eagerly on.

A little smile curved his lips as he read. Mr. Challoner, it appeared, was almost a national hero. Recognizing his two visitors at once as criminals he had with the utmost coolness asked them in, intending to lock them up and telephone for the police. But unfortunately he had himself been overpowered... Bah! What rot! Rezaire skipped it angrily... Ah! The valet, the man who had nearly killed him. He was in hospital shot through the lung and not expected to live. That was Sam again. Rezaire shuddered. But where was what he wanted to see—the description of the fight, the statement of Sam's arrest? He turned the page anxiously, but he could find nothing.

There had been no eye-witnesses, no reporters and there was no official statement. Why? Surely they would announce the fact that they had captured one of the most dangerous of the gang? But there was nothing there. Had the paper been issued before the statement? A new fear took hold of him. Supposing Sam had not been captured after all and that was why it was not in the papers. Then his fear vanished as the real reason came to him. The police were withholding it because they had suffered heavily, too heavily perhaps to justify at first sight the capture of one man. For Sam was a fighter and had seemed half mad then with the lust of it. Rezaire would always remember his last glimpse of that face as the outside lift rattled him down to safety.

He flung the paper down in disgust. There was one thing that he wanted to see more than anything else and it was not there.

He glanced out of the window again and then suddenly looked out more intently. Some distance away there was a light, not the light of a house, but a moving light, as of a car on a road, which appeared and disappeared between the trees. Perhaps that was the main road to Lyndhurst. The moving light was again cut off by trees and houses, reappeared again closer. He watched it as the train went on, catching occasional glimpses. Yes, it certainly was a car, and on the main road, which appeared to be gradually converging on the railway. He remembered now from the map that the Southampton-Lyndhurst Road crossed the railway at Lyndhurst Road Station. But was that light the police car? He could not tell; he could see nothing but the light appearing and disappearing between the houses that lined the road. Behind he now could see the light of another car.

The cars certainly were going very fast. He could see that more easily as the rail and road converged. He was reminded suddenly of his mad ride of that afternoon, of Dixon at the wheel. What had happened to Dixon, he wondered. Probably on his way to London by now under custody—unless by chance he was still in the police car, to which he had seen him being led.

The train suddenly began to slow down. They were nearing the station. The road too was very close. The gardens of the houses that lined it now reached back to the railway itself.

Rezaire nerved himself for the last act of his drama. If the police were there, if those two cars did belong to them, it would be a close thing. At the end of this act the curtain would fall on success or failure, for in a few hours now he would either be safe on his launch or in the hands of the police. He drew down the blinds of his compartment and settled himself so that he could see through a chink without being seen.

The line of houses came closer, ending at last in one big house with a garden and tall trees that filled the angle. Then came the final convergence of the road with the railway at a level crossing. Rezaire peered out, anxious to see whether the police had arrived or not. He could see nothing at the level crossing, and wondered where they were. The entrance to the station was at the far side and the gates would have been shut long before they could have got across. Perhaps they had driven into the coal or freight yard which was on the near side to them.

Then suddenly he saw standing by the side gate to the level crossing two constables and a plainclothes man. In the freight yard just by a lamp he saw also the two cars. His heart leaped into his mouth. So the cars had been the police cars after all; and these men were waiting where they thought the rear of the train would halt, for they had last seen him on the buffers and probably thought he would still be there ready to jump off as the train stopped. The police had arrived and he must act instantly.

Swiftly he ran to the far side of the carriage and opening the door dropped out as the train came to a standstill, closing the door behind him. Then remembering his success with the freight car he bent down and crawled right underneath the train as it lay up against the platform. Peering out between the wheels he saw that fortune had indeed aided him in this maneuver, for the opposite platform of the small country station was empty, save for a porter who had his back turned and some people in the waiting room. No one had seen him get out. Above him on the down platform he could hear banging of doors, excited shuffling, and moving of feet, shouts, voices, a repetition almost of the search at Totton. The detectives, relying on the surprise of their quick move, evidently hoped to catch him just as they had caught Dixon at the previous station. He heard two men run hastily through the carriages to watch the far side, saw their legs as they descended.

With beating heart he commenced to crawl forward, as he had done before, along the track underneath the train, keeping well to the side in the sheltering shadow of the platform.

CHAPTER XXI

AT LYNDHURST ROAD

Rezaire crawled on painfully. His hands were cut by the sharp stones of the ballast, he was soaked in oil and filth, but he persevered. His one fear was that the train should move on again, leaving him disclosed, before he got to where he wanted, but he had every hope that it would be delayed a long while by the detectives. Not having seen him get out anywhere, though they had stationed men all round, they would not let the train proceed till they had searched it very thoroughly indeed.

The banging of doors and stamp of feet in carriages above his head continued. He could hear passengers asking questions, could hear impatient noncommittal replies. There was a buzz of excitement as the news got about that the police were after one of last night's gang. Women stood about in a high state of pleasurable tension; men got in the way, offering their services, and were refused.

Rezaire crawled on. At the end of every car he had to wait and judge his time before covering the gap between the two where he was no longer so well sheltered and where the light from the station lamps struck down onto the track.

At last he came to the end of the cars. Just ahead of him, he could tell by the wheels, was the tender of the locomotive. He paused for a minute. He had reached the point where caution was necessary. He was now well away toward the far end of the platform where the people and the lights were fewer. He gathered his courage to crawl on under the locomotive, though his vivid imagination at once brought back his ever present physical fear, making him terribly afraid of the big hot pulsating monster just above him. He feared all manner of things; boiling water, jets of steam, red hot coals, anything might come upon him from above as he wriggled slowly forward... He had to lie flat and draw himself forward with his hands.

At last he was clear and out in the open just in front of the engine. Before him stretched the track illuminated by the headlights; to left and right the deserted ends of the platforms. On the left the country was bare and open, but to the right as far as he could make out were trees and forest. That way perhaps lay safety. At this juncture he had to leave the shelter of the train and strike out away from the station to Beaulieu. He wondered if he could cross the track to the right without being seen, and get into the friendly darkness beyond. He peered round the off side of the engine, and scanned the other platform. There was only the one porter on it and he was now watching the scene opposite. But the engineer was leaning out of that side of his cab whistling. Even as he looked he called out to the porter who, getting down onto the line, came across and stood talking to him. If only, Rezaire felt, he could distract their attention for one moment he might get across unperceived.

He peeped round still further. The fireman also had his head out now on that side, talking to the porter. The slightest sound or movement would give his attempt away, unless he could get their attention riveted in the opposite direction.

He had an idea. He picked up a big stone and, hidden behind the front of the engine, hurled it well up in the air and away, aiming it to fall directly among the people further along the main platform. As soon as it had left his hand he peered round the corner of the engine to see the result.

But nothing had happened. He had thrown too far to the right and by the sound landed on the roof of the station buildings. The clatter passed unnoticed. He threw another. Again without result. He picked up a third and bigger one, and this time there was a crash and a cry from a woman. Just what he had intended had happened. The crowd, already strung up to a state of excitement, suddenly collected round the woman. He moved to the other side. The engineer and fireman had left the far side of the cab, and the porter was moving down the line to see what the disturbance might be. It was Rezaire's chance and he took it.

Gathering himself up, he ran swiftly across the track, scaled the far platform, was across it like a flash, and into the deep shadow of a siding just beyond. Passing behind a car standing there he mounted an embankment on the far side and moved on into the night, leaving behind him the station buzzing with the search like a hive of disturbed bees.

He came to a thick hedge which he could not scale or break through without much noise, and was forced to creep along this to the right where he suddenly arrived by a gate at the open yard in front of the station. Here and there were two cars standing at the entrance and Rezaire instantly guessed that these must be the police cars which had now come round from the level crossing gates to the front.

He was about to beat a retreat when suddenly he stopped in amazement. There were three men sitting in the back of one of the cars and to his astonishment, under the station lamp he recognized the middle one as Dixon. Dixon with his head, now bandaged, sunk between his shoulders, a picture of dejection. What on earth was he here for, he instantly wondered. He thought that he would have been lodged in jail at Southampton by now.

Then he realized what had happened. They had put Dixon in the car at Totton, expecting that they would capture his companion also the next minute and take them both together to Southampton. Then when Rezaire had made his dash for the train, they had had to start off so hurriedly in pursuit by road that they had not time to get their captive out and so they had brought him along.

He stayed watching for a moment. Deep in his heart a vague feeling of pity for the man who had stuck to him and helped him so well was taking shape. He wondered whether he could not do something for Dixon. Perhaps, he thought boldly, he could stride out and hold his escort up with the revolver while the others were inside. But this picture faded from his mind as soon as formed; his courage was not great enough for that, especially when it was only on behalf of another. The police might refuse to be held up, might shoot back…

Even while he turned the matter over, a man suddenly ran out of the station and spoke hurriedly to one of the policemen in the car, with the result that the man got out and the two went back together. They were hardly out of sight when Dixon, who, despite his air of dejection, had evidently been waiting his opportunity in desperation, suddenly sprang to his feet with a yell and jumped straight out of the car.

He fell to his knees on the far side owing to his being handcuffed, but was on his feet again in an instant, running hard for the shadow, the constable a few feet behind him. The other two reappeared at the door of the station and instantly took up the chase.

It had all happened in the wink of an eye. For the moment Rezaire forgot in his excitement that he had just thrown the police off his own track, and in his desire to help his comrade jumped forward and called out: "This way, Dixon!"

Dixon heard the voice, swerved to the left and ran straight for him. Rezaire could see his face white in the lamplight and his eyes, wildly glaring, noted mechanically the gleam on the uniform of the men behind. At the same instant he realized how, by his altruistic folly so unlike his usual calculating selfishness, he had betrayed his own whereabouts. He half turned to run away himself at the realization, then checked himself. He was a fool, but he must see his folly through. Then Dixon was after him, crashing blindly into the shadows, muttering strangely to himself as he ran.

He reached out a hand to the wildly flying figure, catching at his manacled wrists to support him. Together they ran blunderingly through the darkness, crashed through a hedge into a garden, out again into some trees across a cart track. A big building, with lights in the windows, like the back of an hotel, loomed over them on the right. Behind them the police were running too, following them in the dark by the noise they were making.

"Quietly, quietly," urged Rezaire in a fierce whisper. "Run quietly, you fool."

Dixon got a hold of himself once more and tried to step quietly, muttering queerly to himself. They slipped with less noise past something that looked like piles of sawn up logs and came upon a shed in a corner overshadowed by trees. Into this Rezaire drew his companion even as the first of their pursuers burst through onto the track they had just crossed at the back of the hotel. Behind, in the direction of the station, they could hear further shouts and knew that all the detectives were now on their track.

The first man stopped uncertain for a moment on the edge of the road, paused to listen, was joined by the two others.

"Which way?" snapped one of them.

"Dunno, sir."

"Dunno," replied the other, evidently a sergeant. "You damn fool, Peters, you'll be on the mat if he gets away. He was in your charge. Come on quick! One of you down that way…"

The voices stopped. Footsteps went down the lane. Other men came up. There was a pause. A short distance away the delayed train, journey resumed, puffed past. Through the open doors of the shed they could see the car windows still filled with curious heads.

Footsteps and a voice on the road broke the silence once more: "No sign that way, sir, and no noise."

"Perhaps they're in hiding, if they haven't got away through the trees."

"There are three men of ours already out in the trees," put in another.

"What's that shed there?"

Dixon muttered something between his teeth. Rezaire heard the chink of his handcuffs as he moved.

"Be careful," he whispered. "What are you doing?"

"Getting my gun," was the answer in a strange sobbing tone. "Get it out of my pocket for me."

"Don't be a fool!"

"Must have it," muttered the other. "Get it for me or I'll shout out."

Reluctantly Rezaire took the automatic out of his pocket—the capture and pursuit had been so swift that the police had had no time to search him—and put it in his hand. The voices outside drew a little closer. Further away they could hear a woman talking volubly in broad Hampshire dialect, explaining how she had heard someone run through her garden.

"Don't be a fool," urged Rezaire again. "Don't shoot at them."

"Yes, I will. They shot at us," came back the wild whisper. "Besides, it's our only chance."

"It's not…" But even as he spoke, Rezaire realized that Dixon might be after a fashion right. His hope that they would not be discovered had failed. Their opponents were even now approaching the shed.

Fear came upon him and he laid a restraining hand on Dixon's arm.

The other shook it off angrily.

"Damn it! Leave me alone," he snapped, and again Rezaire sensed that something was seriously wrong with his companion. The man seemed to have changed, to be mad with the fear of capture. Perhaps the blow that he had received had affected his brain, for he was quite different.

"Gently, gently," said Rezaire through dry lips, but Dixon only answered, this time in a low whining voice: "They'll surround us. If we shoot we can fight them off."

He moved away and the next minute a loud report echoed in the little shed.

A warning shout came from outside; the sounds of hurried movement; a whistle.

"They're in there."

"Look out!"

Dixon fired again.

"That'll teach you, you—" he called, again the note of madness in his voice. And then a moment later: "Come on and take me, and to hell with you!"

Rezaire, trembling with fear, flung himself on the ground. He knew what to expect. The detectives who were after them now were the same ones who had pursued them in London. They had him marked as a dangerous man and would not hesitate to shoot.

He was right. As he clung to the foul smelly mud he heard two answering shots. There was a zip of splintered wood, the whine of a torn bullet ricocheting over his head. Dixon laughed loudly, like a maniac, and fired twice more.

Lying there Rezaire was even then wondering what to do. The fact that they were being fired on was for the moment keeping the police from rushing them. But as soon as the situation had been appreciated by the leaders and they had organized a plan, the game would be up. In the meantime could he not creep out, get to the nearest ditch, or into the shadow of the wood, and so away unobserved while Dixon held them off? He crawled to the door and looked out. He could just make out the dark mass that was the edge of the forest, quite close, if only he could get to it. But had he not heard someone say there were three men in the wood?... Perhaps they were surrounded after all. Another shot whined over his head and again he flattened himself to the ground in terror.

Suddenly a choking cry rang out inside the shed, followed by the soft crash of a collapsing body close at his side. Fearfully he put out a hand and felt—Dixon's limp form lying beside him. His fingers came away warm and sticky. Dixon was shot—killed—as he would be too if he stayed. Mad terror came upon him in the darkness. Seizing his revolver he emptied it wildly around him at his unseen foes—to keep them from rushing the place. The next minute on hands and knees he crawled rapidly out of the shed and in a minute was crouched in the shelter of a big pine tree some yards away.

He paused a moment here to master his fear. Voices and movement seemed all around him and yet he did not appear to have been observed. Behind him a shot or two rang out. The police had not yet decided to rush the supposed hiding place of the two criminals, thinking they were still both there. But in a minute a plan would be arranged. He must get away, must put as much distance as he could between himself and them before that time.

He made his way quietly to another tree where he paused. A twig cracked loudly a little distance away. He knew that his enemies, those that were in the wood, were nearby. As silently as a cat he made his way further into the forest, pausing every now and then to listen. The trees stood up about him, straight and silent, and when at last he judged he was out of hearing he broke into a run, setting his direction by the noise, faint in the distance, of the train that was on its way to Beaulieu Road station.

Behind him somewhere in the darkness were the police and—what at the moment he was even more afraid of—behind him too was the shed with the limp body of Dixon—warm and sticky as had been his hand, before he rubbed it with terrified loathing on the damp moss under the trees.

CHAPTER XXII

THE ROAD TO BEAULIEU

Rezaire ran blindly on for some distance further; then he paused and looked back once more. He could hear nothing; the shots appeared to have stopped. By now they would have discovered Dixon's death and his flight. They would then be after him once more. What if they should catch him when he was so near safety! He stumbled onward, the word ringing in his brain. Safety. Safety. He pulled himself up with a jerk. He must not let his mind wander. Suppose he were suddenly to go half mad, like Dixon had, out here in the lonely New Forest. A thing that might very well happen, for in addition to the strain of the last twenty-four hours, he had had nothing to eat since one o'clock at Basingstoke, no rest, except the few hours' sleep in the prison cell and in Mr. Challoner's flat. God! He was weary. Weary in body and mind. If only he could lie down here under the big trees and sleep, sleep, sleep. He got hold of himself with an effort; he realized how near he was to a breakdown now that the immediate and instant danger had been removed.

Making his uneven way forward he came upon the railway line again, a deep cutting on his left. Cautiously he scrambled down to it and looked round. His way lay to the south he knew, and the railway, judging by the stars, went south. If he followed the railway along he was bound to come to Beaulieu Road Station, whence he could take the road to Beaulieu. He set his face southward and began to walk swiftly along the track.

The starlight glinted on the long steel rails, stretching away in front of him. The ties passed away beneath his feet. He cursed the men who laid the railway for not putting the ties a full pace apart so that he could walk swiftly along. As it was, he had to take three short paces on the ties and then one on the uneven ballast—three and then one—three and then one…

He began to be mesmerized by the railway line and the ties, as a hen is mesmerized by a chalk line. It suddenly seemed to him that he had been walking for hours and hours along this line, walking nearly all his life. If only he could rest—rest and eat. Even the cold comfort of a prison cell seemed alluring, for it meant rest for his limbs, freedom for his brain from the constant tension at which it had been working for the last twenty-four hours.

Three and then one… Three and then one… On he went, his mind a machine that seemed every minute about to break down. He was the only one of the old gang left. Viv was gone. Dixon was dead. Harrap probably dead too. Joe in prison. Sam in prison… His brain suddenly roused itself to new activity, and to his old fear. Why had not Sam's capture been in the paper he had picked up in the train? Had the police purposely forbidden it to be mentioned, or had Sam escaped after all; impossibly, incredibly escaped, and was even now after him with that wicked knife? He knew Sam well enough to realize what to expect if Sam were to catch him alone after what had happened. Sam was an artist in cruelty; it was in his blood. He would take a slow revenge and at the end—death. Rezaire's tortured nerves, spurred by his imagination, writhed and flickered so that he almost shrieked aloud. For a moment he paused, half expecting Sam to leap upon him out of the high shadowed walls of the forest on either side of the railway line.

The warning rattle of a train in the distance recalled him to himself. He crawled into the bushes, crouched down while the train approached. Clouds of smoke, red touched from the furnace, jeweled with sparks; lighted cars streaming past in rows; rattle of wheels over rail ends; then sudden cessation of the roar, as if cut off with a knife, and a red light disappearing in the darkness. The train had passed. Rezaire got on the lines again, and went on; but this time with less fear. The sudden contact with ordinary life had in a way refreshed his mind, upon which the loneliness of the forest had begun to work.

He went on some distance, leaving the trees behind him as the country became more open, until he heard the trickle of a stream, and descending found that a small river flowed under the railway.

He stopped and drank greedily, wondering as he did so whether this might not be Beaulieu River itself, upon whose bosom some miles away was his launch.

Refreshed, he got up and resumed his way along the embankment, till at last the rails dipped into a cutting once more and the signal lights of Beaulieu Road Station came in sight.

Upon this he halted for a while to study the sky. The railway was at the moment running south and he knew from what he remembered of the map before he had lost it that Beaulieu itself was south and east of the station, and about three to four miles away by the main road. He took a further look at such stars as he could see and noted that heavy clouds were coming up, then scrambled up the steep embankment and struck out into the country, leaving the cutting behind him. His idea was to make a detour round the station and houses, whose lights he could now see plainly to his right, and join the Beaulieu Road well south of that danger spot. There would be, he felt sure, someone on the watch for him at the station even if they were only porters or local constables warned by telephone from Totton or Lyndhurst Road. The country was open moorland of grass and dry heather, with here and there a clump of fir trees. A south wind had got up and was blowing freshly from his right with a hint of rain.

After some while he came out into the main road to Beaulieu. Beaulieu and safety! He sat down on the edge of the ditch and rested a moment; for the journey across country had been hard. His hunger gnawed at him like a wild thing. If only he could get something to eat! The fresh wind sprayed his face with first drops of rain. But he did not care. He was on the road that led to freedom—though he felt certain that he had not yet done with the police. But even as he loaded his revolver in case he should need it, he felt strangely elated.

To his right he could see some distance away a light which at first he took to be a house. But it moved, came waveringly nearer, and he saw that it could only be a bicycle. He got up from the ditch prepared to hide once more, when an idea struck him. Here was a man on a cycle going to Beaulieu. Well, he had a revolver in his pocket; the cycle should change hands.

He stood up in the center of the road and signaled to the newcomer to halt. The cycle came to a standstill, and a man—Rezaire could not see his face—got off. The next minute Rezaire flashed his revolver in the light of the lamp that the man might see what it was and then dug it into his ribs.

"'Ere, what's matter…" began the other, a country man by his speech, but Rezaire cut in fiercely: "Never mind what's the matter! I want your cycle, or I'll blow a bullet into you."

"Want my cycle!…" vaguely repeated the man, uncomprehending, yet half afraid.

"Yes," snarled Rezaire, trying to inspire him with fear. His hand grasped the handle-bar. "And this,"—he dug him mercilessly in the ribs—"is a loaded revolver."

"What d'ye mean?" again faltered the man, recoiling from the thrusting weapon.

"Quickly now! Don't start talking. And don't think"—Rezaire's quick brain forestalled any possible attack—"that you can hit me, because if you do, this pistol's got a light trigger and will simply go off into your guts."

Still plying the country man with the irresistible persuasion of the steel barrel, he snatched the bicycle from him and backed slowly away for a pace. Then: "Now turn your back and walk away from me. If I see the slightest hesitation or if you turn round and try to follow me I'll put a bullet in you. I can see you quite plainly against the sky."

For a moment the dark figure stood there irresolute, the driving rain striking down across him. Then he turned and walked slowly away. Twenty paces off Rezaire heard him break into a lumbering run.

Hurriedly he pocketed the revolver, mounted the machine and set off as fast as he could toward Beaulieu.

The rain, now coming down fast, whipped his cheek and the side of his face as he rode doggedly onward. He had not far to go now. The little fringe of light from his lamp slid before him on the muddy yellow road barred by bright spears of rain.

He rode on for two miles across the open moorland road, occasionally looking behind him. Once he passed two yokels coming from Beaulieu who bade him good-night, and once a farm wagon, plodding surlily along in the dark; but no one had overtaken him from the direction of the station.

He came to a gate across the road and a few houses by the side, and could not understand it. Had he gone wrong, got into a private park? He stood irresolute outside for a moment; then gently approached and lifted his cycle cautiously over. He did not want to arouse any people, or to let them know he had passed. Then he clambered over himself and resumed his journey. The road was evidently still the main road, but now traversing a park.

He had not gone far before he glimpsed the reflection of bright headlights somewhere behind him. This was what he had feared. He flung himself off his machine, putting out the light as he did so, and dragged it quickly into the side of the road behind some bushes. Here also amid the dripping sodden foliage he himself crouched. He had hardly left the road before the powerful headlights of a car swung round a corner.

Cutting remorselessly through the rain the car went past. Rezaire could not see who was in it, but he was taking no chances. He suspected it was the police who, reaching Beaulieu Road, had been put on his track by the cyclist. He watched the red light fade away in the direction of Beaulieu, then remounted, though this time he did not light his lamp.

A bare ten minutes later, when he was on the outskirts of Beaulieu, he just had time to throw the bicycle in the ditch once more and tumble after it himself, before the car re-passed him at a very high speed. This time he was almost certain it was a police car, for he could see it was crammed full of people and he had had a momentary glimpse of a helmet. He got out and stood for a moment sodden and desperate on the road. He was soaked through to the skin by the pitiless rain; he was cold, weary, and above all, hungry. How hungry he was! He vowed that he would not pass through Beaulieu without getting food somewhere, even though he knew it awaited him on his launch. How he longed for that launch, its little cabin, food, warmth—perhaps even Viv. It was curious how his thoughts were running on Viv whom he thought he had finished with forever. It almost seemed to him as if their break had never been, as if their relations were once more the same intimate ones that had existed before—in the days when there was not much that he would not have done for her, selfish and self-centered though he was.

The first houses of Beaulieu appeared, dark masses on his right hand side. To his left, close by the road, was a wide reach of water—the Beaulieu River again, in which, farther south, half a mile through the village, lay the motor launch. He stopped to relight his lamp. He did not want at this last minute to be summoned by the local constable. He debated with himself for a moment and then realized that his only course was to cycle boldly right through Beaulieu. He could not risk a detour, even if there was one—for while he knew the road he wanted on the far side, he did not know any other way of getting to it. He would have to chance there being anyone abroad on such a bad night. He lit his lamp with difficulty, and rode down into Beaulieu, light flickering in the rain.

He turned to the left into the main street and almost immediately was aware of a figure standing in his path. He set his teeth to ride nonchalantly past, when the figure loomed up clear in the feeble light. His heart came suddenly into his mouth as he recognized the uniform cap and oilskins of the village constable. For a moment fear and indecision held him irresolute, caught unawares, not knowing what to do to circumvent the grim figure before him, which stood for prison, for failure of all his plans, and destruction of his hopes.

CHAPTER XXIII

A BOLD MOVE

Only for a moment though was Rezaire dismayed; the next minute his brain was functioning again with all its usual vigor and alertness. He played boldly as was his custom.

"Ah, constable," he said easily, walking straight up to him. "Any luck yet?"

The policeman, already warned to look out for a man on a bicycle, had just been about to stop the newcomer and interrogate him when the unusual question pulled him up short.

"What luck?" he queried suspiciously.

Rezaire, skating brilliantly over the thinnest of ice, affected to take this the wrong way.

"Oh, I've had none myself yet," he answered, "but they told me that you might have had by now."

Though his heart was hammering with excitement and suspense, he leaned easily on his bike in the now slackening rain.

"Where do you come from?" asked the policeman bluntly, not to be put off, switching on his torch.

For a fraction of a second Rezaire hesitated. His hand had been forced before he was ready. He had hoped to draw the man's confidence further by his assumption that they each knew all about one another. Hurriedly he changed his front—now to play the part of a man who has just realized that he and another have been talking at cross purposes.

"They said they'd told you..." He took a desperate chance which he had not intended to do till he had learned more. "Detective Inspector Harrison of Scotland Yard said he'd seen you when he came up just now."

Inside his pocket his fingers gripped his revolver, ready to whip it out in an instant should his bluff fail. He was guessing wildly, building on the single glimpse he had had of a policeman's helmet in the car that had passed him twice. For if it had been a police car surely they would not have been to Beaulieu without speaking to the constable. He hurriedly threw out a supplementary sentence—just as the constable's lips opened.

"Perhaps it was your colleague he saw—if you have one?"

"No, it was me," said the constable slowly, and Rezaire's heart leaped with joy. He had drawn a bow at venture, but he had hit between the joints of his opponent's harness. "But they didn't say anything about you," added the policeman. "What's your name?"

"My name's Ferguson," replied Rezaire glibly. He was now on safer ground. The fact once established—for it had not been denied—that Harrison and the detectives had been there, he knew very well how much they knew and what they would say. He ran swiftly on, pouring out what he intended should be confirmation of his identity, skillfully allaying the other's suspicions. He laid particular emphasis on the terrible time he had had in his pursuit across country—to explain the condition of his clothes.

"There are three of us on cycles—Mainprice and Waring are the other two—sent out to watch the roads round here. He's reported to have come this way after stealing a bicycle. We've to watch the Lymington, Hythe and Exbury Roads." He reeled off the names of places he had seen near Beaulieu on the map.

The constable's last suspicions vanished at this display of knowledge. He had been much overawed at the visit of the Scotland Yard men half an hour ago and here, apparently, was another. He was gratified at the near escape he had had of making a fool of himself. He had for a moment thought of arresting the newcomer when he appeared like that on a cycle out of the night.

"Is he likely to come this way, sir?" he asked at length, and Rezaire could have laughed aloud in triumph. By the last word he knew that he had won. His luck and his "infernal cheek" had held good.

"Can't say. It'll be a good thing for you if he does. Promotion, eh?" He chuckled affably.

"Well, yes, sir. You see, we don't get much to do down here and to 'ave a man like that—name in all the papers—let slip by the London police," he added with gusto—"and brought to your doors so to speak…"

"Better be careful! He's armed and desperate."

"I'm ready for 'im," responded the constable darkly, and Rezaire laughed.

"So am I," he replied. "And I want to catch him as much as you. It means something to me too. Well, I must be off. If you see either of the others tell them that Ferguson has taken the Exbury Road." He got on his cycle and rode off whistling into the night, leaving the constable, pleasantly intrigued, to step back into the shadow and resume his watch.

Rezaire rode off across the bridge in high spirits despite the cold and wet. Such had been his elation and self-confidence that he had almost asked the policeman where he could get food, but decided against it. The bold man could skate over thin ice if necessity arose, but only the fool stayed on it too long. It would not do to get tied up with the constable and then find that the police car had returned. But have food he must and he had already determined to raid the nearest house and get what he wanted at the point of a revolver. For it was now eleven o'clock, the launch would be lying at the quay about half a mile away ready to move off at a moment's notice, and the fact that safety was in his grasp had made him reckless.

He passed the gate of Beaulieu Abbey, then the stretch of river on his right, and went on up the hill till he came to the turning. Somewhere down this narrow road was the house called "Joyner's End." He did not know the ground very well; but a few days ago he had studied a large scale map fairly thoroughly and knew that there were private houses standing in their own grounds on either side for about a quarter of a mile along a twisting road. The last house on the right was that called "Joyner's End," and somewhere just beyond it, and behind it, was the quay he sought.

He paused at the turning and looked back. The rain had stopped and the moon had also risen. Not a soul was in sight. Behind him lay all the hairbreadth escapes and dangers of the last twenty-four hours; before him lay only safety. And in that moment the pangs of hunger took him again. He must eat, must eat and drink to restore his body and brain, lest like an overwound clock they should both snap and run down, even as Dixon's had.

Putting out his light, he hid the bicycle in the roadside and tiptoed up a little path to a cottage on the opposite side of the main road which slumbered in silent darkness in a small garden. He moved to the back, tried a door and windows, found one that was latched only and with his knife forced the catch.

Climbing quietly in, he found himself in what by the smell and the glint of the moonlight outside on plates and pots appeared to be a kitchen. He felt directly for the cupboards where he discovered a loaf of bread and cheese and a jug of milk. The next moment he was eating ravenously.

A sudden instinct warned him of danger, even before he heard the slight noise outside. He sprang to his feet and at the same moment the door was flung open. In the dim light a big figure in white was facing him. Rezaire could see that it grasped a weapon of some kind—a poker probably. A broad country voice asked him angrily what he was doing.

Rezaire, despite a fleeting temptation to pause and see whether he could not bluff this new opponent in some way, even as he had bluffed the policeman, did not stop to argue. Still clutching the loaf of bread, he went as quickly as he could. The other made a rush at him as he scrambled through the window; he felt the poker whistle past his head and crash on the window ledge. Then he was over and stumbling through a bed of some tall flowers. The owner of the cottage was shouting and cursing from the window, but did not attempt to pursue. By that time too Rezaire, slipping out through the hedge, had regained his cycle and set off again down the road opposite, white barred under the moonlight through the trees. He dismissed the incident from his mind. For now that he was so near to his launch these smaller things did not matter to him. As he rode he finished the bread which he still held in his hand.

He passed the gates to houses on either side, as the road bore first to the left and then to the right again. He would soon now come to the house he sought, the last one behind which lay the quay. It was wonderful to think that all his troubles lay behind him, the police, prison, Sam and his knife.

The next moment his ears, strained to the highest pitch, caught the hum of a car somewhere away behind him, but on the main road. He looked round uneasily. He could not see it, but soon he could make out the reflection of its headlights now on the side of a house, now on the branches of trees. Was it the police car, he wondered, and, if so, how was it that they had come down here after him once more? He had thought they had been thrown off the scent after they had scoured the Beaulieu Road, and it seemed rather strange that they should have returned here. He was certain the Beaulieu policeman had not guessed who he was and telephoned to them and he did not see what else could have given him away—if after all it was the police car.

He dismounted, for safety's sake, and stood looking back. Despite the nearness of his journey's end, he must exercise a certain amount of caution or he would give the hiding place of the launch away.

The lights were going along the main road just beyond the bend. He could see them flashing in and out among the trees. At the corner they seemed to halt; the next moment he realized with a sudden quick beat of the heart that they had swung onto the same road that he was. The lights were gleaming on the road surface just round the bend in the road and would be on him in a minute. As quick as thought he turned and rode on round the next bend, where he stepped aside into the open gate of one of the houses that lined the road, flung his cycle into the hedge and crouched down himself in some bushes.

It was the police car after all. It must be. No other car would have turned down that side road at this time of night. Yet, how had they known?...

The gleaming headlights spread their beams among the trees at the beginning of the road, moved slowly onward. Crouched among the wet leaves, he hoped that his bicycle was well hidden. He had only flung it into the back of the hedge that bordered the road without stopping to see how thick it was. Should the lights strike on any portion of it the reflection would give its hiding place away. He moved slightly and the laurels rustled together.

The car was coming very slowly, almost as though it was searching for him itself. Already it had rounded the first bend and was reaching the next. Through the shrubbery to his left he could see the two big headlights, like two eyes, though at least they could not turn aside and scan the country CHI either hand. But behind he knew were other eyes, keen and watchful, and hands that gripped revolvers.

The leaves and twigs in front of him grew bright under the touch of the approaching beams; the shadows moved athwart his vision. The car crawled slowly along the wet white surface of the road, looking now to his strung up fancy like some baleful animal that was tracking him out by a sixth sense. He felt suddenly that his presence must be known, that the car would stop when it came opposite him, feeling by instinct that he was there.

It came nearer and nearer; and his heart was in his mouth, for he could now see just in front of him the end of the handle-bar of his cycle projecting right through the hedge. The light was full on it; would the keen eyes in the car see it too?

The lights moved on. He heard a voice from the dark mass behind the beams—saw the glow of a torch. The car drew level at last and he could almost have cried out with relief, for the light had passed the danger point and the bicycle had not been seen.

The next moment he only just choked down a quick exclamation of fear. For a few yards further on a voice called out something and the car came to a sudden halt. What had they seen? Surely not the handle-bar of his cycle, for that they had already passed. He peered through the bushes, watching them intently. It was, as his imagination had suggested, almost as if the car was trailing him by scent. A couple of men were out in front of the car looking at the road surface. Then the car began to back.

The truth dawned on him suddenly. Fool that he was to have lingered there waiting for them to pass. For they would not pass; they were indeed tracking him—by the mark of his bicycle wheels on the fresh mud. They had seen that the tracks came to a stop and were backing now to where they had last been seen. In another moment they would find the place where he had turned aside, the discarded cycle—and his hiding place.

CHAPTER XXIV

SURROUNDED

Rezaire rose to his feet and began to tiptoe silently away from the road. He passed quietly through a bed of flowers and found himself on a lawn on the wet turf of which his feet made no sound. Before him the dark mass of the house loomed up and he turned to the left. He was not quite certain now where the quay side was, except that it was beyond "Joyner's End," the last house on this road. But as he left the lawn he heard a shout of triumph from the road where the car, slowly backing, had at last brought the handle-bar of his bicycle within its light.

The air instantly seemed full of noise. They must almost have known that they were very close on his tracks. He could hear the rustling of laurel bushes, the scrunch of feet in the drive, Harrison's voice bawling to someone apparently on the main road to come on up, to someone else to take his men on to the far end.

He broke into a run. It was going to be a near thing, for the launch must get away without being noticed. Besides,—a new and horrible fear gripped him,—supposing in their search for him in this neighborhood the police were to find the launch and there lay wait for him?

With this thought uppermost in his mind, he ran on and burst through a hedge into the garden of the next house. Behind him the night was alive with sound—the shouting of men, the baying of dogs belonging to the various houses, the rustle and crack of bushes and twigs. From the various commands he heard, it was evident that some sort of preconcerted plan was being put into action. Bearing to his left he came upon the road once more and seeing that it was deserted he got on to it; for there he could run better, and by now the lights of the car were hidden round a bend further back.

He had run barely a few paces before a slight noise or even some instinct made him swerve aside to the right once again and double himself up in the bushes. He was not a moment too soon, for there overtook him from behind man after man on bicycles. Rezaire lay there and wondered as the dark figures went swiftly and silently by. They did not seem to be searching for him; it was as though they were carrying out some special orders. Scotland Yard had indeed begun to get the situation in hand. There must have been over a score of police and detectives by now searching for him in this small area. Why had they all concentrated? Was it just luck and good work on their part, or was there something behind it? Something that had given them a clue?

The men on the cycles went past—with the exception of the last one who dismounted some distance away and stood there in the shadows. Away to the left he heard a cough and knew that another one was in that direction. He realized then what they were doing. They had drawn a cordon along the road, to prevent him crossing it. He was now hemmed in in the area between the road and the river, which was in places not fifty yards away. At one end of this area, in the direction of Beaulieu, he could hear the moving line of pursuit, gardens being searched, windows being thrown up, altercations, threats, expostulations, in progress. His capture was evidently far more important than damage to gardens.

He began to work himself silently backward into the hedge in which he was crouched. He was halfway through when a twig snapped loudly against his side and he paused, heart in mouth. Footsteps came nearer along the road; a torch flashed; a voice cried: "Who's there?"

Desperately Rezaire gave up the attempt at silence, wriggled backward into another drive, fled away up toward the house, his footsteps loud on the gravel. Shouts again split the air, whistles blew, but, ominous sign, the man who had discovered him did not leave the road upon which he was stationed.

Swerving to the left as he reached the buildings just in front of him, Rezaire darted into a yard under an archway, past a wooden erection like a garage. A dog chained to his kennel suddenly sprang to life a few feet from him, barking furiously. Within the house a Pekinese was also yapping in answer. He sped through the yard, almost ran into the wall of another building, turned, heard renewed barking as someone entered the yard behind him, and plunged wildly into the open doorway of the first outhouse he saw.

He moved swiftly across this in the darkness. The place smelled like a stable or a barn, but he was seeking only to conceal himself when suddenly out of the blackness someone dealt him a blow on the forehead.

For a moment he staggered, hand to head, then hit out wildly—to realize that no human agency had dealt him that blow; he had but run into a post standing upright out of the floor which had come between his outstretched hands. Still slightly dazed he caught hold of it for support and the next moment discovered that it was not a post but a ladder—a ladder leading upward.

Without hesitation—for already above the barking of the dog he could hear the footsteps in the yard outside—he ran up it. Even blacker darkness and a smell of hay greeted him as he crawled over the edge at the top. He guessed he was in a loft of some kind. Remembering how he had got onto the roof in Carlyle's house—ages ago it seemed now—he caught hold of the end of the ladder and tried to draw it up after him. Luckily it was light, and by exerting all his strength he managed to drag it upward bit by bit.

But not without noise. The grating scrape as the ladder passed over the edge sounded very loud in the darkness, but he worked on madly, unheeding. It was better he knew to get the ladder up and let his pursuers wonder what the noise had been, than to leave it there, a glaring notice to point the way he had taken. The last few inches scraped over the edge and the ladder fell with a thump on the thin wooden floor. He lay panting by the edge, peeping over into the black void below—a void that now was suffused with light from the cautious torch of a man who stood in the doorway.

For several minutes the fellow stood there. The beam travelled up and down the walls, along the floor, and up to the roof. Here it hung for a moment poised, as if it were considering, on the black opening to the loft where Rezaire lay, head and shoulders drawn back out of the light. Then it resumed its wandering and finally went out altogether. Rezaire lay quite still. Knowing what he would have done under similar circumstances, he did not move or peer over to see if the man had gone, with the result that he was not caught when a moment later the rays of the torch shot out into the darkness again without warning, this time straight at the opening to the loft. He lay as still as death, the beam of light passing over and above him to fall on a pile of loose hay that lay against the side.

But the other was not yet satisfied. He advanced with his torch right into the building and stood flashing it about in likely hiding places. The dog gave tongue outside once more and another dark figure appeared in the doorway to join him. They stood together for a moment talking in undertones, then Rezaire's quick ears caught the word "loft" and knew that they were suspicious of the place where he lay hid.

"Must be up there," one of them added at last, in slightly louder tones.

"If you saw anyone at all go in?"

"Ah! I'm not certain of that."

"Well, where's the ladder? We'll soon see." They looked round for a bit and, not finding the ladder, conferred once more: "Looks as though he couldn't be there," replied one.

"How do you make…" began the other, when suddenly he broke off in mid sentence, saying in a quick whisper: "Look!"

There was a dead silence. Rezaire, wondering what on earth it was that had thus suddenly attracted their attention, craned over as far as he could with safety. Below him the men were standing quite still, but he saw that the hand of one pointed to the far end of the building where in the beam of his torch was something that moved.

At first to Rezaire's startled imagination it appeared to be snow, then he realized that it was only dust falling from the roof, the little specks dancing in the rays of the light. Dust falling from a crack in the ceiling, or rather from a crack in the floor of the loft above. For a moment the same processes were at work in the minds of all three men, the two on the ground and Rezaire. Then each realized what that sudden slow movement, which now had almost ceased, meant. There was someone in the loft who, by moving slightly, had sent a shower of dust, hayseeds, meal, and such like, down through the floor into the light of discovery. But while to the two detectives it meant but confirmation of their suspicions, to Rezaire it meant far more. For the dust had fallen from the other end of the loft, away from where he himself lay. It meant that there was someone else in the dark loft with him.

Vaguely he heard the detective say in loud tones: "Well, there doesn't seem to be anyone here," and go out noisily, but even while he accepted at its true value the ruse, obvious enough to him, who knew they had seen the dust, his brain was busy with the new problem. Who was the other person in the loft? What was he doing up there? A detective? Very improbable. Some person on their lawful occasions? Then why the concealment? A criminal? But what other could there be down here at this particular time? Was it just some chance burglar or pilferer that he had run up against? Rezaire almost laughed as he thought of the bewilderment of the local Bill Sykes on attempting to outwit the village constabulary and finding a score of detectives from Scotland Yard on his heels.

But all these thoughts flashed through his mind in a few seconds, even while he had got quietly to his feet. For he knew he was not safe where he was; the detectives would return shortly with help. He ignored for the moment the unknown in the loft with him, and, moving quickly and silently, began to explore his end of the loft for some way out other than the dangerous one of descending the ladder.

Half-way he stopped dead as his practised ears caught the sound of movement at the far end. He stayed still listening intently, and heard a scraping sound, repeated once or twice. He moved up closer. He was not afraid. Who ever this strange personage might be they had this much in common, they were both evidently trying to avoid meeting the police. He moved cautiously toward the sound, and rounding a pile of hay saw the faint outline of a patch of sky, some aperture looking out into the night.

The patch seemed to move and waver, and he then realized what was happening. Something was partially obscuring it, moving in front of it. Then it was clear once more and he heard the scraping again much fainter. In a flash it came to him what had happened. The unknown had found the way out for which he had been looking, had got out of the small opening and was now getting away down the outside in some fashion. He tiptoed quickly to the aperture and looked out. There just by the small opening was a water spout or pipe or some other method of getting to the ground, and halfway down it was a dark figure silently descending.

He wondered again who it could possibly be, then suddenly his hearing was caught away to the other direction by a faint sound in the bam below. There were men there again; perhaps they had got a ladder from somewhere; he must be quick.

He swung himself out and onto the descent which, proving to be the projecting beams and uprights of the barn, was much easier than he had at first imagined. He could not now see the other figure that had preceded him. It had reached the bottom and gone off into the night, and Rezaire forgot at once about it in the more urgent matter of his own escape, as the lion ignores the jackal caught in the same net.

He reached the ground in safety, stole through some bushes and emerged into a well-kept garden at the far side of the house. The moonlight gleamed on a smooth lawn, on trellised archways and stone walls, paved winding pathways and long flower beds, all silver under the beams. Away out on the far side he thought he once more caught a glimpse of the shadowy figure that had been in the loft with him, and wondered what on earth the fellow, whoever he was, was doing. He hoped and prayed fervently that this unknown would not find the launch or, by inadvertently leading the police to it, give away his own escape. An idea flashed across his mind that perhaps he might turn the presence of the newcomer to account. The fellow might, in fact, be the saving of him by attracting the attention of the police while he got away. For the police were only after one person and did not know there were two somewhere in their trap. Then a movement behind him at once recalled his thoughts. Someone was approaching through the bushes at his back. Further, he could now distinctly hear others in the loft he had left, where soon they would discover his absence.

He moved on into the garden and sped across a short length of lawn to a bed of shrubs, where he crouched down. A man came to the edge of the bushes behind him and stood looking out silently over the garden. A moment later another appeared visible in the moonlight to his right. Behind them, standing up dark against the sky, Rezaire could see the house and outbuildings that he had just left. He realized with a sudden thrill of joy that he was now very near safety, for that house was the last on the road and was therefore the house called "Joyner's End," near which somewhere was the quay. But where exactly he did not at the moment know, for he had rather lost his bearings. He decided that the best thing to do would be to get down to the riverside and work along it till he came to the quay, and there lie in wait for a suitable opportunity. For he knew well enough that he could not get away in the launch in a moment of time. If he only escaped by the skin of his teeth it would give the police an opportunity of perhaps stopping him elsewhere. Inconsequently he thought of the sea journey to the Channel Islands in the small boat and realized, now that he had run it so close, how much he had been dependent on good weather.

He began to move slowly along the bed of shrubs till he reached the end. Here he paused and looked back. He could not now make out the two figures he had seen in the bushes, but he knew that they were there, still watching, probably joined by others. He dared not get up and run, for the garden was full of moonlight and an upright moving figure would be noticed at once. He left the actual shelter of the shrubs, but still, he hoped, concealed by them from actual vision, and began to crawl across another piece of lawn, wondering whether he would be seen.

He crossed it in safety and reached a ditch and a bank. Here he suddenly realized, to his dismay, that he had completely lost his bearings. He could still just make out the house, but did not know in what position he was relative to it. The river, he thought, ran in front of him across an open field, but he dared not cross this directly. Some way to his right was a mass of dark bushes; to his left the ground was more open. He turned at length, after a little deliberation, to the left and under shelter of the bank ran along till he reached a hedge.

He was just pushing boldly through this when a voice and a torch suddenly challenged him out of the night, a few yards away. In a flash he realized what he had done and dropped to the ground, even as the searching beam shot out into the hedge around him. He had borne too much to the left and, just as he had done before, had come out again on to the road, where he had for the second time been seen by one of the men stationed there.

Before he could do anything, the man ran up, flashing his torch this way and that. In sudden desperation Rezaire leaped up and struck out at him with the butt of his revolver. The man sank down to the ground with a cry, but the next moment footsteps and challenges rang out on either side as others, also stationed on the road, hurried to the scene.

Rezaire, heart beating wildly with fear, had just time to get to his feet and run, crouching down, back in the direction he had come in the shadow of the bank. Behind him he heard voices, saw lights; torches were flashing to right and left, but once again he was not pursued. As he made his way along his brain suddenly grasped the significance of this last, which had not before dawned on him. Why was he not pursued? Because they thought they had him safely. They had missed him so often before by direct attack that they were this time adopting different tactics. He was being gradually surrounded like a wild animal being taken by trappers. They had prevented him crossing the road, they had in all probability stretched a cordon across the open country in front, they had driven him out of the shelter of the last houses and gardens. Men on the road, men behind him, men in front of him; he was being slowly encircled on three sides—and the fourth side was the river. The river meant safety to him, but did they know it? Surely they would not have left the river bank unguarded. Surely by now they must be pushing down the bank from either end to make the trap complete, cutting him off from the quay and safety?

He got up and ran blindly along the ditch away from the road and in the direction of the thick undergrowth that he now realized must fringe the river. He must reach the quay before it was too late.

CHAPTER XXV

AT THE QUAY

Sick with apprehension Rezaire reached the bushes at the end. He had realized the new methods that were being adopted to ensure his capture and indeed had now abundant proof of their working. He could hear noises all around him in the still night air, a smothered cough here, a step on a gravel path there, vague sounds from the men who were slowly stretching their net round him.

If only he had realized before what they were up to, he could easily have outwitted them. If only he had not delayed seeking food in that cottage... Behind him on the road a shrill whistle blast sounded twice—no doubt an indication that he had been located, or a sign to begin the final closing-in.

He came to the bushes, big masses of briars, small trees, long dead grass, all matted together, plunged in, trying not to make any noise, and arrived at last at the water's edge, marshy and muddy, with undergrowth growing right down the banks. The quay could obviously not be here, it must be farther along to the left, though he could not see it. He knew that it was fairly near a big hollow tree standing in an open space—so his letter had informed him. He paused and listened intently. On his right he could hear distinct sounds as of men working cautiously along the river bank. Some way off he saw the gleam of torches and once he heard a curse. They were closing in.

He turned about and struck away from the water. A twig or two snapped, his boots squelched in the mud. He must get further downstream, but he could not work through the bushes without making a terrible noise. Panic came over him as he began to wonder whether the men further down who were working up-stream had yet got near to the launch and the quay. Almost any minute he expected to hear the sudden outcry which would show that it was too late.

He left the bushes and regained the field once more, hurrying noiselessly along the edge on the soft turf and looking for a path or gap in the undergrowth a little further on. The slow unendurable suspense, helped by all the strain of the last hours, was beginning to have a terrible effect on his nerves; far, far rather would he have suffered the sudden rushes and wild moments of danger than this terrible remorseless closing in of the trap, and his inability to find the one way out before it was stopped.

Skirting the bushes and avoiding the moonlit openness of the field, he almost ran into a building before he realized it was a hen-house on the edge of the field. A sudden outcry of startled fowls arose from within and he left it hurriedly behind, cursing angrily. A little way further on he at last found what he was looking for, the end of the mass of undergrowth and a path leading toward the river, a lighter line in the dark shadow that cut into the thick mass of brambles and trees towering above his head. Glancing back for a moment he could, some way back, almost make out the relentless line of men advancing upon him in the moonlight from the direction of the road and the house.

But these did not matter for the moment; these he could escape; his main fear now was of the parties on either side working down the river bank, the points of the pincers that were seeking to close on him. Sick with anxiety, he turned down the path, stepping cautiously and quietly in the darkness. Other paths intersected the thick mass, running this way and that, but he kept his direction and soon came out into a little clearing, lit by the moon. Beyond it were but a few trees and between them he could see once more the light upon the face of the river now almost at full tide.

He passed like a wraith across the clearing and silently through the trees. Then he could have shouted for joy, but that his enemies were so near. Away to the right in an open space stood the big hollow tree and in front of him was another small open space, this time right on the bank of the river, where a flat square piece of ground like a table jutted out into the swirling water. It was the quay; and there by the side of it was a long black mass. His launch! France! Safety! It lay there, a protective shadow with a faint subdued glow of light hovering over it from the closed-in cabin—the goal of all his hopes. Already he could distinguish the dark figure of one of the crew standing on the quay side waiting for him. To board it, push silently off down-stream and start the engine when out of hearing would be but the work of a minute.

With joyful heart he was about to traverse the last few yards that led to freedom, when a sudden quick sound smote his ear. It came from the left and just behind. There was someone in the bushes quite close. He kept as still as possible, verifying his suspicion. Then he heard it again and terror gripped him. Was it the party that he feared, working along the river bank, and nearer than he had thought? If so, he dared not board the launch this very moment; he would assuredly be caught, since his pursuers were too close to allow of a get-away. He must first distract their attention momentarily, and draw them off if possible.

He stole back to the edge of the trees and from the shadow peeped out into the little clearing he had just crossed, white in the moonlight. The noise, subdued, yet intermittent, came from just the other side, as if someone were trying to move silently through brambles, having lost the path. Then he realized that it was too far round to the front to be the particular party of detectives that he feared, since now that he listened intently he could hear them too, both parties of them, on the river bank on either side.

For a moment he stood there wondering, then suddenly it came to him who it was. It must be that stranger who had been in the loft with him, a short while before—the other apparent fugitive from justice. That unknown was of course in the trap too… He gasped suddenly as he realized the possibilities of the situation, remembering how the thought had flitted through his mind before, that he might turn the presence of this other to account. Here ready to hand was the means of distracting for a moment the attention of the detectives to ensure his making good his own escape. This unknown man, now moving in the shadow just to the right, should draw off the police while he himself went free.

No sooner had he decided than he was putting his plan into effect. Swiftly he moved round to a new position, and peered through the bushes till he could just see the stranger, the dark figure of a man. Then with a smile to himself Rezaire deliberately trod loudly on a twig and called in a low gruff voice: "Now then, who's that?"

The effect was instantaneous, and as he had hoped.

The man gave a convulsive start, a low cry, and fled swiftly across the clearing away from this sudden new danger—straight in the direction of the detectives, coming up the river bank. Rezaire chuckled at his ruse. The capture, or at any rate the noise and sudden distraction, would just give him the time that he needed for his escape. Then the chuckle froze suddenly on his lips, and he gave a little gasp. For the flying figure had halted as it reached the hollow tree and turning swiftly was lost in the shadows. But it was not that which had made Rezaire gasp. For as the figure turned, looking back across the clearing, the face had been clearly visible under the moonlight.

It was Viv!

Viv! Rezaire sprang forward. His lips formed to shout her name, but at that moment there came to his ears the louder noise of the party of detectives beyond. Instinctively he turned and ran in the direction of the quay, driven only by the instinct of self-preservation.

He reached the quay and then for a moment his footsteps faltered. If only he had known it was Viv, they could both have got away. But now it was too late. Vivienne, whom at the very first he had helped to escape, had almost reached safety, and then he had unknowingly betrayed her to save himself, for she could not remain undiscovered for long. He could have cried aloud at the irony of it all.

Then he pulled himself together. Why should he regret it, just because it was Viv? Had he not carried the gang on his shoulders long enough? Vivienne, Harrap, Sam, Dixon, time and time again he had jeopardized his whole safety for their sakes... He moved onward, listening for sounds be hind him. Soon he would hear the sudden outcry that would herald her capture.

A figure detached itself from the shadow of the boat.

"Mr. Carlyle?" it queried, and he automatically answered "Yes."

Safety at last. He was at the launch now, he could almost see into the little cabin, dimly lit, but at the same moment he realized in an instant one thing. He could yet save Vivienne,—but only by sacrificing himself. He could see it all in a flash. He would rush madly down the river bank to where the other detectives were slowly advancing, would be captured; the chase would be called off, Vivienne, well hidden, would be left alone, and could escape afterward, for, as far as the police knew, they only had the one quarry in their net. For him, capture, ignominious capture, and prison—but Viv would be safe. He could save her—*if he sacrificed himself.*

He stood on the plank leading to the launch. To turn back meant the end of all the struggle, which he had at last brought to success; it meant imprisonment, failure—and all to save Viv. To go forward meant safety—freedom—life.

He put one foot on the little deck. He looked into the cabin where in the shaded light he could at last see figures,—the men who would be his companions to freedom.

Then with a little gasp he turned impulsively, his mind made up, and ran desperately back into the darkness, plunging noisily along the river bank to where the detectives were closing in upon him...

* * * *

But even at the last Rezaire had proved true to himself and his character, for it was not to save Vivienne that he had turned back. The real reason was that he had just seen clearly one of the figures awaiting him in the cabin.

It was Sam. Sam, who, how he knew not, had escaped and found his way to the launch. Sam whom, despite his threats, he had betrayed. Sam with his cruel anticipatory smile, and his long evil knife....